One Trade Too Many

TJ Arant

. . . And we are here as on a darkling plain
Swept with confused alarms of struggle and
flight,
Where ignorant armies clash by night.

Matthew Arnold, "Dover Beach"

Contents

Chapter One

OCTOBER IN NASHVILLE MEANS that Vanderbilt is already out of the SEC football race. It's too soon for basketball, and the weather is still nice, so the students get drunk and go to watch the Commodores get beat by Auburn or Alabama or Georgia, then spend the rest of Saturday maintaining a fairly stable buzz. The Greek kids hit the parties at the houses, non-Greek kids grab a bite at Rand or Branscomb, then head to wherever their beer and liquor flows from, and the whole place settles out around 2 a.m.

It was three in the morning. There was a little breeze, but even that didn't disturb the quiet of a campus sleeping it off.

Looking up or looking down, it's all the same, he thought, or at least it would be in the light. Dark now, but Patrick knew more than what he saw in the light ahead of him. The Kirkland tower was an MC Escher print come to life. He knew. He had the Ascending and Descending print hanging above his desk in Carmichael East, a reminder of his academic treadmill. It only appears that he is making progress. In reality, he was just making movement.

But not tonight. He pulled the hands closer to him and got the face situated. Tomorrow, when the concert on the lawn below is in full swing, they'll be tripping on Mickey. And all because of Patrick.

Behind him, his silent compatriot carried the ropes and staple gun.

The idea had sprung fully formed into Patrick's brain. Zappa and The Mothers of Invention would play on Alumni Lawn. It was a freebie. There would be a massive crowd. And every one of them would look up at Kirkland Tower and see it.

Howell had lifted the surveying tools from the Engineering School's storage and used the bricks on the tower as the measures. Raines had created the hands, face, and body, no mean feat for a pre-med chemistry major. And Patrick? Patrick had worked the locks that got them inside. No alarm. No security system. Just the locks, and Patrick had taken care of that problem. For two nights, they'd come inside to test again, to make sure they could get into this most secure place, this tower, this citadel.

Two hundred thirty-four steps, the last dozen a ladder. The flashlights had given out about a hundred steps ago. Now they were relying on the feeble twenty-five watt bulbs that were placed every hundred feet or so. Patrick unlatched the trapdoor on the tower roof and moonlight flooded in.

"You ready?"

"Yeah. Let's get this done and get out of here. The place gives me the creeps."

Patrick fixed one end of the rope to his harness, passing it through the protection bolts he had fixed into the side of the tower. He then ran the rope runs through the protection to his co-conspirator who would serve as belayer. The belayer wore a harness with a belay device attached, and together they threaded the rope through the belay.

This was the part that Patrick feared the most. They hadn't worked this together, as a tandem. But they'd both played these parts before. He just had to trust.

"You know your part," he said, but he meant it as a question. His hands were sweaty in the cool night air. He hoisted himself up on the roof.

"I got this. Here's the gear."

Patrick took the face and hands, secured them, and took a deep breath. He took the staple gun, put it in the backpack. "Here goes nothing."

Over the side of the tower he went, through the small cornice and brushed passed the "V" inside the shield at the very top of the tower. The night air freshened and for a moment he thought he felt a bit of a sway in the rope. He gripped and tried by force of will to still his body. His legs came to rest against the side of the tower. The swaying stopped.

"Everything ok out there?"

He took a breath, afraid to look one way or the other. "Ok out here."

"Great. Get to work."

Patrick lowered himself cautiously. The stone topper was much bigger than it seemed from the ground. Ten. Twenty. Thirty feet he descended. He stopped as he reached the brick portion of the tower. Howell had made the calculations and he had checked them himself. Another twenty feet down on the bricks, and he should reach the clock face. He felt the rope tighten, then slacken, then his movement slowed as he lowered himself closer to the goal.

The line tightened again. "Let's go a little at a time," he said. His voice sounded loud in the early morning air, suspended high above campus. He looked down for the first time, scanning to see if anyone was there to hear. The movement spoiled his fragile balance, and he almost capsized, but he recovered with a foot on the tower and a grimace.

"A foot at a time, then," came the answer.

Foot by agonizing foot he descended. "What the hell am I doing up here?" he whispered. But soon he was face to face with the Kirkland tower clock, and it was time to go to work. "Tie it off," he said.

In their planning, it had been clear that the work on the clock's face would be at close quarters. Now, suspended one hundred forty feet in the air, it became clear just how close the work would be. Patrick was up against the face, and would have to reach both up and down to accomplish his task.

He took a gloved hand, the one with the single finger, and reached to affix it, like a glove, to the minute hand nearest him. Then the other gloved hand, attached to the hour hand, thankfully still close but lower and to the left. Again, he found himself about to spin, but this time he used the hour hand to steady himself. He tied both off.

The face came next, and he pulled himself higher, using the wooden face of the clock to support his weight. He pulled the staple gun free, and with eight quick punches, two in each of the four corners, the face was fixed.

Now for the part that was nice to have, but not necessary: the rest of the body. Reaching behind him into his backpack, he withdrew the rolled finale. Patrick held the right side with the staple gun until he could twist himself into place, holding the body with his left hand. Then he made quick work, stapling the body, again in four bursts at each corner, and left the legs to unfurl underneath.

"Done," he said. "Coming up."

"Everything in place?" came a voice that sounded too far away.

"We're good."

Patrick slipped the staple gun inside his backpack, then gripped the rope with both hands. "Don't fail me now," he thought. "Not after we've come this far."

Pulling himself into a walking position, he began to make the trek to the top of the tower. The holds he had placed on the way down he now collected as he made his way back up. A foot, then two feet at a time, he came in due course to the cornice. He straddled the summit, and rolled over onto the rooftop. "Damn," was all he said.

He lay there, heart pounding, for a minute. "Remember Batman and Robin? Walking up the side of a building? Swear to God, that's what I was just thinking."

"You may be Batman, but I'm not Robin. Let's go. We need to get out of here."

The two intrepid pranksters went down the ladder, one at a time. Patrick put the repelling gear into his pack, then tossed the rope aside. "Leave it." Two hundred forty two steps, in reverse order, like an Escher print.

Parsons was outside. "Come on," he whispered. "Let's go have a look."

The three conspirators walked toward Alumni Lawn, as if they were just three undergraduates returning from a late-ending party. But they needn't have worried; there wasn't anyone awake on campus to see them. When they got just far enough away to be able to see the clock on the tower in the moonlight, they stopped. For a moment, there was utter quiet. Then one, then the second, and finally the third began to laugh, quietly at first, then loudly, then like drunken sailors on extended shore leave.

"That's a damn piece of art, if I do say so myself," said Patrick.

"Damn straight," said Howell. "Damn fucking straight."

There, over Vanderbilt's stately campus, was the Kirkland tower, with its clock, symbol of all that was Vanderbilt. A keeper of time, and yet timeless. And tonight, as it kept the time, it had transformed into the world's tallest Mickey Mouse watch, complete with Mickey's face and his body, his legs unfurled down the tower. Now, as the hour reached four and the bell began to toll, Mickey's hour hand gave an underhand peace sign, while his minute hand, held straight aloft, extended the middle finger salute.

"Time for a well-deserved nightcap," said Howell. "Back to my room?"

"Sounds like a plan. Patrick?"

"I'll be over in a bit. I just realized the flashlights are still in the tower."

"Leave them," said Howell.

"Easy for you to say. Mine was part of my college package from my parents."

"You have sentimental feeling for a flashlight?"

"No. It has my name stenciled on it."

"You mean, like your mother put your name in your underwear for summer camp?"

"Something like that." He winced. "Go ahead. I'll catch up."

Patrick turned and jogged back to Kirkland, opened the outside door, and looked ahead. The tower door stood open.

The door should not have been open, he thought. Didn't we close it all? And why was there light inside? The whole place should have been dark; the pitiful light bulbs were much higher.

He pushed the door aside, further open. And the light abated. Why was that? Was his mind playing tricks on him? What had appeared light only moments before was now enveloped in dark.

He saw a shape in the corner, away from the staircase. How had they missed that? It appeared to be a pile, perhaps of clothing? No doubt it was there. What was it?

He heard a crack behind him, the sound of something, perhaps a person? A soft sound, like a footstep. Then another.

Patrick turned, but knew immediately he had turned the wrong direction. The sound behind was still behind. And as he tried to correct, the same as the way he'd tried to correct on the outside of the tower, he heard a sickening splat, the moment before he felt it, the moment before he realized that the sound and the feeling were one, and that they were his entirely.

He heard himself say, "What are you doing here?"

As he felt his body sink onto the floor, in his mind he saw Mickey's face. And then he thought he saw his middle finger. And that was the last thing he saw.

Chapter Two

We had been drenched by sweat, then we were in the river, and then we were baked dry, the mud covering us like a foul, crunchy coating, as if we were a meal for a giant who didn't much care what we tasted like as long as we went down fast and easy. The delta sun was too far overhead, and our legs were beginning to wilt under it. The day had been unreasonable, and the night could not approach quickly enough.

I wasn't walking point. That was Eaton, and he moved as if he saw snakes everywhere. Which is to say he wasn't moving at all. "Come on, Corporal," I said aloud to myself, "Act like you've got a little gumption." To my rear, I could hear somebody razzing the FNG, the new guy who had been with us for a week, and who hadn't picked up anything yet except a budding case of jungle rot on his feet.

"Come on, yourself, Jackson," Eaton whispered through clinched teeth, "There's something up ahead. I can feel it."

"Then hold up." I raised a hand, and so did Eaton. "Hold up," the message went rearward, voice to voice. Our unit quieted.

The elephant grass rose up around us like stakes in a VC booby trap. Sharp, impenetrable, the edges like razor wire, the grass reached for us and snagged our boots, sliced our cheeks, caught us inside its sinewy maze. It invited us to kneel, then give up, pray to it for shelter.

"They're out there," Easton whispered.

No sound came. If there had been animal or bird or insect sounds, they had collapsed into the ground as surely as animal and bird chatter goes to ground when a hawk begins to circle. The air itself went still, refusing to move. The sun intensified, and then dipped behind a cloud, as if it too wanted nothing to do with what played out below.

A sound behind me rumbled, soldier's gear dragging on the ground. Hisses from behind, soldiers' attempts to quell the sound. Suddenly next to me, FNG drops his pack and stands up. He was about six-two, and his head just cleared the grass. "I want to go home," he said. "I'm done."

I grabbed his pants waist and yanked him down to the ground. "Quiet." I looked at him and saw my own face: frightened, angry, and tired.

We stayed there, locked down. I don't know how long. Then we heard it.

I thought it was the chop-chop-chop of a Huey, but there was no LZ anywhere near. However, the sound didn't stay that way. It was the distant pop of NVA artillery. Pop. Pop. Pop-pop-pop. Was it there? Yes. But no corresponding boom. The boom that let you know it was coming for you. In the movies the rounds make a whistling noise. Only the ones that are going over your head, missing you, make that sound.

I didn't hear that sound.

I waited for the boom, the sound that would tell me that we're dialed in, in the target area. FNG looked at me with terror. "I want to go home." He had his hands on my shoulders, pulling me down. "I have to go home."

Then it came. The boom. And another boom. Smoke and fire were everywhere. Men screamed and would scream no more. The quiet of the prequel was broken, and I heard the cries.

Medic! Over here!

The elephant grass cut me as I tried to move toward my men. My face bled. FNG was behind me, crying. Boom. And then another boom.

I ran through my unit, all lying strewn in the smoke. Devastation lay everywhere. The grass had sliced me and I bled. From my wrists. From my face. The jagged grass had cut my uniform to tatters and, underneath the mud-baked crunch, my torso was sliced. FNG kept bawling, wanting to go home.

Boom.

Boom.

"No," I screamed. "No more."

I sat bolt upright in bed, soaked in sweat.

A fist pounded the door. "Jackson." Another boom. "Are you in there?"

***

I recognized Don Mercer's voice. Don is a campus cop, second in command. He's also a vet like me. I took a deep breath to calm my insides. "Yeah," I said, "I'm here." Then I yelled it, "Coming, for Chrissakes."

I live in an east facing garage apartment and, when I opened the door, I had to shield the morning sun with my hand. Mercer ducked under my arm and came in. Five-seven with a belly that will eventually become a paunch if he doesn't watch it, Don's brown face looked like he'd been chewing a problem for a while. The jaw muscle just below his left ear jutted out, a sure sign that he was stressed.

"What's up with the early roll call, Don?"

He turned and stood in the middle of my one-room place. "You look like hell, Jackson. You know what? Anymore, you always look like hell."

I stood by the door in my skivvies with yesterday's t-shirt half twisted on my body. My hair is long, down to my shoulders and a little greasy. I felt my beard with my hand, and I could tell that it was skewing to the right, since I lay on my left side. "I can't help what I look like, Donnie. What the hell do you look like first thing in the morning?"

"Better than you," he said. "Why don't you look into a steady gig? You should be more than tapped out from the Pitts business. Don't you need money?"

Almost a year ago, I helped a father learn more about his murdered daughter. That was the Pitts business. Before that I was an Assistant Dean at Vanderbilt, where I'd used GI benefits to get a degree. Before I was fired, anyway. And before that? My job was infantry in Vietnam. One tour. One tour too many.

"I don't need much, Donnie." I crossed the studio apartment to the bed. I shook the covers so that they made a semblance of order, then sat on the edge of the mattress. "Have a seat, officer, and tell me your troubles."

"I'm dead serious, Jackson. You can't keep living like you are."

I panned the room with my left hand. "How can you say that? I have all that I need. A place to sleep. A place to eat. A place to wash dishes." The sink was full. Of dirty dishes.

"As if you do that with any regularity."

"I've been busy," I said. "And over there, where you are welcome to sit, is my reading chair, where I while away countless happy hours."

"Where you sit and drink," he said, picking up the glass on the side table. He sniffed it. "Bourbon."

"Elixir of the Kentucky gods," I said, yawning. "And since I grew up right on the state line, the gods of my youth. Ezra Brooks, Jim Beam, TW Samuels. Holy Trinity. Father, Son, and Holy Ghost. Patris et Filii et Spiritus Sancti." I ran my hand through my hair, straightening it a little. "World without end. Amen."

"Are you sober?" It is a conversation Don and I have had a few times. Most of the time he's not asking the question. He's making the statement. As in, you're smashed.

I had to laugh. "Don, your door-banging was in the middle of my nightmare. If I wasn't sober, I would not have been having this particular nightmare."

He sat in the chair by the table, putting the glass back where it had been. "Damn it, man. If you need help, go see somebody. Drinking won't make it go away."

"I'm not trying to make it go away, Don. I'm trying to live with it." I didn't say what I really meant. Without drinking to relax me, I stay paralyzed. I can't do anything. At least when I'm drinking, as long as I can even it out, I am not paralyzed. The edge comes off. I can do things, such as explain a dead girl's life to a grieving father.

"Not the way it looks to me."

"I'm pretty sure you didn't come beating down my door to check on my drinking. What's up?"

Mercer lit a cigarette and took a drag. "We had an interesting night on campus last night." He raised an eyebrow and looked at me sideways.

Interesting is always a euphemism with Don Mercer. It can mean anything from "this is unusual" to "this is beyond screwed up." I nodded. "Sounds like a typical Vanderbilt weekend. You have the concert over there this afternoon, too. Zappa, right?"

"God, yes. Don't remind me. But truly we had a one of a kind night last night. Someone broke into Kirkland and went up into the clock tower." He held the cigarette up in front of his face, ninety degrees to the floor and considered it, as if it were an object he wasn't familiar with.

I whistled. "Really? I think that action is the Holy Grail on campus. How'd they do it?"

"That's not clear yet. But the why is clear. They put Mickey Mouse hands on the clock hands, and Mickey's face on the clock." He stopped staring at the cigarette, apparently convinced that he recognized what it was after all.

"Well, that would be one for the books. Good for them, whoever did it. I assume they got clean away."

He flicked ash into the ashtray. "One didn't. We found him dead at the base of the stairs." I must have registered surprise even though I was trying to keep a poker face. "That's right. We've got a dead Vanderbilt undergraduate. Patrick Vincent. You know him?"

I had been Assistant Dean, but not for almost two years now. Still, I knew him. He had been an orientation advisor, a VUceptor, they called them. He had been full of energy, and more than a little full of fun. "Bright kid. From New Jersey, I think. Engineering student?"

"That's the one." He took another long drag, and French inhaled what he exhaled.

I sighed. Students always think they're bulletproof. Until they're not. "Did he take a fall? I assume those steps are treacherous."

"He had his head stove in with a crowbar."

"How do you know it was a crowbar? That seems pretty specific. Unless it was just sitting there."

He flicked another ash, this one half missing the ashtray and landing on the table. "Yeah, it was there all right. In the hands of the murderer, we think." He stuck the cigarette in his mouth and took the ashtray in hand, raking the missed ash in with the other.

"That doesn't make any sense, Don. Why would the murderer still be there, with the murder weapon in hand? Unless your guys got there just as it happened?"

"No, we got there much later. This morning, in fact. McCarter was on foot patrol and came across the open door in the bottom of Kirkland. He went in and found them." He paused, then added, "You know how McCarter is. He pushes every door, even if it's always been locked. This one flew open. It wasn't locked."

"I don't understand. Why would the murderer hang around with the crowbar for hours?" In the newspapers, if you kill someone you want to get as far away from it as you can. That was true in combat. I couldn't imagine it would be any different anywhere else. Unless you're sick, why would you hang out with the body?

"I don't know. Got coked up and crashed? That's the theory right now."

"But why?" I asked. "Why attack a kid? Are you telling me that someone came on campus, found the door open, and, having a crowbar handy, took it to a kid he didn't know?"

There was a long silence. Mercer took his time stubbing out the butt. "I didn't just come to tell you about the Mickey Mouse hands and the dead student."

I stopped short. "I figured you wanted to know if I knew Patrick Vincent. Could tell you something about him."

"We've got that angle covered, Jackson."

"Ok. What, then?"

"The cokehead who crashed? The one with the crowbar?"

"Yeah?"

"He's an interesting character. His identification says his name is Thompson."

"Common enough name around here."

"That's not his full name. And it's not that common at all. His name is Thompson Trade."

Chapter Three

Wordlessly, Don and I got into the VU police cruiser. He had the good sense not to ask until I was ready.

It'd been years since I'd seen my older brother. I remembered him as he was when he left for Middle Tennessee State. Eighteen and ready to fly. The first of us to leave. Our sister, Swanson, was still at home, pining for the chance to leave. Thompson, named after our father, was "the smart one." She was "the sweet one." And I was "the one who'd farm." No one ever doubted that Swanson would leave. Same with Thompson. Never any doubt that I would be the one to stay.

He was also the good looking one. Large wide-set brown eyes with thick dark eyebrows, above a handsome nose, Thompson had the sort of infectious smile that made everyone around him happy. He had dimples when he smiled, and a small cleft in his chin, like a young Cary Grant. It was all topped by hair that went easily into any style that was current.

It would have been hard to be his little brother if he'd wanted it to be. But he didn't. He was always fair and kind and willing to include me. Besides, my growth caught his by the time I was seven. After that I was the bigger, younger one.

But that all changed when he left for Murphreesboro. He grew silent. He didn't call. He didn't write. Daddy was so worried that he drove from Dimsville to MTSU just to see if Thompson was all right. Daddy came back, and didn't say much to us. Just said that Thompson was welcome to come back when he wanted.

That's what he said to Swanson and me. I don't know what he said to Mama. All I know is that her face soured and never sweetened back up.

Thompson was her favorite, the one who looked like Daddy. And Daddy, Mama said, was the handsomest man she'd ever seen.

After fall semester, Thompson's steamer trunk showed up on the front porch with shipping due. A day later, Mama got a letter from him. It said he was dropping out of school and headed to California. He said he'd be in touch.

I'd been to Vietnam and back, Swanson had died in a Christmas car wreck while I was in country, I'd been through college, got a job, got married, been fired and divorced. Now, I guess, he was back in touch. And in jail.

Mercer must have read my thoughts. "Does it sound like something he'd do?"

The police radio had the usual Metro chatter. It was a Sunday morning. There were scattered discoveries of Saturday night mischief. It was nothing serious.

"Who knows? It's been ten years, Don." I rolled the window down and put my elbow on the door. It was warming up. It would be hot, for October, for Nashville.

"You never talked about him."

We were heading down West End, then onto Broadway. Except for the few people heading into the 8:00 Mass at the Cathedral, there weren't many people on the sidewalk. Nashville isn't enough of a big city for that. On a Sunday morning, early enough, it's no different than the smaller towns all around. The God-fearing folk are getting ready for church, the night set is still sleeping it off.

"Nothing to talk about. He broke my parents' hearts. But life went on. My life certainly did." I noticed a solitary man, brown paper bag hiding a bottle in hand, sitting at a bus stop. He'd be waiting a while. But he didn't look like he'd care. "Has he seen a judge yet?"

"Metro booked him. It will be a murder charge, so there was a quick bit before the night magistrate." He turned at 15th Avenue North and then onto Church. "They can hold him forty eight hours before an arraignment hearing." He stopped at a red light and looked at me. "You know he won't get bail, right?"

"Sure." Unless he'd made a fortune out west, neither he nor I could swing bail on a murder rap. Mama might want to try, if she heard about it, but she couldn't do it. And I wouldn't.

Mercer parked in the police lot just off 2nd Avenue North, and we went into the Metro jail. There has been talk of building a new jail for a couple of years, and the current jail was the best argument for it. The building was dark, felt damp, and had a feeling of 1930s criminal justice. Which is to say: it felt like a place where they really might throw away the key.

We wound our way along corridors, led by a Metro police officer, until we came to a row of cells. The hallway was lit by flickering florescent tubes that were black at both ends. These light could flick out, and nobody would bother to change them. The floor was cement and hard and cold. I could hear someone moaning.

"Wait here," the officer said.

"Nice place," I said to Mercer.

"Just like the Hermitage Hotel. Nothing but the best for the County's visitors."

When the officer returned, he said, "You can come with me."

We walked to the end of the corridor. He punched a code and the lock gave way. The barred door swung open and he motioned me inside. "Ten minutes," he said, "And I'll be back."

The door shut behind me.

There, looking a little frightened and a little angry, was my brother. He sat on the mangy cot, squinting up at me.

"Hey, little brother. Been a while."

I took a long look at him. He wore what the county gives you after they finger print and strip search you. Just a faded yellow jumpsuit and flip flops. Just a stripped down version of something related to me, a long time removed. "That would be your fault, not mine."

"Fair enough." Even in the faint light, I could see his face was drawn, his eyes bloodshot. Say what you would about me, he looked worse. "I was over your way last night, but I guess you heard about that."

"Yes." I paused. I had a lot to say to him and I didn't know where to start. And I wanted to say it so it'd be a fair fight. From the looks of him, though, he was already a whipped dog. He didn't need me to beat on him. "You need anything?"

"Don't suppose you have a line or two on you?"

"Of cocaine?"

He smiled. "Just a little joke, Jackson. Unless, of course, you do."

"That's your drug of choice?"

He shrugged. "It makes me feel alert, confident. You know? The way I used to feel. Powerful. Able to do anything."

"Leap tall buildings at a single bound."

"Yeah, Jackson. That's it. Able to do things." He rubbed his nose on his sleeve. "How's Mom?"

"I don't get back there much." That's not true. I don't get back there at all. "You broke her heart, you know? You know that?" My voice was louder than I wanted it to be. It echoed in the cell.

I wanted him to stand up. I wanted him to argue with me, or get up and push me in the chest, tell me that I didn't know what I was talking about. I wanted him to give me a reason for what he did, to justify all the hurt. The little brother in me wanted him to explain it, make it right.

But he didn't do any of that. He put his head in his hands and then moaned. His was the moaning I'd heard before, except this now was a low, nearly silent moan, as if it came from deep inside him.

"Why'd you do it, Thompson?"

He lifted his head. "Do what? Leave Tennessee? Or do what they said I did last night?"

"Let's start with why did you leave in the first place?"

He looked at me but didn't meet my eyes. He gaze seemed to fix in the middle of my chest, as if he needed something to focus on.

"You know I couldn't stay. We talked about it all the time."

"You and Swanson did. That's right. You talked about getting out into the world."

"Dimsville, Tennessee is not real, man. We never thought it was real."

"Seemed real enough to me. Daddy and Mama were real. The farm was real."

He waved his hand at me, dismissing the thought. "Come on, Jackson. Even you, you who were going to help farm the place, even you knew that it wouldn't be big enough for you."

"It might have been. If things had been different."

"Different? You mean, if I'd got my degree and done something around here? If Swanson had stayed around?" he grimaced. "It wasn't ever going to get any bigger, any more exciting. No matter what happened."

"Why'd you have to run so far, Thompson? Why'd you have to never write, never call?" I realized I was sounding like a ten-year old. I decided I wasn't going to sound that way again.

He stood up slowly. Shorter than I was, he had always been a kind of wiry strong. Now, the jail clothes hung off him, badly fit to a body that didn't look wiry or strong. "Y'all don't want to hear from me. Truly, you don't. I don't have anything to say that any of you want to hear. Hell, I don't have anything to say that I want to hear myself."

He turned away from me and walked to the back wall of the cell. He bent at the waist and leaned on it with his hands outstretched, a version of the search-me pose he'd probably assumed last night.

"Did you kill Patrick Vincent?"

He stayed in the position he'd assumed. "Is that the boy's name from last night?"

"Yes. Patrick Vincent. Twenty years old. Senior engineering major. They found the crowbar that killed him in your hands. Did you kill him?"

"Does that sound like me, Jackson?" He took his hands off the wall, turned toward me and sank to a squat, leaning against the wall. "Have you ever known me to be violent? Toward anybody?"

"I haven't known you, or anything about you, for ten years. When I knew you, you didn't do cocaine. You didn't look like you do now."

"And you haven't changed at all. Have you, Jackson?"

"We're not talking about me." Again, too loud. Again, an echo.

"Fine," he said. "We're talking about me. And I don't know what happened last night. I came in on the bus. I did a few lines and got a little bottle of Seagrams." He looked at me through hooded eyes. "I find it takes the edge off."

I knew a little about that.

"I came over to campus. I knew that you had a job there."

"How did you know that? You haven't been in touch with anyone."

"I ran into a VU alum out west. He asked if I was related." He stood, a little unsteady. "It's not that common a name. Our name."

"So you came to campus."

"By the time I got there, it was late. I found this building that looked like a main building."

"That'd be Kirkland."

"And a door in the back was open. I just followed along until I came to what looked like a passage with a door. It was open. I was just looking for a place to spend the night."

"And then what?"

He looked at me with distant eyes. I thought he might begin to cry. He walked toward me and stood directly in front of me. He looked tired, and completely out of reach. "I don't know. The next thing I knew, an officer was handcuffing me."

"Did you kill Patrick Vincent?"

He put his hands on my shoulders and sniffed. "I don't know. I can't imagine I did, Jackson, but I don't know."

Chapter Four

WHEN I CAME OUT with the jailer, Mercer was gone. "He got a call. I don't know anything else." Fine. That's the way it goes sometimes.

I made my way back across 2nd and down Union to Printers' Alley, which was as good an excuse as Nashville had for a serious honkytonk district. Places like the Brass Rail and the Black Poodle were famous, at least in the South, for the sort of anything goes stripping and music and steaks as you could get anywhere outside of Memphis. I was heading for the Oscar, where I knew a guy who could give me a drink, even on a Nashville Sunday.

The Oscar was a place that relied on the popularity of its neighbors. Heaven Lee was stripping at the Black Poodle and that was good for The Oscar. The mayor and other politicos would show up at the Brass Rail, and that was good for The Oscar. It was good because there were only so many seats at the good places. The Oscar wasn't a good place, but it had seats.

Billy Wendell was the manager of The Oscar and he lived above it in a little flat, not a lot unlike my garage apartment. I threw rocks at his window until he looked out, at first mad, and then just dejected.

"Open up, man." I said it conversationally. Just in case someone was listening.

"Really? What time is it?"

"Time for honest people to open up the bar."

Ten minutes later I was sitting in The Oscar and sipping a bourbon. Billy was making coffee and cross-examining me.

"You're telling me your long-lost brother is in town, and he's sitting in jail for murder?" He poured a cup of steaming coffee from the pot. "What the hell do you even do with that?"

"I stop for a drink with my oldest friend in the neighborhood. Then I head back to campus to see whether it makes any sense."

Billy parked himself across from me at the bar and blew on his coffee. "You figure he didn't do it?"

"I have no idea." The bourbon was burning the back of my throat. Or maybe that wasn't bourbon. Maybe it was the situation. "I just know that, even if he's a complete shit, he's my brother. It's not like anyone else cares."

"So you're going to get in the middle of it?"

"Do you see another choice?"

I had another bourbon and left The Oscar. I walked what was better than two miles back to Vanderbilt, and went between the iron gates that framed the opening to campus. I edged around to the back of Kirkland Hall, found the glass door open, and walked right to where the entry to the tower staircase was.

Kirkland was the icon of Vanderbilt, the one building that every generation would describe if you asked them about Vanderbilt. Other buildings had been built, and some were iconic themselves. But it was not always so.

Kirkland stood as the central building on a 74-acre campus at the beginning of VU's history, and it housed everything--classrooms, labs, the library, and even a museum. Originally, it was just the main building. Like many campuses as they were getting started, it was iconic because it was all there was.

But there was an epic fire at the turn of the century, and the two-towered, Victorian Gothic burned for two hours, from the top downward, as frantic students carried or tossed out books and lab equipment from the lower floors. The clock in the south tower was engulfed in flames but survived just to the noon hour, struck thirty times, then fell to the rubble. Afterward, the building was rebuilt in an Italianate style with a single tower.

That's what the Kirkland Hall tower meant. It was the sort of place that enterprising students could aspire to mount, even to put Mickey hands on the clock. It was certainly, now, the kind of place a murder could take place. I just wondered if it was the kind of place my brother could murder someone in.

I pushed the doorway open. Inside there was a kind of confusion that you see when someone or some group of people has been given a series of orders, mostly conflicting. It's the sort of scene where "do this" and "do that" move in different directions at different speeds for different purposes. At the center of all the confusion was the interim Chief of VU's police department, Clint Fish. Where the former chief, a retired Military Policeman with an orderly mind and a kind spirit, would have attacked the crime scene with a plan, Clint Fish threw as much spaghetti against the wall as fast as he could. That had been his MO as a Lieutenant, and one a rung below Don Mercer, and that was his MO now, as the interim chief appointed because his father-in-law was connected.

Clint's salt and pepper hair was wet with sweat. Mercer stood off to the side, letting his interim leader screw up what was left of the crime scene.

"Metro has done everything we need done," Mercer said over the general hubbub. "All we're doing is fouling the scene if they need to come back."

"I'm in commend, Don, not you." Fish's skinny frame made the Chief badge an outsized and ridiculous statement on his chest. His shoulders stuck out on either side like hangar points that held the shirt straight. "Dust over there for prints," he yelled at the shift sergeant, Broyles. "Yes, there," he said to an inquiring look.

Mercer caught sight of me. "What are you doing over here, Jackson?"

"Trade?" Fish turned to me. "You should not be here. Your brother is the prime suspect. Get out of here this second." He was the sort of man whose voice got squeakier the louder he got. Right now, it was in Barney Fife territory.

"I'm just here to tell Mercer thanks, for not waiting for me."

Mercer rolled his eyes.

"I'm serious, Trade. If you don't leave this area immediately, I'll have you arrested."

"For what, Clint?"

"For interfering with a police investigation." His voice squeaked past the Fife register. Broyles looked at him, then at me. "The prints, Broyles?"

"Looks to me like you're the one interfering with Metro, Clint. Me? I'm just here to talk to Don."

"Talk to him outside, then." He kicked a piece of yellow tape aside. "Go ahead, Mercer. We don't need you here."

Mercer motioned to me and we went outside the entry door. "You know you shouldn't be here," he said.

"Why not? I'm not a suspect. I can't very well help my brother if I can't see the crime scene, can I?"

"If you're smart you'll let this thing take its course. You'll just muddy everything up."

"Nobody is going to look out for my brother's interests in this, Don."

"And you're not a detective. You're a guy with his own set of problems, Jackson." He gave me the look that says he's done discussing it. I've seen him give it to seniors who were full of beer and mischief.

"What's a detective anyway? Somebody who doesn't know the answer and wants to find out. Not like the detective that sees the obvious and closes the case."

"Nobody's closed the case on your brother."

Sure. That was the right answer, the legal one. But they had him with the murder weapon next to the body. They'd made their minds up. It was given to them on a silver platter. And even if Clint Fish spent a couple of days playing pretend, it wouldn't change anything Metro had decided. And you could bet they had decided Thompson Trade was made for it. And the District Attorney would take it from there.

"Right, Jackson? You know I'm right."

"Here's what I know, Donnie. It looks like a slam dunk. And things that look like a slam dunk are treated like that's what they are. If I don't get in this, Thompson's toast."

Mercer drew closer and jabbed a black finger into my chest, lightly. "Here's what I know. You better keep your nose out of this."

He turned and went back into the tower entry. I turned the other way and went outside.

***

It had been a long, confusing day. I put a dime in a pay phone and dialed a number. "Feel like a little company?"

The answer had been the one I wanted to hear.

Betty Henderson was the apartment superintendent of a complex where a Vanderbilt coed had been killed the year before. I had leaned on her for company then, and a couple of times since. We went together well without having to go together all the time.

I knocked and she answered in a tie-dyed tee shirt, one of those psychedelic patterns you used to see a few years ago, and a pair of spattered painter's pants. She held up a paintbrush.

"I'm all done. Come in, stranger."

We kissed, and then I put my arms around her, and we kissed again.

"Mmm," she said. "You come to talk or you got something else on your mind?"

"Let's see how it goes."

We made drinks and she put Smokey Robinson on the turntable. "Tears of a Clown," I said. "Haven't heard that in years."

"Just like Pagliacci did, I try to keep my sadness hid. Damn, got to love Smokey's writing." Betty was a would-be song-writer. She was probably working in the wrong town. More a Memphis girl than Nashville.

"How's your writing going?"

"Not as good as my painting. Finally got around to re-painting my kitchen." She pulled her legs up under her on the couch. "And you?"

"I have some interesting stuff on my mind."

She put her elbow on the back of the couch and faced me. "So let's hear it."

I gave her the rundown. Thompson. The whole family back story. Mickey Mouse and the clock. A regular three ring cir-cus.

"Kirkland's bells have a ring," she offered.

"Could be. Or could be Kirkland is the circus tent and we're all the three rings inside. I just don't know."

"You really think your brother didn't do it? I read stories about cokeheads doing awful things, not remembering them."

"True. But he's my brother. He deserves a chance."

I got up and flipped the album over.

"So there's one thing I don't get, Jackson. Why did he come back? To Tennessee."

"I'm afraid we didn't get to that." At least, Thompson didn't get to it.

"Why? I mean, I get that you've got unfinished business. But why not find out why he's here to begin with?"

"I don't know," I said. "Which is the way I feel about all of this so far."

The conversation stalled. I didn't have much to say that I hadn't already said. I didn't like the job Thompson basically had handed me. I didn't like the way Mercer was acting. It felt too much like I was falling into a hole and I didn't know how deep it was. Like they say, the trip down isn't bad, but the landing is a killer.

The conversation stalled too because Betty and I had unfinished business. We met when a tenant had been killed in her apartment upstairs. The flirting then was serious enough, but it didn't take off.

"So," she said.

"So." I got up and walked to the table where the bourbon was. She followed.

There was a silence between us.

It was the place we'd come to several times over the course of our friendship. We began hot, then cooled, then heated up again. But it had never really been consummated, not in the way that you'd expect. When I was ready, she wasn't. When she'd been ready, I wasn't.

Most people would have said the hell with it and gone ahead, hell for leather, and banked the experience--one night, one time. Hope the spark caught and there'd be a flame.

Or said the hell with it and given up.

We weren't most people.

I had finished my drink. The cool, moist glass felt slippery in my hand.

"When you got here, I thought you had more on your mind than talk."

"A kiss is just a kiss," I smiled.

"Don't Bogart, bud."

We were both standing by the bourbon. I reached for the bottle at the same moment she did. Or maybe she reached for my hand. I let her get there at the same time I did.

"Should I make you one?" I nodded toward her empty glass on the side table.

"And then what?" Her hand was warm against my cool, wet one.

"And then drink it. What do we usually do with bourbon?"

She took her hand off mine and put her hands on my hips, pulling close to me. I could feel her body from my thighs to my chest. Her hands went behind me, and she pulled me closer.

"I don't think I want bourbon." I could smell paint in her hair and the dried sweat on her forehead. It didn't smell bad. Not at all. "What do you want, Jackson? Bourbon?"

I could have told her that I wanted not to over-think everything. I could have added that bourbon helped me not over-think it. A psychologist will tell you that alcohol breaks down inhibitions. But what if what it breaks down is paralysis? What if the thing that makes you weak is the thing that makes you normal?

"I would like to go into your bedroom and see the secrets on your wall."

She snorted, involuntarily. "The secrets on my wall? What does that mean?"

I put both my hands in the small of her back, and she pulled me closer. It felt like the right time, the right place.

"It's a city full of secrets, Betty. I've got some. You've got some. I think my brother may have one or two."

"Are you talking about making love, or are you in Metro jail with your brother?"

"I'm talking about you and me. You're upfront with me, Betty. You always have been."

She stepped back slightly and took both my hands in hers. "And?"

"Your bedroom is where we've never been. You still have some secrets, but they will be there for me to see." I leaned down to kiss her, brushing her lips with mine. "Show me your secrets, Miss Betty. And I'll show you some of mine."

"Yes," she said. "Absolutely."

Chapter Five

IT TURNED OUT THAT Betty's secrets were safe with me.

In the morning, I let myself out while she was still sleeping. I felt light, lighter than I had when I'd walked over. The walk back home led me through campus. The brick walkways were covered in red maple leaves as the sun rose, peeking between the yellow leaves that remained on the trees. At intervals, benches were completely covered by leaves, a sure sign that no one had passed through the academic part of campus during the home football weekend.

As I got closer to Alumni Lawn, I could see the remains of the concert—beer cans smashed, cigarette packs crumpled, the detritus of three or four thousand people enjoying the music and each other. Plant Operations would attack all this, from leaves to beer cans, and in another hour there would be no sign that this was anything but a neat, orderly campus.

That's the way it goes. The kids tear it up. The adults, the ones paid minimum wage, put it back together.

I looked up to Kirkland tower. There was Mickey, his bird-flipping finger at eleven, his peace sign at seven. Yeah. Neat and orderly. Underneath the appearance, or in this case, above it, there are always signs of chaos.

I cut across West End and ducked into Krystal for a cup of coffee and a square burger, and ate my breakfast on the way to the apartment. After a quick shower and shave, and a much needed change of clothes, I was back on campus before Mickey's finger was half past.

I knew Art Blake, the Dean of Students, was always up and at 'em before making his eight a.m. appearance in the office. I banged on the door of his West Side Row apartment, and waited.

Blake is six-six, has a handlebar mustache, and could make a good living intimidating students, if that's the way he wanted to roll. Generally, though, the way he rolled was as a straight shooter. If you didn't want the truth, you steered clear of Blake. I used to work for him. He fired me because he had to. You can't have an Assistant Dean who puts his wife's lover in the hospital. Even if you sympathize.

"Well, Jackson," he said when he opened the door, "I'd have thought you'd be here before now."

"Next day isn't good enough?"

"Given the circumstances, no." He held the door open, and I went in.

Art's a bachelor and his small, four-room apartment is plenty of room for him. A kitchen and bedroom in back, a living room and office in front, the small two-story house was a mirror of the other four in the original campus plan. First residences, then offices, then turned back into duplex residences with an apartment upstairs and one downstairs, they served as prestige addresses for groups of students or, in Art's case, for the Dean of Students. Living on campus meant that he was, as I had been, usually called at all hours of day and night.

As he had been in the early morning hours when Patrick Vincent was found.

"Can't say your brother looks all that much like you."

"He's the smart one." I sat in the rocker near the television in Art's office. "At least that's what we said."

"And what were you? The stubborn one?"

I wanted to say I was the smarter one, since I wasn't in jail. But I restrained myself. "They say he did it."

"What do you want them to say? He was next to the body. He had the crowbar. You want them to say, 'well, look here, an innocent man next to a dead body.' That's not going to happen."

"Who were the other guys with Vincent that night?" I pointed at Blake. "You've got toast crumbs on your shirt."

He brushed the crumbs and sat in the banker's chair behind his desk. "Don't know yet. I've got my staff working on that." He would have, too. More than once, I'd received a call in the middle of the night from Art with the instruction to have an answer by eight. "Ten to one they're engineers, though." He resumed his assault on the toast.

I had to agree, if history was any guide. If there was a prank that required more than a passing knowledge with mechanics or thermodynamics, an engineering student was likely at the heart of it. "Think that Axel Ronningen knows anything about it?"

Blake stopped mid-bite and looked over his toast at me. "Professor Ronningen still isn't over the last time you and he crossed paths." He finished the bite and chewed, talking at the same time. "So if you're thinking you'll just have a chat with him, my advice would be to abandon that idea."

Axel Ronningen was an intense teacher, a brilliant researcher, a pied piper to a certain kind of student, and one of the most insufferable shits I've ever met. "He's at the bottom of every complicated prank on this campus, one way or another."

"He also threatened to ask for a restraining order the last time you spoke. You remember that, right?"

I motioned toward his chest. "Crumbs." He mumbled something and brushed them onto the plate. "Yes, I remember. But that was in another country. And besides the wench is dead."

"Is that a literary quote?"

"At the very least, it's an allusion. My point is that Ronningen may have information about the other pranksters."

"If he does or if he doesn't," Blake said, getting up with the plate and walking toward the kitchen, "leave it to my staff to sort it out. If there's anything there, we'll give it to the police." He said over his shoulder, "And they'll do what they will. I don't anticipate a reason to share it with you, Jackson."

"No?"

"No," he said, as he entered the kitchen. "You'll be wise to stay out of this. You're too close to it. And you'll probably screw it up because you are."

That's right, I thought. I am absolutely too close to it. And I may well screw it up. And I damn well will talk to Axel Ronningen. "Thanks, Art," I called as I walked to his front door. "I'll let myself out."

I heard him as I exited through the screen door. "You stay out of it, Jackson."

***

I walked over to Rand Hall to use a campus telephone. It was the one place I was sure would have a campus directory. I called the Engineering School and did my best undergraduate imitation, asking for Ronnigen's office hours. He wouldn't be in until 3:00. I could wait until then.

Instead of an early lunch, I decided to visit West End Methodist and went around to the back, where the gym is. I've made a habit in the last year or two of coming here to watch guys play basketball, although I don't play anymore. I'm a step too slow for the younger crowd and can't jump, so there's no use in even trying. But there's a pace to the game played pickup style that shows there's still grace and beauty in the world.

The game I play these days doesn't have grace and beauty in it. My game is to keep my mind from tearing itself out of my head. Most days, I can keep the level about right, but it takes a knowledge of just how far I can go before I swing the other direction. Some days, it's just the basketball that takes my mind off it.

An older guy I know used to come in here when I was an undergraduate. He sat in the corner, all coat and cigarette smoke smell. Between games one day I sat near him, and he said he came in to pray, but he came to the gym because he felt too dirty for the sanctuary.

"What do you pray for?" I asked him.

"I pray somebody will find me and take me home."

I thought it was a creepy answer, and I checked myself back into the game. Then one day he didn't show up. I wondered if he got his prayer answered.

I wonder what my prayer is.

A couple of hours later I took the long way to Hannigan's, greeted Mrs. Hannigan at the bar and went back to a back table with a bourbon and a Tennessean. The mayor, as usual, was hogging the front page with a half page photo. Honest to God, either the guy has an ace PR operation or the editor owes him big. The inside was a muddle of national news that didn't matter and state news that did, but didn't get much coverage. And the sports page was all about UT. They had a new coach, Johnny Majors, and they were .500 for the season, but the rest of the schedule, until they got to Vandy in the final game, looked like a rough slog.

I had a second bourbon and a cheeseburger before I decided it was time to take the measure of Axel Ronningen.

His office was on the third floor of Olin Hall. What I remembered was that he was a mechanical engineer, specializing in materials. He had been a big deal because of his work on composites, discovering something about carbon fiber that had made him a boatload of money. He had a horrible personality before the money. Now, it was worse.

The door was partially open and I pushed it the rest of the way. Ronnngen sat hunched over his desk, squinting at a mechanical drawing. His red hair circled a bald spot on the back of his head that would get bigger over time. Now it looked like it had a fighting chance. Freckles still dotted his face and hands, and I knew that, when he looked up, there would be a cracked tooth on his lower bite.

After about thirty seconds, he looked up. "Yes?" You could see the recognition spread from his eyes to his brain as he slowly sorted where he'd seen my face before. "What do you want?" Heavy on the "you."

"You remember me, then?" He remembered me because I had questioned him until he gave up the students who'd managed to get a VW Beetle on top of the flat roof at the entrance of Branscomb Quadrangle. I don't think he liked that I'd tricked the first name out of him with the oldest trick in the book—announcing that I was going after the brightest kid in the class as the ringleader.

"I remember. I don't remember your name. I also remember that the Dean fired you." He pushed back from the desk and stood up. "Are you allowed to be on campus? I seem to remember that you nearly killed someone."

"He lived. And I am allowed on campus."

"Then get out of my office. I don't want you here."

"How many of your gang put Mickey on Kirkland?"

He moved toward his telephone. "Why do you care? You don't work here anymore."

"Must be some of yours. It's not as mechanically challenging as getting a car on top of a roof, but it's much more derring-do. They'd have to know how to design the dimensions of the mouse, get the ratios just right, then have an idea how to scale safely and attach the stuff. Sounds like a gear head to me."

He put his hand on the telephone. "Just because it's inventive doesn't necessarily mean that an engineer was involved." He looked over my shoulder, but I could have told him that none of his colleagues were on the floor. "Students climb things all the time."

"I just need a name, Axel."

He picked up the phone. "I'm going to call Campus Security. I do not want you in my office."

I don't know what he expected, but he froze as I slammed his door shut, shot across the room, and grabbed the telephone out of his hand. "Stop," he yelled. "You're hurting my arm."

"Then tell me what I want to know, Axel." I had his wrist in my hand. I wasn't twisting it. But I was pretty close to it. "Give me a name, and I'll leave you alone." I twisted a little. "Who was Patrick Vincent's collaborator on this?"

"Let. Me. Go." He said it deliberately. "I will have you arrested."

"No," I said, "you won't. You're going to give me a name. And you will not want to talk to the police about it because they will want to know why you didn't give the name to them in the first place." It was a bluff, but it sounded like it made sense.

I let the wrist untwist but I kept it in my hand.

"What do you say, Axel? Do you want to play ball?" I twisted hard enough to make it hurt.

"Howell," he said. "Howell Parsons is Patrick's best friend."

I let his arm loose. He pulled away.

"Thanks, Axel. You just saved yourself some misery."

He rubbed his arm. "Just get out of here."

Chapter Six

HOWELL PARSONS WASN'T THAT hard to find.

I called my friend Wendy Williamson, still Assistant Dean of Students just as she was when I worked with her, and asked her to pull up the master list of residents. She did, but with a warning. "Art already knows Parsons was in on the prank. If you go over there, you might trip over him."

Parsons lived in Barnard Hall, which could best be described as scruffy. Why a senior, who could have lived in Carmichael Towers or over in one of the new apartments on the south side of campus, would have lived in arguably the worst location at VU was a head scratcher. Shotgun hallways, gang showers, and a level of housekeeping that left something to be desired—all this was why Barnard was home to unlucky sophomores, guys who didn't have frat brother upperclassmen who could let them coattail into a suite somewhere else.

Parsons' room was on second floor, and as soon as I was on the hallway I remembered why I was more than ready, when the time came, to abandon dorm life altogether. With the smell of stale cigarette smoke, stale beer, and overripe laundry, I didn't see how anyone could study, sleep, or conduct life's business there. Unless they just got used to it.

Parsons' room was 217. I knocked and went in when I heard a sleepy "Yeah" invite me in.

Stretched out on the bed was a young man about 5-9, with a shock of curly brown hair that was long on the sides and back, and receding already in front. He had the kind of large straight teeth that told me they had been harnessed back into order by a regimen of expensive orthadontics. He wore only a white pair of boxer shorts. Indeed, that was the general look he had about him. A prep school boy with all the advantages, slumming it for a few years, before graduating and going back to the country club set.

"Who're you?" Above the bed was a full-size rebel flag, with little Gray Confederate army hats, the kind you'd get at a novelty shop, hanging on the two nails at each top corner.

I pointed at the flag. "You a Civil War buff?"

"You mean the War of Northern Aggression? Yeah." He sat up on the bed. "Who're you?"

"I'm a friend of Professor Roningen. He told me you were part of the crew that put Mickey on the tower." I smiled. "Nice work."

"Ha. Old Axel figured it out." He pushed hair behind his ears. "Unless it's all over campus because of Dean Blake."

"Blake knows, then?"

"By now he does. Damn Head Resident came down here asking a bunch of questions. But he already knew. If you knew Patrick was in it, you had to know I was along for the ride." He got up and pulled on a Rolling Stones t-shirt. "Who're you again?"

"My name is Jackson." I didn't figure putting the Trade on it would help. If he knew Thompson's name, it really wouldn't help. "I'm a graduate student in education, over at Peabody," I lied. "I'm doing research on college pranks, and lo and behold, one arrives right on schedule."

He grinned. "No shit? You're writing about stuff like that?" He pulled some clothes off the wooden desk chair. "Please sit down, Mr. Jackson. What's your first name?"

"Jack." I shortened it. People who didn't know me sometimes called me that, thinking I must go by it.

"Well, nice to meet you Jack Jackson. I'm Howell Parsons. But you already knew that."

I sat. "It's a shame about your friend. Patrick, isn't it?"

The smile left his face. "That is a sad thing, man. Patrick was amazing."

"The prank was his idea?"

"We all had the idea, but Patrick was the one who put it all together. We thought it would be such a groove if Mickey was overseeing the whole concert crowd. Kind of a gigantic fuck you to the University, you know?"

"I get it." Parsons seemed to want to talk, so I let him. "How did you put it all together?"

"Like I say, it was Patrick who was the real mastermind. I lifted some surveying tools from Olin, and used them to develop the dimensions of Mickey so he would fit perfectly."

"Amazing. How?"

"Well, the one thing you know is the dimensions of a brick. With binoculars, you just count. Then you use geometry to calculate the size. It's simple, really." He seemed to deflate. "God, Patrick was absolutely the best."

"He's the one who went up?"

"He's the one who jimmied the locks. He's the one who went over the side. I thought that was the craziest thing. I mean, repelling down the side. Carrying all the parts of Mickey. Carrying the staple gun. I mean, a hundred things could have gone wrong. But with Patrick, I mean, he was charismatic. He could convince you that you could do anything." He realized, I think, he was talking faster and faster. He stopped for a second, took a deep breath. "Damn shame, man."

"Who had the other side of the rope?" I asked. "Or did he anchor it and do it alone?"

He hesitated. Maybe he hadn't given up the third accomplice to Blake. "Uh, I don't know if I should tell you that."

"I understand," I said. "But I'm just researching. I'm not going to get him in trouble."

He looked like me might tell me, but he shook his head.

"And you?" Since he was already identified, he could tell me that, at least.

"Oh, hell, man, I was the lookout. I never had to leave the door where you get into the tower."

"And nobody came by while you were there?"

"Quiet as a mouse," he said, then laughed. "As a Mickey Mouse."

I wondered if he'd seen Thompson, earlier or at all. "So it's just weird that this guy shows up later, right?" "

A male voice boomed, "Perhaps you'd like to make yourself presentable, Howell. There is about to be a lady present."

I turned to see a tanned, silver haired man in the doorway. If he got a single word description, it would be impeccable. He wore a navy suit that fit him exactly, a blindingly white shirt with a rich red tie. I could see a glimpse of a gold watch on his wrist. He was tailored in the way that you think bankers and lawyers will be, but seldom are.

"Hey, Mr. Pettibone. How's it going? You bring Grace along?"

The impeccable man entered as Parsons was pulling on a pair of jeans. "Don't you ever clean this pig sty? I have no idea how you live here." He was holding a book, and he handed it to Parsons with his fingertips, as if some of the disarray might infect him. "This is the book I told you about, the one written by Fitzhugh Lee." He seemed to notice me for the first time. "The memoir that General Lee did not write," he said, then turning back to Parsons, "I think you'll find it highly edifying." He turned back to me, but said still speaking to Parsons, "General Lee is presented as he was, as the truest exemplar of a gentleman and patriot."

I might have added, "But he lost, right?" I didn't.

"Thanks, Mr. Pettibone. I'll get right to it." He looked around the impeccable one. "Where is Grace, anyway?"

"She stopped in the doorway of one of your neighbors. Someone she has a class with, I believe." He still looked at me—pony-tailed, bearded, and too old to live in Barnard Hall. "I am William Pettibone," he said, extending his hand.

"Jack Jackson," I replied, keeping up the fiction. "You're a Civil War buff too, I see."

He looked at me as if he were trying to decide if I was friend or foe. He decided on somewhere in the middle. "I am a Southerner, Mr. Jackson. A true Southerner. I believe that the war of the last century has been consistently misrepresented, and that the South has been made the villain in a historical set piece."

I must have looked a little confused, because Parsons jumped in. "Mr. Pettibone is, among other things, head of The Pettibone Institute. It's a think tank for the South, right Mr. P?"

"The Institute funds activity that promotes the history and culture of the South. In fact, I'm here for Professor Elsey's lecture on the Southern Agrarians tonight. The Institute is sponsoring the lecture series. It's entitled, "The South as a Counterbalance to Destruction.""

"Wow." It's all I could think of to say.

"The South," he continued, warming to his subject, "has always represented the highest values in the nation. Morality. Chivalry. A culture both gentle and rich."

"I guess I wasn't taught that in school," I said.

"Exactly," he said. "Exactly, and more's the pity. The false narrative that the North had to take action against a slave-holding south to eradicate slavery runs counter to fact." He looked up as a leggy woman with shoulder-length hair entered.

"That's why The Institute is producing the biggest exhibition of all time, downtown at the Arena. We call it South Rising, and it will feature everything from Southern music to

Southern politics to Southern economics. All things Southern, in their natural states."

"Daddy, I don't know who you're preaching to, but it can't be all that comfortable for him. Besides, you might want to get a few sponsors and exhibitors first." She was tall and slim, and she wore jeans with an embroidered wool poncho finished with fringe. She smiled a brilliant smile, the sort that occurs in nature only once in a great while, and always without the benefit of an orthodontist's skill. "I'm Grace."

Yes, she was. And elegance, style, and beauty too. If she had wisdom covered, I'd be impressed. But I was pretty impressed anyway.

"This is Jack, Grace. He's doing research on college pranks for his master's thesis at Peabody."

"Pleased," she said. "I hope the rest of your subjects don't have the tragedy of ours."

"Yes, yes," said Pettibone, "Patrick. Such a tragedy. Do we know if his parents have arrived?"

"They're not coming," said Parsons. "They're having his body sent home."

"I would have come, if I were them," said Pettibone, "if only to lay eyes on the bastard that killed him."

"Daddy," Grace said. Her tone and look indicated that it was rude to say such a thing in front of a stranger. If she'd only known.

"I was just saying to Howell as you got here, that it's weird this guy just shows up out of nowhere, right? I mean, Howell was on lookout for, how long?" I turned finally to face Howell.

"Like, an hour? Something like that."

"And here's a stranger comes in, takes the crowbar away from him, then stays for the night? How weird is that?"

There was a long silence as we all thought. At least I believe they were thinking. Pettibone could have been thinking about his haberdasher. Grace could have been thinking about a nail appointment. Howell could have been wondering when about the last time he did laundry. But probably not.

But it turned out to be Howell who was thinking. "You know," he said, "I'm not sure Patrick had a crowbar with him."

All three of us were in unison, then Babel broke out.

"No," he said, "it's not like that. Patrick had brought a crowbar during our reconnaissance. We didn't know if we would need it for anything. There's a whole stash of tools there. He was going back to get all that. That's why he went back. The flashlight had his name on it, for God's sake. And there had been a crowbar in all that. I'm just not sure he had it with him."

"Well, that's simple," said Grace. "Somehow this addict got in after, and found the crowbar. Maybe Patrick startled him or something."

"Whatever the case," said Pettibone, "the wretch has been caught red-handed." He crinkled his brow and looked at me. "Vermin, sir, pollute the land."

Vermin, sir, which makes me the rat you don't want to mess with.

Chapter Seven

People deal with death in interesting ways. In combat, you could go weeks without anything happening. You might have some sort of enemy engagement, a kind of hit and run with VC, say, and somebody would get wounded. We'd make the Purple Heart jokes, same as when somebody got a bad rash and had to be medevacked. Then someone in the unit would get it bad. Maybe it'd be the sort of thing where they were still talking and breathing, or maybe they'd already stopped talking and breathing.

There was a hole there. And nothing filled it.

Everybody dealt with it his own way. One guy would get off to himself, be alone for a while, and yeah, maybe cry a little. Another guy would get stoned and get lost from it all. Other guys would sit around and tell stories about the missing guy, laugh a little, be quiet for a while, kind of like a wake. And still others would raise hell like the party is just getting started. Some guys, and this got to be me after a while, just went on with the business of war.

It was clear that Patrick Vincent was the glue that held the prankster party together. I hadn't seen Raines Durst yet, but it was clear enough that Howell Parsons was the guy who would talk, laugh a little, and do the wake thing. Durst's girlfriend, Grace, was just going on with business, like her father. It sounded like he had a lot of business to get to.

The longer I go, though, the more I see those dead soldiers. Richardson, who caught it on a night patrol my first month in, the first guy I saw go down. Slater, who we lost in the middle of the hottest August I ever experienced. Bone Pile, who detonated a toe popper, lost his leg, then bled out before he got to a surgeon. And Elias Miller, who got shot by an MP during R and R in Vung Tau, victim of a misunderstanding, a mistake.

Maybe they were all misunderstandings. Maybe it was all a mistake.

More and more often, I see the mortars coming in. I hear the confident chatter of the AKs. I imagine I hear voices in Vietnamese, whispering, all around me. I taste screams in my mouth, and hear the rapid lop-lop of a Huey Slick, and its turbine slowdown, whining like the last gasp of daylight. And then the total sense experience of dark. And danger. More and more, I sleep to this. Or rather, I don't sleep at all because of this.

I knew it was going to be a bad night. It's one thing when you go to bed and wake up with the dreams. It is another entirely when the dreams start while you're awake.

I spent the night walking up West End, hitting every bar for a drink. It was a Monday night, and nobody but the regulars were in any of them. I hit the Hideaway on Elliston, then Hannigan's, before moving out to West End for Top Hat, The High Life. I finally ended up at Linda's, which is not a place I go. It's too rowdy and rough on the weekends, and too much like a cat's litter box during the week.

It was midnight when I got there and Bobby was at the tap. He used to be at High Life but he's regressed. We go back a few years, back to when he served an underage freshman a few beers before the kid wrapped his father's Oldsmobile around a light pole. Nobody was hurt, but the car was totaled and the father wanted Bobby to pay. But because the father wanted his boy to be a doctor, and because I explained how hard that would be if there was a DUI in his discipline file, the father backed off. Good thing too; medical schools don't look in our discipline files.

Since then Bobby and I have a relationship that is different from bartender to drinker, although he thinks more of it than I do. He's called me a couple of times for advice on handling the student who mistakenly comes into Linda's instead of High Life next door, although half the time he just calls me Slick because he can't remember my name. He needs advice because, by the time they get that far down West End, they're already looking for trouble, whether they know it or not.

It was a slow night, but that just meant Bobby had plenty of time to talk. And he already knew about my brother. He said he was sorry about that.

"Thanks, Bobby."

"Tough spot to be in, for sure." He pushed a draft toward me with a bourbon. "Got a lawyer yet?"

There's a good question. "Public defender, I suppose." I put the bourbon down fast, and took a sip of the draft. "If he's even been arraigned. They are supposed to do it in forty-eight hours, but the district attorney can wait on all kinds of things."

"You been to see him, right? Shame to be in jail with no kin around."

"I saw him yesterday. I spent today trying to figure out who else was in that tower."

He refilled the bourbon glass, even though I said no. I said no with my hands and my head, so I guess I should have said something. "I saw the dead boy's picture in the paper. He used to come in here now and then."

You could have knocked me over with a feather. "Really? He doesn't seem the type."

"Oh yeah, him and several of his buddies."

"No offense, Bobby, but what the hell are engineering students doing in Linda's? Used to be, you're calling me because undergrads are here by mistake."

"It don't offend me none, Slick." He refilled a plastic cup with a draft for a dodgy looking character with a John Deere cap and carpenter overalls. "There's a motorcycle club . . ."

"You mean a gang?"

He shook his head, but only to the right, toward the John Deer cap. "Not a gang. They're a group that likes to ride. A motorcycle club."

"And Patrick Vincent was part of this . . . club?" That was hard to square with what I knew.

"Naw, him and his friends didn't ride. They just palled around, I guess you could say."

"I don't get it, Bobby. What was the connection?"

"They call themselves the Sons of Shiloh. They kinda want to refight the Civil War. Well," he said, fidgeting with the tap, just below the Budweiser knob, "Not exactly refight it. They mostly want to shout 'the south is gonna rise again,' and play Sweet Home Alabama on the jukebox." He looked to make sure the John Deere hat had left. "Actually, they're pretty nice guys, for the most part."

"Any people besides the boys hang out with them?"

"You know how it is, Jackson. Any Thursday, Friday, or Saturday, it's damn near full in here. I can't keep up with who's who."

"But you noticed the boys. Who else stood out?"

"Actually the reason you notice the guys is the girl they were with."

"Tall girl?" I could imagine.

"Tall and fine," said Bobby. "Real looker. She stands out in the crowd."

I described Grace Pettibone's impeccable father. "Ever see him?"

"That doesn't ring a bell, Slick. I don't remember the last time I saw a suit in here."

I spent the better part of the rest of an hour listening to Bobby tell me the ins and outs of Linda's, of all its regulars and half its sometimes denizens. The man in the John Deere cap left by the front door halfway through the tale, and the other, few and sad drinkers were pretty much ready to leave by 1 a.m. I certainly was.

I made my way back down West End, the path in reverse. There was something in the notion of a motorcycle club that attracted Patrick, Howell, and Raines that make no sense at all. And yet, Howell had been visited by Grace and her father, who dropped off the biography of Lee.

I knew one Civil War historian, at least one who was an amateur enthusiast, and I knew he was probably up.

Art Blake was up, and he was polishing off a very good bottle of Maker's Mark when I arrived.

"You have been busy," he said, pouring me two fingers and pointing one at me. "And I'm not sure I approve."

"What can you tell me about the Battle of Shiloh, Art? I remember that it's important somehow. I just don't remember why."

Art got the look he only got when the bourbon was excellent or when someone asked him about history. And just now he had both. "Shiloh was important." He took a sip and savored it. "Grant's army had taken Kentucky and they moved south to consolidate Tennessee. But Johnston's Confederate force attacked at Pittsburgh Landing."

"That's Shiloh?"

"Exactly. The Confederates drove the Union army to the Tennessee River, and there was considerable carnage. General Johnston was killed, and General Beauregard took command. His forces were exhausted and night was coming, so he pulled off the assault, intending to finish Grant off the following morning."

"I take it that didn't happen."

"You take it correctly. Buell's army arrived to reinforce Grant, and the next morning the Union forces counterattacked, and with superior numbers and firepower they held the Confederates off until they boys in Gray retreated. Grant declined to pursue them further, but the Union forces won the day. Or rather, the two days. At the time it was the bloodiest battle in American history."

"Why would a bunch of bikers call themselves Sons of Shiloh? If it's a loss."

Blake sat with his eyes closed and his nose just over the glass. "If they're Tennessee boys, and they must be, Shiloh was where the battle for Tennessee was lost. Everybody talks about the eastern theater of the war, the battles at Antitam and Bull Run and Gettysburg. But the western theater pretty much collapsed after Shiloh."

"So you name yourself after that loss?"

"Like many things in the South's past, it's not the facts that matter but the myths. You had the death of General Johnston, whom Jefferson Davis believed was their finest general. Yes, better than the sainted Lee. There was General Beauregard, also legendary. And there is the image of Grant on the other side, the hated, drunken, miserable general who couldn't get anything right, and yet won. And Sherman was there too, on the Union side, and you know how the South feels about him. If you ask me, to be a Son of Shiloh would pretty much encapsulate what it means to be a Southerner, if you think the South is going to rise again."

"Embittered, but with a story about how you're better?'

"Yeah. That's about it."

By the time we finished the Maker's Mark, it was 3 a.m. I went home and stripped off my clothes, opening the window so the October night air could get in and freshen the place. Earlier I had been afraid that my past would come back to visit me in the night. But thoughts of Shiloh must have put me in the middle of a different war, one that was just as cruel but one that was not mine. Or the bourbon had driven my fears away. Or both. I fell asleep with the air, almost liquid, like water washing over me, and I slept until the morning air, warmed by sunlight, resurrected me, and I awoke.

Chapter Eight

THERE ARE DAYS I don't love Nashville. The days when you end up dealing with the faux hipsterism of the country music business, or at least the kind of hangers-on it attracts. The days when, since I'm located right by Vanderbilt, you deal with entitled preppiness masquerading as working class. Or the days when, as an unemployed veteran of an unpopular war, you get tired of the limitless gall of the employed, of those who weren't there, and of anyone who crosses my path. Because when I have a bad day, I don't go light.

But on the bright sunny days when I do love Nashville, there's no place better. The temperature is just right, not the cold of the North or the heat of the Deep South. The sky, with apologies to Carolina blue, is the perfect shade. The food is comfortable and the tea is sweet and there's plenty of it. And the people, on those days, have pep in their step and can put it in yours too.

So it was that I awoke on Tuesday, bright and sunny as the day in front of me. How that happened, I have no idea. In anticipation of a bad night's sleep, I had drunk enough to knock me cold into the weekend. But I had a good night's sleep, a clear head, and a task in mind.

What was the connection between the merry pranksters of Kirkland tower and the motorcycle club, Sons of Shiloh? And I thought of the one motorcycle-riding friend I had. Don Mercer.

I walked over to 25th and Garland, the corner where the VUPD was located. Inside, thankfully, the interim chief was involved on the phone with a parent who had demanded to speak with the man in charge about a spate of parking tickets. My guess was that Clint Fish was going to find being Chief, even for a little while, to be a lot less glamorous than he thought.

Mercer was sitting inside his cramped office, clouded in cigarette smoke and scowling at his typewriter. Clearly, he had not awakened on the same side of the bed as I had.

"As you were, Lieutenant," I said.

He jumped. "Jesus, Jackson. At least make a little noise."

"Sorry. Thought you guys always had your head on a swivel."

"Supposed to be peaceful in here."

"Yeah, you looked really peaceful." I motioned toward the typewriter. "Tough report to fill out?"

He leaned back and scratched his back against the chair, not so much like a cat as like a bear. It didn't give him relief apparently, because he did it again before answering.

"It's not a report. You know the student who does Sunday dispatch for us?"

"Are you kidding? Everybody who's been through here knows him." He was a born-for-the-first-time cop, starting with student patrol all the way up to Sunday dispatch. He all but saluted Mercer, which drove Don crazy.

"Well, he's asked me for a letter of recommendation. I really want him to get the job."

"Check that. You really want him to leave his current job."

"Right. But the problem is, I really can't think of much to say about him that's positive. I could say he's a pain in the ass."

"Determined and persistent."

"Sure. I could say he drives everybody crazy quoting procedure. Which by the way, since he's never been in the field, he really has no clue."

"A student of procedure, with a gift for memory that belies his lack of field experience."

Mercer clinched his jaw, then laughed. "You're right. Let me scribble some of this down."

"He's someone whose absence will be noted by all."

"Hey, that's pretty good." He wrote for a few moments more, tossed the pen down in triumph, and leaned back with his hands behind his head. "Well done. Well, at least done." He leaned over to crack the window and let some smoke escape. "Seen your brother?"

"No. But I've been nosing around a little."

"I wish you wouldn't do that. Clint will have a fit. Hell, he's already had one. And Blake won't be pleased with you either."

"My brother is in jail, Don. I can't afford a lawyer for him. He can't afford a lawyer. About all I can do is ask around. It's what I do."

"You're going to end up on the wrong side of Metro before this is over with." He shut the window again. "It's just letting heat in. Look, Jackson, let the machinery take care of this."

I knew that the machinery had all it needed. "That's not why I came in, Donnie. What do you know about motorcycle clubs?"

"I know they're usually white and don't let people my color in. Why?"

"Do you know the ones around here? The ones in middle Tennessee?"

"Sure. There's a bunch. Or are you talking about the one percenters?"

"I don't know. What's a one percenter?"

He lit another cigarette and passed the pack to me. "The American Motorcycle Association says that ninety-nine percent of riders are law-abiding citizens. There are one percenter clubs. They're not law-abiding."

"Sons of Shiloh?"

"Local boys. I think it may have started up in Clarksville, but it's a Nashville bunch for sure. There might be a few of them that harbor one percent aspirations, but they mostly ride and drink and raise hell on the weekends." He cracked the window again. "Damn ventilation in this house. How come you're asking about them?"

"The Kirkland burglars drink with them sometimes at Linda's."

He whistled. "Really? Those guys are bikers?"

"No, I don't think they have a motorcycle among them. But they drink with them."

"In the cop trade, we have a term for that."

"Yeah? What is it?"

"A fascinating but completely irrelevant fact."

I blew cigarette smoke in his direction. "I'll see you later, Lieutenant."

"Here's another one for free. You will discover that Vanderbilt students also sometimes eat in restaurants with aspiring country music stars. Excuse me, I should have said, where aspiring country music stars are also eating."

I got up. "Later, Donnie."

I left just as he was telling me that students could also be found in the same lines at banks with grandmothers who had German last names. He was choking with laughter. On cigarette smoke.

***

When I was a freshman, an older one at 20 with a tour in combat, I had to take a couple of English courses. Everybody did. I lucked out by getting not one of the graduate assistants, but a young Assistant Professor named Bruno Prince. Besides being a kind man to a clueless freshman, he was invariably interesting, especially about his field of research, Southern Literature.

He had come to Vanderbilt, and Vanderbilt was interested in him, because of that passion. Vanderbilt was the origin point for the great group of Fugitive writers--Ransom, Tate, Warren, and the like. Prince was interested in later writers, but the marriage had taken.

I found his office door in Vanderbilt Hall open, and Bruno was riffling through his filing cabinet with uncharacteristic fury.

"Anything I can help with?"

His tie was loosened, and he had rolled his sleeves up. His light brown hair looked like he had run his hands roughly through it, back and forth, and it was lying on his head in a way that a comb could not have intended. "I'm just. . .", and then he looked up. "Jackson Trade. Come in, sir. Please, come in."

We shook hands and he pulled his desk chair around to the front of the desk, facing me. "You've lost something?" I tried to look helpful.

"No. Well, yes. I am presenting at the Modern Language Association meeting in December, and I wanted to reference some notes I made last year when I spoke at Tulane. The file folder is not where I knew it to be. And I am searching. But no. Enough." He gave a small smile, the kind that signals kinship. "Is it true what I heard? That your brother is in jail over this student death?"

"I'm afraid so, Dr. Prince."

"You're not a student. Call me Bruno." He looked through thick glasses. "I'm so sorry. I wish I could do something to help."

"Actually, you may be able to help me, in a way."

"Tell me how and I will do my very best."

"You're an expert on the South."

He held up both hands and shook them. "Not so much. I have a bit of familiarity with Walker Percy, and a passing bit with Faulkner, but the South escapes me as much as it escapes everyone else."

"But you have some knowledge, at least, of what makes the South tick. About why people want, as they say, for the South to rise again."

"I think that phrase is a little tired, if you want to know the truth. But it stands for something that's real, even if unacknowledged."

"That something was lost?"

He put the file folder he was holding onto the desk, where there were many such folders. Some held class notes, and others, doubtless, the notes for articles he intended to write. He took a deep breath and looked past me, out the window.

"I have a colleague at another university who calls it The Southern Rage to Explain," he laughed. "But it's real, this feeling that something was lost. Something valuable. Something priceless, really. Ground down in the blood of battle and then squeezed dry by the post-war years, in the interest of making the country homogeneous."

"The Confederacy as a noble lost cause."

"Oh sure, there's that. Lee as a saint. Stonewall Jackson as some kind of working man's version of Lee. Only in the South have towns put every dead general and lots of dead colonels on a bronze horse in the town square." His eyes returned to me, intense. "I don't really mean that, though. What I mean is the idea of a superior culture, the gentry, even in an odd way, the royalty that the United States never had, except in the South. Washington. Jefferson. Even in his roughhewn way Andrew Jackson."

"If it was so superior, why is it gone? Why did it lose?"

His eyes returned to their usual, less intense and happier state. "Well, there you go, Jackson. Many a Southern night on a wood slat porch has been devoted to analyzing just that."

"And are there answers?"

"As many answers as the minds that debate it. But they all have one thing in common."

"Yes?"

"The Yankee devil who's not worth the spit of a Southerner." He stood up and looked around his disheveled office. "I'm sorry. What a mess this is." Then, as if a thought had suddenly leapt into his head, he said, "Why on earth do you want to know about the South." He chuckled. "What's that great line in Absalom, Absalom? "Tell about the South. Why do they live there? Why do they live at all?"

"As I recall, that novel ends badly for just about everyone."

"Not an untrue statement, although you could say that, in a way, those aren't really characters. They are constructs to explain a region that can't stop investing in itself, in what its history really means. But why are you asking now?"

"The Kirkland pranksters believe in all this Rise Again stuff, I think. I don't know what it means."

"It means they're like half of the student body and three-quarters of Nashville."

"As a friend of mine says, a fascinating but irrelevant fact?"

"Most likely. But if I were you, if you really want to understand, I'd go to the lecture tonight. The one sponsored by Pettibone Institute. If half the South's job is to awake from its history, the other half of the job is to stay sound asleep in it. I expect you'll hear the sleepy part tonight." He resumed his search for the missing folder. "Being so far out is probably why the Institute one step ahead of the bill collector."

"Aren't all small nonprofits?"

"True. But being far out doesn't help."

***

The Pettibone Institute had managed to book the second-floor room in Alumni Hall because Grace Pettibone was an officer in her sorority and the sorority was officially sponsoring the lecture. There was a decent turnout for a Monday night, and the room was nearly full. Gray haired professorial types sat interspersed with polo shirt and khaki'ed fraternity types and sorority types in dresses and espadrilles. There were a few McGill Hall types--what the rest of campus would call freaks--lounging near the back. Toward the front I saw Grace and her father.

The speaker was Dr. Lawrence Elsey, once a Vanderbilt professor but now on the faculty at LSU. He was a historian, but he had made his reputation being a gadfly on the subject of the Civil War. If there was a way for him to be provocative, he would find it. That was the rumor. I suspected the crowd tonight was there largely because word of mouth promised a show. Or maybe because there was a reception after.

Elsey certainly appeared ready to perform. He had on a tan pincord suit, penny loafers, and a blue paisley bow tie. He was a short man, mostly round, topped by short dark hair parted in the middle. He wore glasses that were perfectly round and wire-rimmed. He resembled a cantaloupe on sticks. I suspected a reedy, nasal voice.

Pettibone introduced him as the nation's leading voice on the nineteenth century South and a truth-teller like no other. When the applause died down, I could not have been more shocked by what I heard.

Instead of a nasally, sallow cantaloupe, Elsey transformed before us into an animated, rich baritone fruit of a different color.

He had a story to tell. That's about the best I can say.

His story was about a nation within a nation. The nation was agrarian and lived modestly within its means. But it was assailed by another part of the nation, determined to gut the

South, to live off the South's largesse, and to make the South its slave.

In his telling, the South did not want slavery, but had slavery foisted on it from the beginning. But the Civil War was not fought over slavery. Instead, in his telling, it was fought over whether states had the sovereign right to say they'd had enough. In his telling, the Constitution was a contract that could be broken.

His rich voice went through peaks and valleys, telling his story first as epic, then as tragedy, as the South was defeated, the slaves were freed, and families were ruined. "Ladies and gentlemen," he intoned, head shaking slowly in sadness, "even through all this, there was something different, something valiant, something intangible and incomprehensible about the South. And the North knew it. And the North decided that it too, whatever it was, must be destroyed."

And then in his telling, the weapon became education. "The South lost control of the education of its young people. The school books all came from the North, and told the North's story. It is said that history is the tale told by the winners. That is certainly true, but in the case of the American South, its story was to be totally eradicated, so that no state and no region, ever again, should rise up to take a stand."

The room was still. Even the McGillites in the back were listening.

"This struggle, this noble endeavor, was to beat back industrialization, to quiet the ever-striving of what is called progress, but which is really only the immoral and ravenous thirst of the craven god, the god who cannot speak but can only devour. It is all or nothing for this god, and the South stood in the way. And so, when the South was defeated, this god decided the South must also be destroyed.

"But in pockets throughout the South, and in the minds of all true Southerners," he concluded, "there burns this white-hot knowledge. That the South is true. The South is right. And that the South will rise again." He raised up his right hand in benediction. "To live and die in Dixie."

The crowd applauded politely, except for a few scattered here and there who stood and clapped wildly. One McGillite stood in the back but not to applaud. He shook his head and walked out.

The reception afterward was across the hall, and most of the attendees stayed, the students for the food and drink, the others for chit chat. I took my bourbon and stood near Pettibone and Elsey. A third man, not nearly as round as Elsey or as impeccable as Pettibone, was engaged in conversation with them. He had the skin of someone who worked with his hands for a living, as well as the brawn, but he had the voice I'd expected of Elsey, and his words came out in a thin, almost whining tone.

"Mr. Hanna works for me, Dr. Elsey," said Pettibone. "So I'll take responsibility. I'm sure he doesn't really mean that."

"The hell I don't." Rodney Hanna's thin whine broke above the general murmur in the room, and everyone briefly stopped talking. When he said no more, the crowd returned to its chatter.

"It would not have been that easy," said Elsey. "And I don't believe it was really possible, except in a metaphorical sense, to reignite the conflict."

Hanna tapped his foot in front of him and gnawed at a piece of Melba toast. "But if you say," he began, and stopped, aware that I was listening. He shot me a look. "Can I help you?"

Pettibone composed his face into a friendly smile. "It's Mr. Jackson, isn't it? I'm so glad you could come tonight. Dr. Elsey," he said, "this is Mr. Jackson."

Elsey gave me an unexpectedly firm handshake. "You're a student of the South, Mr. Jackson? I know that some of these younger people are here because of Mr. Pettibone's daughter. But you are a bit older, I suspect."

Twenty-six isn't that old, but I got the point. "I just met Mr. Pettibone and his daughter. I thought I'd come and see what all this was about."

"And what did you think, Mr. Jackson? Was it worth your time?" Pettibone wore an expression halfway between kindness and condescension.

"I don't do much on Monday evenings. Maybe have a bourbon or two," I said, holding up the glass. "But it was interesting."

A shout from across the room interrupted things. "Hey, Jackson," came the cry, and then two undergraduate males, students I knew in my year as Assistant Dean, pressed forward.

"Friends of yours, Mr. Jackson?" said Pettibone, somewhat more toward condescension now.

"Of course, we're friends," said the one on the left, whose name I could not recall. "Dusty and I are old friends of Jackson Trade."

Hanna and Pettibone exchanged glances, and Hanna put his hand on Dusty's shoulder. "I'm sorry, fellows. You'll have to excuse us and your friend. We have business."

"It's ok," I said. "Good to see you fellows. Let me buy you a beer at Hannigan's sometime, ok?"

"Sure, Jackson," said the one whose name I couldn't remember. "Good to see you." He looked back over his shoulder as he left, clearly not used to being told to leave in quite that way.

"So," said Hanna, "it's Jackson all right, but it's Jackson Trade. You any kin to Thompson Trade, the scum that killed the Vincent boy?"

There didn't seem to be much use in denying it. "My brother."

"And you are snooping around Howell? And my daughter? Toward what end, Mr. Trade?" The condescension was gone now, replaced by something a bit sterner.

"I don't think my brother did anything. Howell Parsons was there that night. I wanted to know what he saw."

Hanna had moved behind me. I turned a little to keep him in my line of sight.

"And my daughter?"

"If you recall, you and your daughter arrived while I was talking to Parsons. I don't have anything to do with you and her."

Hanna and his whiny voice were in my ear. "You need to keep it that way, Trade," he said quietly. "You could find yourself in a very bad way if you don't."

"What Mr. Hanna means is that you deceived us, and I can well imagine it was intended to gain some advantage for your brother. Once deceived, fine. Twice? That will not happen."

"No need to threaten."

"Threats work," said Hanna.

Pettibone, ever reasonable, added, "It's not really a threat, Mr. Trade. It's a simple statement of expectation. You will disappear. If you do not, it is you who will have violated expectation. That is not a threat."

"That's ok," I said. "I'll see myself out."

"Make it fast," said Hanna.

Dr. Elsey," I said and bowed bricfly. "I wish you a good evening." I took two steps toward the exit, then turned. "By the way, Mr. Pettibone, do you know anything about the Sons of Shiloh?"

He shifted his weight and looked at Hanna, then Elsey. "I don't think so. Are they a civic group of some kind?"

"More like a motorcycle gang," I said. "Just wondering."

I felt Hanna's glare all the way out of the room.

Chapter Nine

THE QUICKEST WAY TO get me to do something is to tell me not to do it. I was that way as a boy, and I stayed that way until I found, in the Army, that I needed to do what I was told. But the strain of stubborn could not really be erased then. I just found other ways to do the thing I should not do.

It was easy enough to ignore Pettibone's indignation and Hanna's threats. It made sense for a father to protect his daughter. It didn't make much sense at all, though, for Hanna to threaten me over it.

So I found myself the next morning hidden from view, sitting on a little bench I'd moved behind a bush, near the student union, waiting for Grace Pettibone to emerge from Cole Hall. I had a fresh pack of cigarettes and a tall Styrofoam cup of coffee. I figured I could hold out as long as my bladder did.

The night had been clear and all heat had left overnight. I could see my breath when I first sat down. I had on my old jean jacket and had parked a Vandy baseball cap on my head.

I didn't have long to wait. Grace and another girl, much shorter and far plainer, came down the steps and made for Rand Hall where the cafeteria was. I followed at a distance, watched them enter Rand, and later, watched them use their meal points to get coffee and toast. I stayed just hidden from view.

They parted, the shorter girl headed downstairs to the mail room, Grace setting off toward the library. When I followed her in, I lost her for a moment. Then I caught sight of her, in all her height, thank goodness, walking toward the 21st Avenue side of the building. I caught up just in time to see her entering the Special Collections area.

I knew the area from my time as an undergraduate. I was doing a research paper on housing at Vanderbilt, and I used the University Archives housed there. I knew the space well enough to know that I couldn't hide from Grace in there. Too small. Too open.

I took up my post at a carrel where I could view the door. After two hours had passed, I decided there might be a better use for my time.

I went home, fired up the Impala, and drove downtown. I parked in the visitor lot, and showed my driver's license to the officer at the front desk. I told him what I wanted and he picked up the phone. Fifteen minutes later I was sitting across from my brother, holding a phone attached to the one in his ear, a sheet of plexiglass between us.

"Food ok here?" I didn't know exactly what to say. I hadn't had much practice with him.

He nodded. He'd had a shower but not a shave and he didn't look like a month of good food and rest would set him right. "Can you get me out of here?"

"You know what you're in here for, right?" He nodded again. "I didn't even ask what your bail is set at. Because I know I can't raise it."

"What about a lawyer? Can you get one for me? They sent me a kid. Looks like he just graduated law school." I hoped his kid lawyer made better eye contact than Thompson did. He looked around my face, but never in my eyes.

"I don't have money for bail. You think I have enough for a lawyer?" He was once my idol. Now he was someone I didn't even know. "Why'd you come back, Thompson?"

"Doesn't matter," he said. "Wouldn't have if I'd known this." He gestured with his free hand. "All this."

I could sympathize. If he hadn't been there that night in Kirkland, what would have happened? "Do you even know what happened?"

He held the receiver at the top, next to his ear, and placed his elbow on the counter top. For a second, he looked exactly like Daddy would, right before he would deliver bad news about the tractor or the combine. "I don't remember anything, Jackson. I'm sorry. I've tried and tried. It's just a black hole to me.

I didn't have anything I could do for him, not anything that made a difference. I would have liked to go back ten years, back to before everything went to hell. But there wasn't anything I could do. Even if I tried and tried. "I'll keep looking around," I said. "It's the best I can do."

Before I left, he said, "Jackson?"

"Yeah?"

"I'm sorry."

What are you supposed to say? "Yeah. I know."

The day moved slowly, and I was back at the library by 4. I looked inside Special Collections and, as I suspected, Grace had long since finished whatever she was doing. I went in and leaned on the service desk. A young woman with a Chi Omega shirt came out of the back, blond and smiling and ready to help. Which is what she said.

"My friend was in here today, and I think she left some notes for me?"

Her head shot backwards and her eyes opened wide. "I don't know anything about that," she said. "I just came on an hour ago. But I can check?" She really, really wanted to help.

"Please do. We're trying to get a project going for class. But I don't know what she's got in mind."

"What's your name?"

"Jackson Trade." I smiled my best smile back. "Her name is Grace Pettibone."

"I'll just be a minute," she said, and moved with speed toward the back.

The reading room was empty, which was my experience of it before. Only serious scholars really needed the Special Collections area, and while it was quiet, most undergrads opted for the Reserve Reading Room. If they opted for the library at all. Me, when I was an undergrad? I went for an empty classroom in Furman or Calhoun.

After a few minutes she returned. "There wasn't anything left for you."

"Damn it," I said. "She said we would work in shifts. I have a job over in Housing during the day."

She looked sympathetic. "I know. I've had bad research partners before."

"Is there any chance you could look up what she checked out today? Just so I don't do the same thing over again?"

"Of course," she said, brightly. "Let me go look at the logs."

I killed time while she looked by looking out the window at traffic passing on 21st Avenue. By the time she returned I was through with my game of "which car I'd buy." My old oil-burning Impala was in worse shape than every car I'd seen.

"Ok," she said. "Here we go. She checked out the Diaries of Corporeal Gilbert Adkins, CSA. Then later she took the Artemis Williams Papers. Does that help? What are you two doing? An upper level History Course?"

"I get the Adkins stuff. What are the Williams papers?"

"He's also a Confederate soldier. So this is pretty high level research you're doing."

"Oh, I don't know about that," I said. "We're just trying to write about what it was like if you were a Confederate soldier." It was the best line I could come up with.

"I guess," she said. "I'm just trying to write a paper about a poem. Yours seems more interesting to me."

"I wish I could agree," and I gave a half-hearted shrug. "Ok, so let me start with those two, and I'll see if there's more that I need." I grinned at her. "At least I can catch up to where my research partner is, right?"

"You bet," said the Chi O, and off she went in search of the selections.

It turned out that Grace was interested in a couple of very rich troves of Confederate information. The diaries of Corporal Adkins started off slowly enough, but they picked up once he got to the battlefield. Interestingly, he had been at Shiloh and the way he wrote about it mirrored the worst of my battlefield experiences

The first day was glorious. We took the Yankee encampment entirely by surprise, and they fled, leaving behind coffee still on the boil and hardtack for the taking. A lot of the boys stopped for vittles, but not me. I was hot to get some Yankee blood and I was down on them. Our flank got so far so fast that we were inside their center before we realized it. It could have been a debacle, but we managed to double back and hold our position.

The next day, though, was as bad as the first was good. Grant's army pushed us all the way back to the landing, and then even further back to the old school house. We managed to hold them off, but we took a shellacking, losing many men. I swear I felt the wind of musket and cannon race by my head all day long. How I come to be alive to write this is a miracle I do not understand.

You and me both, Gilbert. You and me both.

But it was not the last of Gilbert Adkins, as the Army of Tennessee made its way back, all the way to eastern Tennessee. The western theater of the war was practically over, only awaiting the final decisive battle at New Orleans, but the rag tag group of Tennessee soldiers stayed their course. In a later letter, Adkins wrote:

It is said that Richmond has fallen, or will fall soon. Davis and his Cabinet have evacuated and are somewhere in Georgia, we hear. If there is a way that we can continue, some sort of nomad government and a nomad army, striking where we can, then I suppose that will be what we must do. Surely in the mountains we could hold out for some time.

On the other hand, to do so would require that the treasury is saved. There is talk that two trains left Richmond; one with Jefferson Davis and the other with the treasury of the Confederacy. If this is true, and if it can be salvaged until we reach where we must be, in order to be safe and effective, then the Cause of our strife may yet be served.

"It must be interesting," said the girl, startling me. "You have barely moved for an hour and a half."

"I admit it," I smiled. "I'm a little nuts for old stuff." I was also struck by how Gilbert had gone from reminding me of my own combat situation to sounding very much like how the VC thought. He might have been correct. A guerrilla strike force, well-funded and armed, might have given the Union forces something to think about. "How about bringing out the other set? The Williams papers?"

She brought in short order a box of folders. "Four linear feet, that's what it says in the catalog. And here is the first box."

There was too much to go through, although there was a key at the beginning of the box's contents. It began with his training, then the papers moved to his service in the first years of the war. There was a set of papers related to his letters back and forth from his father and sisters to him, as well as a good bit of correspondence related to a mix up in his orders that caused him to spend a month in transit to a new unit under Johnson before being returned to Beauregard, then back to Johnson. I could tell that he was in some demand because he was a man with a rare blend of skills. He was trained as an engineer, a builder of roads and bridges, but he was also, by dint of his upbringing perhaps, also a marksman. A sharpshooter. A sniper.

No wonder he was in demand.

I was barely into the first set of papers when the young woman came to tell me the library was closing. "I'm sorry. I know you're just getting started, but they'll be here tomorrow."

I was pretty sure I wanted to be ahead of the game, ahead of Grace Pettibone anyway, when the time came tomorrow. I couldn't check out the papers. I couldn't very well pocket them and leave.

It was clear to me what I needed to do.

I thanked her for her help and I carried the ungainly box back and put it on the counter for her. "You could just leave it here," I said. "I'll be in first thing tomorrow, or if I'm not, Grace will be."

"I couldn't do that. I'd lose my job. Everything has to be put away."

She carried the box back into the collections area, and I left by the front door, the one that empties into the main floor. People were streaming in various modes of urgency out of the building. Some had places to get to, and others moved as if there was no place in particular they needed to be.

I had a place I needed to be, but it wasn't outside the library.

I slipped past the entry to the middle part of the building, took steps three at a time to the third floor, and angled toward the back corner of the building, back where the oldest graduate student carrels were. As an undergrad looking for a quiet place to sleep, I had literally found cobwebs on a carrel back in this area. I had a feeling I wouldn't be noticed here.

I wedged myself under the desk, entirely concealed in the dark. And I began to wait.

Chapter Ten

I KNEW HOW TO wait in the dark. I knew how to wait quietly. In Vietnam, so much depended on not just my ability to do that, but on an entire unit's ability to do it. It was a kind of patience, and it was certainly a sort of discipline, but more than anything else it was a matter of making yourself empty and yet entirely present. It was a skill that came naturally to me and, in the end, it may have saved my life.

Now, in the dusty dark quiet of the third floor stacks, I listened to the sounds of a building shutting down for the night. There would still be functions that continued as if nothing changed. The heat, the ventilation, some of the lights. But most of the library shut down.

And in being shut down it was mostly, I knew, the same as it had been when it was teeming with people. The books, all of them, rested just as they had throughout the day, the knowledge inside them no more and no less transitive than before. A repository of knowledge depends on humans to make it active again. Without humans, or at night in the absence of day scholars, the books wait.

The papers of Artemis Williams waited for me. And I intended to see what they wanted to tell me.

I waited until two in the morning, well past when the cleaning people would have made their rounds and completed their tasks. Earlier I had heard the clanking of a bucket on third floor, but the housekeeper didn't come into the darkened older section where I hid. Instead, the sounds went on down the hall until they didn't come back. I waited an extra hour, and then I began to make my way back toward Special Collections.

Second floor, being the main floor, was lit more than the others, but it was no more than shadow. There was just enough to see by and, if I am honest, more than enough to see, from the outside, a figure lurking inside, if you should be looking. I kept myself low to the ground, and against the wall.

The Special Collections area was, of course, locked, but it was not a hard lock to defeat. It was a simple bevel phalange, the sort that the right credit card or, in my case, driver's license, could open. I popped the bevel and slid inside, shutting the door with a muted click.

I grabbed a little banker's light from a table and went behind the desk. I was hoping that the Chi Omega had been lazier than she should have been, and I was rewarded by the sight of the Williams materials sitting on a cart. She had left the shelving for the next student in the morning.

I plugged in the little lamp, lit it, and sat down next to the cart, pulling two folders out to start with.

Dear Father, one letter began, *the War goes badly. I have on more than one occasion felt the starkest kind of terror, as my fellow soldiers are mown down, as if the enemy has its own scythe and wields it unconscious of its effect. For surely no one could believe that humans should treat their fellow creatures with such cruelty.*

And yet, what will they say of us? We return every shot, every cannon, every bayonet with its fiendish answer. How have we come to this, and what will become of us? I do not know.

There was correspondence in the second folder from later in the war. Between the earlier letters and these later ones, something had happened to Captain Williams. There was an edge to his letters. I could believe that this is in fact what combat does to you. If you live, it requires you to coarsen certain parts of your personality in order to live, and it requires you to refine certain other qualities that are not necessarily desirable in civilization.

There are signs, Father, that our cause is nearly lost. The flood that began at Gettysburg has now loosed upon Virginia, and it will not be long before the horde of blue devils will show us their boot. Be assured I will die like a man, if I must, but I will not be humiliated by the enemy. Let him do his worst, and I will make a heavy penalty for him.

If we only can somehow gather our forces for one last stand. I know not where that stand may be, whether on the Potomac or in the north Georgia mountains. But there are enough of us, seasoned now and dangerous men, who could lift this cause upon our shoulders and carry it into the world triumphant. But we must have time. And we must have resources.

Be of good cheer, Father. That time may even now be approaching.

There was something in both these boxes, the diaries of the corporal and the letters of the captain, which spoke of hope. Even in the near total defeat that was coming, they both believed that there was still a possibility of victory. The mountains held a hope. But it depended on resources, and there weren't resources forthcoming. The Confederacy, as I understood history, was out of money. The Union had outspent them and had more still to spend. Both Adkins and Williams were dreamers, I decided.

I had enough. It was getting close to 6 a.m. and I was beat. I needed a cigarette, or ten. And I needed a drink. I was well past the point of being hungry too. It was time to use the bathroom, conceal myself, and get ready to exit when the place opened at 8.

Which was exactly what I was in the process of doing when the alarm went off. At first I jumped, thinking I must have set off some sort of security alarm. But then I realized I'd heard the alarm before. It was a fire alarm, and it was going off inside the library.

This is not the way I'd like to die—-suffocated by smoke in a locked-up library.

I ran to the lower floor, which exited onto 21st. The doors there were not the kind of crash bar glass doors that we had installed in the residence halls because of emergencies just like this one. Instead, these were oak doors that were dead bolted with a key on the inside. No help there.

I ran back up to second floor. The doors that opened onto Library Lawn were similarly dead bolted. I would have to have a talk with Mercer about this.

If I made it out.

I could hear sirens and saw through the windows a couple of campus police officers crossing the brick terrace on the lawn side of the library. I didn't smell smoke. Maybe it was a false alarm. Maybe I should just hide.

I retreated to third floor, making sure first that there was no smoke or fire on the floor. While I'm a smoker and don't have the most reliable nose in town, I couldn't find anything to indicate danger on the floor. I went back to my carrel, and waited.

Soon, there was a crashing and clatter coming from somewhere downstairs, followed by yelling and cursing. I decided to venture out, trying to construct my story as I walked, silently, toward the noise.

Campus Police had apparently keyed in through the deadbolt, but Metro Fire, clumsily, had managed somehow to break a large window behind the circulation desk. Glass fragments where everywhere, and the din of speech was mostly profane and coming from both sides, campus and Metro alike.

I felt a hard hand on my shoulder. "Hey. What are you doing here?" I was spun around by a firefighter who wore a station 2 helmet and an angry look. "Chief. Come over here."

Clint Fish had likely arrived at work just as the alarm sounded, so he'd not had time to sufficiently make himself believe he was interim chief all over again. He came running at the fireman's call, then slowed to a more appropriate gait. Wouldn't do to be at the beck and call of a fireman.

But when he saw me, he turned red.

"Trade," he sputtered. "If I find out that you have anything to do with this, I will see you tried and convicted."

"Not so fast, Clint. You don't know what you're talking about."

"Not so fast, yourself, buddy," said the fireman. "Can you have this man cuffed and detained until we find out what's going on here?"

"Of course, we can," said Clint. "Turn around, Trade."

Clint Fish gave me a quick pat down, then tightened the handcuffs a little more than necessary. "Go sit over there until we're ready for you."

I did as I was told. "You'll see, Clint. You really should listen to me."

"Shut up."

The library staff began to arrive, and a couple got to work cleaning up the glass. Bubble top lights continued to reflect in the windows, even after full daylight hit. The library was closed to the public for now, and I saw the helpful young Chi Omega peer in briefly through the window. I felt sorry I had impugned her in my mind. Clearly, she just left the shelving work for herself the next morning.

"All right, Mister," said the fire inspector. "You were in the building when the alarm went off."

"I was reading last night. I dropped off and got locked in."

"You did, did you? Where?"

"I was on third floor, in the old section."

"And what were you reading, if I may ask?"

"A novel."

"Which one?"

"Absalom, Absalom. It's by William Faulkner."

"If I were to go up there now, I'd find it just where you left it, would I?"

"You'd find it where I re-shelved it. I woke up and re-shelved it. Then the alarm went off."

"I don't believe a word of it," said Fish.

"Why in hell would I lie, Clint? Do you think I want to be locked in a place with no food?"

"And no drink. No drink is a bigger deal to you," Fish said. "You were in here illegally."

"When an alarm went off," I reminded him. "I take it there was no fire?" I directed my question to the fire inspector, but Clint interrupted.

"It was an electrical short in the system. But you should not have been in here." Fish was a Fife, probably with a single bullet in his shirt.

The fire inspector regarded coolly. "I know you didn't have anything to do with our matter, so I don't care. If he's in cuffs because of us, you can let him go."

"I don't think so." Cliff was warming to his chief role. "You." He yelled toward a Metro cop I didn't recognize. "Take this man downtown. We need to investigate how he got in here. For now, hold him on suspicion of illegal entry."

"Cuff and transport?"

"Yes." Cliff grinned. "Treat him the way you would any criminal."

Chapter Eleven

"I DON'T THINK THERE'S probable cause here, buddy, but I got to take you downtown." He was an older Metro cop whose name plate said "Higgins." His face was what you might call Roman because of the nose, but the rest of his face, from his blue eyes to his whiter than white complexion, screamed Irish.

"I know the drill."

"Been picked up before, eh?"

"No. I've been with Metro when they took a student down."

"You a campus cop?" His eyebrows slanted up with interest.

"Just a pal."

"You're no pal of that chief over there," he said, opening the back of the cruiser. "Watch your head when you get in."

He wasn't in any hurry to get to the magistrate, which, if we were showing up when I usually had, everybody called Night Court. Since the 1960s, the Davidson County Night Court has been the only court in the state that operates 24 hours a day, 365 days a year, with five judicial commissioners, who are appointed by the court, presiding on rotating shifts.

The commissioners, whom everybody calls magistrates, mostly conduct probable cause hearings to see if an arrest warrant is called for, then set the bail bond if it is. They also issue protection orders and deal with committals from county psych units.

During the day, Night Court ends up being the graveyard of junk warrants, and the people who didn't show for court dates get hauled up in front of the magistrate who wants to know, if they knew they had to appear for drinking from an open container, why they hadn't come in, and further, did they want to spend time in the jail for it? It's not the sort of thing you want your county judges spending their days on, and it kept the court calendar from clogging up with the flotsam of petty cases that Nashville had.

On the other hand, Night Court at night was as lively a show as you could get west of the river. Drunks who had gone public, prostitutes who had asked the wrong potential john, and all manner of belligerent men and women, ranging from the barely legal to the nearly dead were likely to show on any given night. For your money, if you were a college student, it was as good a free show as you could find.

I expected to show up after the parade of ne'er do wells from the evening, but I was wrong. Officer Higgins brought me in, still in handcuffs, and we stood against the wall as two Metro cops flanked four long-haired, fidgeting men in double knit leisure suits.

"Are you telling me," asked the magistrate icily, "that you have brought these guys in because they were selling flowers? At the airport?"

"There were complaints from passengers checking in, sir," said the officer on the left, a skinny guy with freckles. "They're pretty aggressive."

"These guys? You mean the guys with the flowers?" The magistrate was a black man who looked too young to have the white hair he sported. His tie was loosened and he'd put his suit jacket on the back of the chair. "Or the passengers were aggressive?"

"The Krishnas, sir."

"If I may, Your Honor?" said the taller man in the center. "We are simply exercising our right to free speech, our First Amendment right. We approach people and ask their names. We want to be personal and engaging. Then we offer a pamphlet, and we ask for a donation. It's true, if they give us a dollar we are trained to ask for two, but we do not think of it as aggressive. We are simply trying to practice good offertory techniques."

"Panhandling techniques," said the other officer.

"I'm sorry." The magistrate scratched his head vigorously, and a shower of dandruff flew through the sunlight. "I thought you just said these men were Hare Krishnas. They have on leisure suits."

"It's a disguise."

"To the contrary, sir," said the man in the center again, "we find that our usual clothing puts people off. So we try to look more like the people we are engaging."

"Panhandling." The skinny officer was staying on his script.

"Has the airport banned them from this activity?" The magistrate was scanning the paper in front of him. He looked up at the officers, looked at one, then the other.

"Well, no."

"Then on what basis did you place them under arrest and bring them here?"

"They're aggressive, sir."

"Have they harmed anyone with this aggressive behavior?" The magistrate was leaning up on his oak desk. Unlike in other courtrooms, the magistrates sit behind a desk, much like a school teacher, and look up at the prisoners standing six feet away from them.

"Well, one guy took a swing at them. At this one here," he said, indicating the man in the center.

"It's true," he said. "A man put his suitcase down and tried to strike me."

"And what did you do?" asked the magistrate.

"I did what any peace-seeking person would do, Your Honor. I ran."

The magistrate leaned back onto his chair and pondered the cosmos. At least, that's the way it looked. After a full minute, he opened his eyes and leaned forward again. "There is no probable cause here. There is no complainant. There are two officers who do not approve of what these men are doing." He leaned his elbows fully on the desk and looked from one to the other of the officers yet again. "But unless you can find something that overrides these men's practice of protected speech, I'd advise you to leave them be unless they actually break a law."

"Yes, sir." There were two unhappy Metro cops in the courtroom.

Higgins nudged me. "This is why you're lucky. Listen."

"Probable cause means that you have reasonable belief that they've committed a crime. You need to have this belief based on evidence. You cannot suspect that something is wrong. You have to have some fact." He paused to see if they were understanding him. "You can't just handcuff people and come in with a story about how they're so annoying that a guy took a swing at one of them. It just won't wash."

"Yes, sir." The skinny freckled kid barely made a sound when he said it.

"Take their handcuffs off. You men are free to go."

"Uh, Your Honor?" The center one wriggled out of the cuffs. "Our car is at the airport."

"The officers will transport you back," said the magistrate. "And they will do it kindly and without speaking." He looked again at the officers. "Understand?"

"Yes, sir."

The magistrate was already looking past them, shuffling papers and nodding toward Higgins. "Next up."

"Let's go," Higgins said to me.

"Case 40497, what's the name?"

Higgins nudged me in the side. "He means you."

"Jackson Trade."

"Middle initial?"

"No, sir. Don't have one."

"Too bad. They don't cost extra." He smiled wearily. "What is the situation, officer?"

"We responded to a fire alarm at the Vanderbilt library. While securing the building with Vanderbilt Police and Metro Fire, Mr. Trade was discovered to be in the building. After a brief conversation, the Vanderbilt Police asked that Mr. Trade be transported here for booking."

"On what charge?"

"Unlawful entry."

"That true, son?"

"No." I wasn't going to go further than that. A lawyer friend once told me that if you're asked in court what time it is, you don't tell them how to make a watch.

"You weren't in the building?"

"I was."

"How did you get there?"

"I walked in."

"When?" The magistrate was writing, but he looked up, one eye cocked at me.

"Yesterday."

He put down his pen. "Listen, Mr. Trade. I've been here since 9 p.m. I've had my fill of unreasonable people and my shift is about over. If you don't mind, I'll stop asking questions and you tell me what happened after you walked in." He smiled. "Yesterday."

"I read. I fell asleep. When I woke up, I was locked in."

"So you spent the night in the library."

"Not on purpose." The first lie I told. But he wouldn't know it.

"Did you trip the fire alarm?"

"It was an electrical fault," said Higgins. "No one set it off."

"Then I'm at a loss to know why the Vanderbilt Police want you arrested."

I shrugged and looked innocent. Open face. No motive showing. Just a guy who likes to read until he gets tired. That's how I imagine I looked.

"Tell you the truth, sir, I think the one Vandy cop has it in for him."

"And is there any reason for that to be true, Mr. Trade?"

"Honest to goodness, Your Honor, I have lots of friends on the force there. I don't know why he'd have it in for me." I gave him the same innocent face. Whether he bought it, I don't know.

But even if he didn't he said, "Free to go. Warrant denied." He looked behind us. "This looks to be the right time for me to make my move. No one is here. Next commissioner comes on shift in ten minutes." He rose and got his jacket off the chair. "Good day, all. And Mr. Trade?"

"Yes, sir."

"I'd stay away from that officer who seems not to like you."

After Higgins unlocked the cuffs, smiling as he did, I ventured outside to the front steps of the jail. I'd spent too much time in the past three days there. It appeared that the Trade brothers were going to be there more still.

I heard his steps before he said anything. When you're as big as Art Blake, your steps tend to announce your presence before anything else.

"Damn it, Jackson. What's going on?"

"Hi, Art. Just trying to plan the rest of my day."

"Did you bail out already?"

"Magistrate didn't find probable cause. Probably because there wasn't any." I lit a cigarette. "Why are you here? I mean, I'm guessing it's me. But why?"

"Clint and Don showed up in my office first thing this morning. They are fit to be tied. Something about you being locked in the library all night and an alarm going off."

I explained what I'd said to the magistrate, which is to say that I didn't exactly tell the whole truth. Just enough of it to make Clint look like the ass he was.

"Let go get my car. I want to have a talk with you."

We found Art's Rambler in the courthouse lot and got in. As long as I'd known Art, he'd had this car, a 1970 two-door that looked big enough for anyone except Art. We drove up 24 toward East Nashville. "Mexican all right?"

I said that it was.

We pulled into Chi-Chi's. It was early enough that we were seated immediately and ate about half the basket of chips before Art looked at me and said, "Tell me the truth, ok?"

I scooped too much salsa for the chip in my hand and part of the salsa drew a line from the bowl to my mouth. "Sure, Art. Fire away."

"How did you get in that library?"

"Walked in the front door like free men and women do. Every day."

"I don't believe you." He crossed his arms and gave me the look that made undergraduates tremble.

"Your call, my friend. I fell asleep and was locked in." I took another chip. More salsa. "Besides. It's your fault."

That broke the look on his face and made him uncross his arms. "How in God's name is it my fault?"

"Well, not yours only. You got me thinking after our talk about Shiloh. So I went over to have a chat with Professor Prince. You know Bruno?"

"Yes," he said, the syllable drawing out at the end, as if he couldn't see where this was going.

"And Bruno started talking about Faulkner. That made me want to go look up Faulkner and I ended up in the library."

Our enchiladas had come and Art waved the waitress away after she left the plates. "Are you telling me that you got locked into the library because of William Faulkner?"

The thing about Chi-Chi's is that the sauce comes from a can. The tortillas come from the freezer. About the only thing that's real and fresh is the lettuce they sprinkle on top, and even it comes with brown edges. I don't know why everybody comes here. I answered with a full bite of chicken enchilada in my mouth. "Yep."

"You fell asleep?"

"That's right."

We ate in silence. Art made short work of the plate, and he took a long drink of iced tea, downing the rest in one gulp. "All right. Let's go."

I left my plate half eaten, we paid, and got back into the Rambler. Or rather, Art wedged himself into the driver's side. He turned on the radio and we listened to WLAC all the way back to campus. He eased into his parking spot next to his cottage and cut the ignition. WLAC went quiet.

"I don't know what's going on. I know your brother is in jail and that has to hurt, even if you're not that fond of him. I know you want to help. And I'll tell you this. I don't believe your little Faulkner story. Clint and Don don't believe it either."

"I can't help that, Art."

He put his hand up to stop me. "Here's what you can help. Stop whatever it is you're doing. You're not going to help your brother. You've already got campus police riled up. And it won't be long, the way you're going, that you'll get Metro riled up." He opened his side of the car, and put one long leg out. "You mess around enough, Jackson, and you'll get me riled up."

Chapter Twelve

THE ENCHILADAS SAT HEAVY on my stomach all afternoon, and by 4:00 I'd had enough. I'd spent the night in a library, been handcuffed and taken to court, then chewed out, at least as much as Art ever chewed me out, and had heartburn.

What I needed was a drink. Probably several of them.

I sat at the Hideaway until I had four empty shot glasses lined up in front of me. One of them I called Patrick and I turned him upside down. One I called Howell and I put him far away from Patrick. One was Thompson, and he was near Patrick. And one I called Pettibone. I don't know if it was the father or Grace, and I didn't really know where to put it. It was the last one I drank.

"Mind if I take those now?" The bartender had let me play my little game after the first drink, but he clearly was done indulging me. "And let me get you some food?"

I waved him off, and put a ten on the bar. "I'm done here."

There was a bit of cool in the air as I stepped out on Elliston Place. It was getting to be dinner time, and students were out in multiples of twos and threes and fours. Some were heading to the Soda Shop, others stopping in at the new gyro place. All of them looked innocent, whether they were sporting the prepster look or the not-quite-a-cowboy look. Or the innocent look, like I looked eight or so years ago, before the war.

Innocent of death.

They had forgotten, if they'd even processed, that one of their own had died. Been murdered. Snuffed out after his crowning achievement.

It wasn't the sort of thing you should be able to forget that easily. But they were young. They didn't see his face right before. They didn't see his lifeless body right after. Most of all, they couldn't imagine that they might have the same fate. They weren't afraid for themselves. For their friends.

For the others in their unit.

I looked in their faces as they passed and wondered if they'd ever be afraid that way.

There was no good reason to stop at Hannigan's. I could have easily gone right past and down West End to another bar. But a creature of habit will do what he does. I was still thinking about innocent faces as three students, two guys and a girl, went into Hannigan's in front of me and held the door open.

I just walked in.

Katie was behind the counter ringing up a customer, but she stopped for a moment and motioned me toward the back. "Your buddy is back there."

I said, "Bring me a bourbon, and start a chicken fried steak plate for me. Collards and pintos."

I headed back to see who my buddy was.

In the very back booth I saw the thick neck and neatly trimmed black hair of Don Mercer. I approached from the rear and put my hand on his shoulder. He didn't jump, but turned his head slowly. "You."

"Katie said my buddy was back here."

"We're not buddies today." He shoved my hand off his shoulder.

"What kind of jive bullshit is that, Don?" I sat down across from him. "Mind if I join you?"

"Your butt's already in the seat." He took a drink of his beer and resumed demolition of a substantial Reuben.

"Art said you're pissed. What gives?"

Don Mercer is not a tall man. Standing up, he comes to about my shoulder. Sitting down, you realize that all his height, and bulk, is in his torso. He is wide shouldered, bull necked, and barrel chested. You wouldn't want to get in a wrestling match with him. I've seen strong undergraduates make that mistake. He oozed power, and he put a muscled forearm on the table as Katie brought my drink.

"Tell your friend that he needs to cut back," he said to her.

"He's your friend. You tell him. But tell him after he pays his tab." Katie was smiling at Don, ignoring me

"Do you two mind speaking to me when you're speaking about me?"

"Mrs. Hannigan would like for you to pay something on your tab tonight. It's getting up there." She gave me a fake smile. "How's that?"

"Sure. That's fine."

As Katie walked away, Mercer gave me a look. He almost launched into a sermon. Or a speech. But he sighed and resumed the destruction.

I lit a cigarette and took a sip. "You were in Vietnam, right, Don?"

"You know I was." He put down the sandwich. "Losing your memory? You . . . ," and then he stopped, shook his head. "Why?"

"These kids. One of their own died a few days ago, and life just goes on for them. They don't give it another thought." I breathed the smoke in deeply and held it. I bent my head back and exhaled. "Life goes on. Daddy sends another check."

"Yeah? What else is new?"

"They've just got this crystal clear notion, Don. Everything's fine. Nothing's wrong. They just go about their day, their night, like the world will never end. There's nothing at all that's gray in their world."

"Black and white. That's the way it is. And sometimes that is exactly the way it is, Jackson." He leveled his gaze. "Sometimes it's black and white. Right and wrong."

"That's not right, Don. Everything's gray. You know that. You were over there. There's not a damn thing that's black or white."

"I'm black. You're white. People say that's pretty cut and dried."

"Yeah." I took a sip. The bourbon was losing its taste to me. Or else Katie had watered it down. "But not over there, Don. And not over here anymore, either. Remember how it was in the morning. The fog? That great, gray swirling fog over everything. And it never really cleared."

"The hell it didn't. What country were you in, anyway?"

"Yeah, the literal fog cleared. But we were always in a fog that didn't lift. And it meant that the rules didn't work anymore. Truth didn't work anymore. You went in, and instead of order, you got chaos. We lost our sense of direction. We got out, and the world didn't work."

"My world works, Jackson. Just because yours is screwed up doesn't mean there's no truth." He finished off the Reuben and wiped the corner of his mouth with a meaty hand. "Tell me why you were in the library."

"There's proof that the world doesn't work. Clint is the interim chief."

"Clint's an asshole. Answer my question."

"I fell asleep."

"You're lying. I don't know why you're lying, but you are."

I knew better than to try the face I used on the magistrate. It wouldn't have worked on Mercer. He'd seen me do it before. I didn't have that many tricks.

The only other trick I had just then was to change the subject. "You grew up in Alabama, right? Huntsville?"

He eyed me cautiously. "That's right. Just outside Huntsville. But what's . . . ,"

"What was it like? Growing up there? I mean, was it integrated?"

"Not that much. Brown v. Board happened in the 50s, but it took a while to get to us."

"So you didn't have much contact with white folks until the Army."

"That's not really true. I just didn't have contact where I got to talk much."

"But growing up in Alabama, you had contact as a black person."

"I'm always a black person, Jackson."

"I mean, you dealt with white people who were treating you, explicitly, as a black person."

"I am not getting your distinction."

"White people in history, at least certain kinds of white people, viewed black people as creatures. Three-fifths of a white person, you know? Things you move around. Creatures with minds and motives, certainly, but almost as creatures you can talk about, even if they're right there in the room."

"I guess. Never thought about it that way. Just thought they were bigots. Or too old to know better."

"Any of them ever talk about the old days, say back in slavery, as if black folks were better off then?"

"Everybody's heard that bullshit, Jackson. Every white person in Alabama probably thinks that."

"But do they really think it? Or is it just a rationalization? Something that the great Lost Nation of the South must have been?"

Mercer sat for a moment, thinking. "I just figured it was bigoted and hateful. You're saying there's something else to it? Something that excuses it? Because that's some real bullshit, man."

"Oh, listen. It is bigoted and hateful. But there's also this sense you get, talking to some of them, that part of the story is something they have to believe. That they were generous and magnanimous. That they were as stately as the plantation mansions."

"Except the ones that believe all that have never been inside a mansion. You're all over the place tonight. Going from kids to truth to mansions." He finished his beer. "You're drunk."

I thought he was about half right and I said so. "But here's the thing, Donnie. They see the mist, and they think they see the truth. Those kids are walking through the mist and they're just happy. You're in the mist, you've seen it for what it is, and you're choosing to see black and white."

"You are drunk."

"But what I see is order turned into anarchy. You've been to Night Court. People are dragged in for no reason except the exercise of the law. Not law with a capital L. Lower case."

"Like me, right?"

"Definitely not like you, Don. But like Clint. Like the Metro guys I saw today."

"What Clint did was stupid. He hates you."

"Clint's just playing out his role. We all are. There isn't truth. There's aren't laws. There's no order in the world. Nineteen year old kids die. And people just go on about their lives. Blind to the world."

"You talking about Nashville, now? Or Vietnam?"

"What's the difference, Don?"

Katie brought my chicken fried steak plate and another bourbon. Don got up and left, with the admonition that I was drinking myself into a bad place. I ate the food but didn't taste much of it. As far as that was concerned, I didn't taste the bourbon either.

As I left Hannigan's I waved as I walked past Katie at the register. "Tell Mrs. H I'll bring a check by tomorrow." More on my tab. There's a lot on my mental tab too.

And there's my brother, sitting in jail. A murderer, they say. Some might say that about me, too. Baby killer, they might say. They wouldn't be right about that.

More mist.

I gave up on my night of crawling the bars. More drinking wouldn't help my sleep. And it wouldn't bring me peace. When I got home, I didn't even undress. I fell on the bed and closed my eyes.

Chapter Thirteen

WHEN I KNOCKED ON the door, I don't know that I was expecting anything. Betty's face told me what to expect.

"Well. Look who's here." She had on jeans and a t-shirt that said, 'Powdermilk Biscuits (Heavens. They're tasty.)' "I wondered if you'd dropped off the side of the earth."

"I've had better weeks." She stood in the doorway and didn't move. "Mind if I come in?"

She gave me a few seconds to wonder, and then moved aside. "Come in."

I followed her into the kitchen, a small room with a large window facing south. She had taken advantage of the position by decorating the room with an array of houseplants, all of which seemed to be thriving. The word 'lush' does not normally apply to kitchen spaces, but it worked here. The paint job was a mellow and rich yellow.

She reached into the cupboard, got a second cup and filled it with coffee from the percolator. "Sit."

"Thanks for the other night," I said.

"Don't mention it," she answered. "You didn't for several days. Four days. Why start now?"

"Betty," I began.

"No, seriously. Don't mention it. I know you've got a brother in jail. I know you have things on your mind."

"I should have called."

"Maybe. Depends on what you want to say." She got up to freshen her cup and stood by the kitchen counter, looking out the window. "Look. We're both grownups. We had something going a few nights ago. It was great. At least, it was great for me."

"Great for me, too."

"And there's no obligation on any of this stuff. You didn't obligate yourself. I didn't obligate myself. Right?"

I sat quietly.

"But a girl likes to think, after that kind of night, there'll be something more than an empty bed the next morning and four days of nothing."

"I'm sorry. I'm bad at this."

"You don't have to be good at this to leave a note and say you'll be busy for the next few days."

"I . . ."

"You don't have to be good at this to drop a dime in a phone booth and say, "Hey, you made me feel good." Her jaw showed that she had it clenched tight between sentences, probably to keep something else from coming out of her mouth. "You and I have danced around each other for the better part of a year, and when we finally make love, you act like a shit."

She turned. We looked at each other.

"I'm sorry."

"That's all you got? You're sorry?" She tossed the coffee into the sink and put the cup down a little harder than she meant to. "Well, I'm sorry too. I'm sorry that you are so entitled that you can walk in and out of here whenever you want to. I'm sorry that I've sent that message to you."

"You haven't sent that message."

"Apparently I have. Because that is the way you have acted for a year. Show up without warning. Take what you want. Usually conversation. Sometimes liquor. One time, me. Oh, I was willing. I have been willing." She turned back toward the window. "I'm not willing anymore."

I sat without saying anything. She stood by the window, looking out. "I guess I should go," I said.

"Yes, please do. I can't have you here right now." She blinked a couple of times. "You know the way out."

That's the thing. I always know my way out. There's nothing, in fact, that I want to stay in, so out is a right move.

I hadn't meant to be a jerk to Betty. But she was right. It hadn't even occurred to me that she might be wanting something, maybe even needing something from me. When I decided to go over there, in my mind it was just the natural thing to do. I wanted to see her. I wanted her conversation. I don't think I was over there to get in bed, but who knows? If it had happened, would I have fought it?

So what did that tell me? It told me that I shouldn't be sleeping with people I liked. I was just going to mess it up.

The other thing it told me was that I was on a roll. Art was mad at me. Mercer was mad. And Betty was mad. If there were another friend I had, that person would be mad too. Trouble was, those were the three I could count on.

Nice going.

I went by Tolman Hall to see if Wendy Williamson was around. I wanted to talk about Grace Pettibone, see if there was anything interesting Wendy could tell me. I also wanted to quiz her about Raines Durst, the third prankster who so far had not turned up in any of my wanderings. But Wendy wasn't in. The way my luck was going, she'd be pissed at me too and wouldn't tell me anything.

I tried next door at Cole Hall, also in Wendy's area, just to see if she might be there. She wasn't, but before I left the desk clerk struck up a conversation. "You were a dean here, right?"

"For a little while."

"And now what do you do?"

"Little bit of this. Little bit of that."

"Well," she said, "you have to make a living. Wendy's your friend?"

"I hope so. Seems like I'm ticking them off, one at a time."

"Is there anything I can help with?" She was one of the full-time daytime desk clerks. But I didn't know her. She had been hired after I was fired. "I mean, unless it's something confidential." She was in her forties, but she was forgetting that. I think she was flirting. I know she was extending the conversation.

"As a matter of fact, it's not confidential at all. I'm just trying to locate a student."

"One of our girls?" She looked a little crestfallen.

"No, not at all. I'm trying to find where a student named Raines Durst is living." I tried to look employed on a paid mission, despite the way I was dressed. "Raines is a witness in an insurance claim that I'm investigating."

"Saw someone back into a car in the parking lot? Something like that?"

"Something almost exactly like that." I smiled my widest and most trustworthy smile.

"Well," she said happily, "I can certainly just look that up."

She did, and seemed delighted to tell me that Durst lived practically next door in McGill. "I hope that helps, Mr.?"

"Jackson." Wendy would be nonplussed to know she knew a Mr. Jackson.

"Come by anytime, sweetie. I'm happy to help."

Durst was supposed to be on the second floor of McGill, room 232. I knocked, but got no answer. Just as I turned to go, a bare-chested young man in bell bottom jeans opened the door across the hall, then shut it just as quickly and clicked the deadbolt. The smell of marijuana smoke told me all I needed to know about that. I knocked. No answer.

"Hey, man," I said. "Don't worry. I'm just here trying to find Raines. Can you help me?"

No answer still.

I knocked again. "Really, man. I don't care if you've been doing bongs since last week. I'm just trying to find Raines."

I heard a shuffling and then a sound that sounded a little like a chair scraping the floor. Silence. Then some hurried whispers. I couldn't make out the words. But at long last a young man, a different young man, opened the door.

This one was my height, about six-two, and of some vague but real ethnicity. Hispanic maybe. Middle Eastern, possibly. He had luxurious black hair to his shoulders, a thick mustache, and dark brown eyes that were faded like bong smoke in a tailwind. He was also completely nude, except for his bathrobe which he wore open.

"Yes," he said with an accent.

"You heard what I said? Raines Durst?"

"Raines lives across the hall," he said, and began to shut the door.

I wedged my foot in between it and the frame. Then I pushed my forearm against the door and muscled my way inside the room. There was no one else in the room. Not the bare-chested boy. Not anyone else. And not a bong in sight. But the windows were open and it was at least possible, and maybe clear, that all had gone out the window and onto the ground to avoid a dorm violation at best, a bust at worst.

"They didn't have to go out the window. I'm not a cop. I'm not with Housing."

"I don't know what you're talking about," he said, finally thinking to close his robe. "I'm going to be late for class. Please get out."

"First, Raines Durst. Where is he?"

"Am I my brother's keeper?" He laughed. "Brother's keeper. That's good." He started laughing, then he couldn't stop.

He was pretty solid but he was stoned. I grabbed the terrycloth belt, yanked hard, then wrapped it around his neck. I popped him in the kidney with my left and he would have gone down, except that I held him up with my right.

"Are you going to tell me what I want to know?"

"I don't know where Raines is." He struggled, but I had the advantage. "Let me go."

The bare-chested guy appeared in the doorway. "Let him go." He said it without urgency and with an almost complete lack of intonation, flat, as if he really couldn't care less. "He doesn't even live here."

"Then what's he doing here?"

"He was the only one who wasn't willing to go out the window."

"Where are his clothes?"

"They got tossed out the window with everything else."

"Are you guys crazy?"

"It's McGill, man." He said it with the same flat cadence. "What do you expect?"

"Could you let me down now?" The one with the accent had more urgency in his voice.

I dropped him and he fell in a heap on the floor.

"Raines Durst," I said.

The one in the doorway stepped in. "This is my room. I'm Eric Williams. Raines lives across the hall."

"We established that. Several times," I said, indicating the one on the floor.

"Oh, ok." The primary effect of weed on this one seemed to make him forget what had and hadn't been said in the most recent past. He sat down on a ratty armchair.

"Durst is always with his girlfriend. What is her name?" He looked at the ceiling, as if it might be written there. "One of the Graces. Let's see. Thalia is one. Uh, Leonardo," he said to the one still on the floor, "What are the other two Graces?"

I was losing my patience. "Her name is Grace, idiot."

"Ha. That's cool. She's not one of the Graces. She is Grace." He looked at me and his arms made a flourish. "There you have it. Raines is with Grace."

"What were you guys doing Saturday night?"

"We had a monstrous pre-concert party, man, I mean, we were rocking until three, four in the morning. Cops came twice to quiet it down." He looked at the ceiling again, not because he thought there was an answer. I think he was just resting his stoned-out head. "Monster party, man. McGill, damn it."

"I imagine Raines didn't get to the party until late."

"Raines didn't get to the party at all. He was sick, man. I mean, like, vomit was happening."

"Durst was sick on Saturday night?" That meant he wasn't one of the pranksters after all.

"Hugging the porcelain god, and not because he had too much liquid happiness. Pretty messy, man." He made a face, stuck out his tongue. "He had the whole second floor potty to himself, man. Until it got really hopping about one. After that, we just walked around him."

As I left, I heard Leonardo, the one on the floor say, "Grace is one of the Graces?"

Chapter Fourteen

I LEFT MCGILL WITHOUT a plan. When I worked at VU, as an Assistant Dean, that wasn't an unusual feeling. McGill was the "freak dorm." You went in, and came out not always sure of what you'd heard. Plus, the Philosophy department had offices there. Even if you knew what you heard you weren't always sure what it meant. One time, an assistant professor told me I was experiencing "the phenomenology of doubt."

He might have been right. I couldn't tell.

Fortunately, I saw a familiar, tall female figure across the lawn. She was moving with the stride of someone who had somewhere to be. I figured I could do worse than follow Grace of the Graces.

She had on a long, clingy top over jeans, and the jeans were tucked into knee high leather boots with heels. Her long hair floated off her shoulders. I didn't know who Raines Durst was, but he must be some stuff to have hooked up with her.

I hung back as she hit the center of campus, Calhoun Hall to her left, as she walked toward Stevenson Center. She was nearly six feet tall with the heels, and she walked with the full confidence of someone who knew she was hotter than you would ever be.

When she turned east, I knew she was headed toward the library. I waited, then went in the turnstile several people after her. I knew where she was headed. I'd spent the night there already.

Since I knew where she was going, I went to the basement where the pay phones were. I dropped a dime and dialed Betty. I got no answer. I wasn't that surprised.

I went up to fourth floor where the 800 Dewey decimals were and pulled Absalom, Absalom off the shelf. That's where I'd said I'd left it, even though that wasn't true. I took it and sat just off the seating area in front of Special Collections, so I could see Grace when she left.

If you don't know the novel, there's a lot going on. There's a brother and a sister, and a half-brother. The half-brother wants to marry the sister (she doesn't know they're kin). The father forbids the marriage, because he does know. The brother decides he is going to allow the marriage after all. But then he finds out the half-brother is also part black. And he kills the half-brother he was willing to marry off to his sister.

It sounds like the South's original sin, doesn't it? You're willing to be ok with incest. But not if there's black blood involved.

Plus one of the narrators is crazy, and maybe two are. But that's just par for the course with Faulkner.

What I remember about the book's theme is that the truth isn't one thing, and it may be no thing. There are too many narrators and all of them are telling the truth. But none of them agree with each other. I remember Bruno saying in class that it was just like the South. The past is always there, and it's always being talked about. So it's always being revised.

In other words, who knows what's true?

Suddenly Grace was on the move and I made haste to follow her. She was out the library and headed south down 21st. It was a cool day and the sun was bright, and it was easy to keep up with her. She stopped briefly to light a cigarette, but she was walking quickly and so was I.

I kept just out of sight. Soon we were in Hillsboro Village, and she crossed 21st at Blakemore and went into the Pancake Pantry.

I pondered my next move. On one hand, there was no real reason to go into the restaurant. I could wait until she came out and resume my chase. On the other hand, I had no idea who she was meeting there. At least I needed to walk by and look in the window, right?

I stood at the corner of 21st and Belcourt and waited for inspiration. Before it could strike, I felt something sharp in my back. A nasally voice said, "Walk straight, Trade, and turn when you get to the pancakes."

Hanna.

This time, I did what I was told.

Chapter Fifteen

I COULD HAVE TAKEN a shot at his head with my elbow. It probably would have staggered him enough to spin him against the
wall. But then again, he was a stout guy. It might have gone
another way.

Besides, he didn't seem to want to slice me right here in the
street.

"Inside, jackass." He pushed and I complied. I didn't know
whether he really had a knife. I've known guys who could get
the same reaction with a well-placed key.

"I don't have a beef with you, Hanna. Why are you all over
my ass?"

"Just go inside."

We went inside Pancake Pantry. On Saturdays and Sundays,
there is no getting in the place. People line up out the door
for what in any other city would pass for ordinary pancakes.
In Hillsboro Village, though, they were prized as the very best
the town has to offer. Maybe it's just people from parts of town
with unfortunate pancakes who want to come there. At any
rate, the coffee is pretty good. That's about all I can afford.

I nodded to a couple of VU alums I knew at a booth, one
of whom gently wagged his fork at me, dripping with maple
syrup. Nice. Very polite.

"Look who I found snooping around." Hanna pushed me
toward a chair at the four-top. "Sit down, asshole."

"Please, Rodney. There's no need to speak that kind of language." The impeccable Mr. Pettibone had found another perfectly fitted suit in his closet, and had accented it with a brilliant orange striped tie. "Mr. Trade, please have a seat."

I sat down next to Grace and across from Pettibone. Hanna completed our foursome, within half an arm's length of me. "Just answer the questions you're asked, ok?"

I'm happy to answer any and all questions," I said pleasantly. "How are you, Miss Pettibone?" I looked into a pair of deep sapphire eyes. I thought, that's not a natural color. But then, she was unnaturally pretty. You could go as far as beautiful, and you might not stop there.

"I wonder why you keep turning up," she said. "That makes me a little nervous."

"You don't look nervous." I found her foot touching my leg, her legs crossed next to me. I moved my leg away.

She smiled. "Sometimes I get nervous when something's unfamiliar. You're unfamiliar."

"Maybe if I keep turning up, I'll become more familiar."

Hanna scowled at both of us, not sure what to make of the banter. Mr. Pettibone looked briefly amused, then changed the subject. "Why do you keep turning up? Grace has asked the correct question. You've been asked, rather politely given the circumstances, to stay away from us. And yet here you are again." He looked at Hanna. "This will be the third time?"

Hanna grunted. "Twice that I've seen him. First since he's been told. So I think that means three strikes you're out."

I waved toward a waitress. "Coffee?" She nodded.

"You're not staying that long, Trade." Hanna tried to get her attention, but she was already at the coffee maker, her back to us.

"Let me ask a question, just to get the pot right. You've got a question out there. Let me put one." When nobody said, "no," I put one out there. "What does the Pettibone Institute do? I mean, other than bringing lecturers to campus?"

"That got anything to do with why you won't do what you're told?" Hanna was a bulldog. I could see why Pettibone might want him around. He got a bone and he just gnawed it.

"Maybe," I said. "Maybe not. How about it, Mr. Pettibone? What's your passion?"

"The Pettibone Institute's mission is to further discussion about the historical South. Not the one-dimensional version that's in the media and, even more sadly, in our schoolbooks. We are interested in spreading Southern virtue, Southern values. We want to correct the historical record. That's why we're leading the effort to mount South Rising."

"I got that much from Elsey the other night. But that's the whole ticket?"

Grace sipped a Coke through a straw. She left her tongue on the bottom of the straw just a little longer than she needed to. "Isn't that enough?"

"Sounds like it's a values thing. But don't these efforts usually have a social program, some kind of economic platform? What the less well-educated would call The South Will Rise Again."

Grace raised an eyebrow and looked at her father, who sat in silence. Hanna's face had not faded from the red it had become outside. The waitress brought my coffee, sat it down, looked at the four of us and waited. "Anything else?"

Pettibone's face reanimated. "No, thank you." He reached into his inside jacket pocket, then thought better of it. "I believed you were interested in the cause, Mr. Trade, and then I believed that you deceived us. I still believe you are up to something, because your brother is the person who killed poor Patrick." I started to speak but he continued. "I know that you have fixed on us for some reason. Grace, of course, is friends with all three boys."

"I'm friends with lots of people," Grace said. Her foot was on my leg again. This time I let it stay.

"You've been expressly warned to stay away from us. And yet here you are. And now you are asking about the Institute." He smoothed the napkin on the table. "The question is why."

"Look, Mr. Pettibone. You're right about my brother. I'd love to help him. But the police have him six ways to Sunday. Plus, I don't really know him. I haven't seen him in ten years. That's a lifetime ago." Pettibone seemed to ponder this. At least his face made that expression, the one where you look away and furrow your brow. Like you're thinking. "Sure, I went to Parsons' room to see what he knew. But that's when I came across you folks. And your very interesting take on Southern history."

"Are you trying to tell me that you're following us because you are interested in Southern history?" Hanna wasn't buying it. He would have preferred to punch me.

"I'm just a Southern boy who's spent his life trying to escape the South. Problem is, there's nowhere else I fit. Sure didn't fit in Vietnam. Don't fit here now that I'm back."

"Yes," said Pettibone. "I hear that is a common fact with our veterans."

Grace was looking at me with what I construed as interest. She smiled when I looked directly at her.

"So the talk the other night was interesting. Your Institute is interesting. The idea of a big to-do at the Arena is interesting."

"And now you're a groupie?" Hanna still wasn't having it.

"It's not a big town. Especially when you're usually on foot, like me. If you weren't within a dozen blocks of campus, you'd never see me and I'd never see you. Can I help it if you're always within walking distance?"

They looked at each other. Finally, Pettibone said, "When you put it that way, Mr. Trade, it seems reasonable. And I suppose it's reasonable that you initially deceived us about your name."

I took a drink of coffee. They didn't seem to be smokers, so I didn't press my luck by lighting up. "So, we're square, then?"

"I still don't like it," said Hanna. His fists were balled up and rested on the table. He was a ball of tensed energy. If it ever got let loose, he might do some damage.

"I'm satisfied that, should we venture beyond your foot patrol, we'll not see you," said Pettibone. "Can I be assured of that?"

"Without a doubt. Now, given that your daughter is on campus all the time, I can't guarantee she won't run across me."

"That won't be a problem." The way Grace looked at me, when she said it, told me that it might be just that. A real problem.

They got up to leave. "I'll pay for your coffee," Pettibone said. And the three of them went as quickly out as I had come quickly, though not exactly willingly, in.

I walked over to the table where Eddie Hiller and Bob Wyatt still sat, pancakes now eaten and coffee well underway. I sat when they motioned me in, and lit my own.

Eddie had worked at VU, but had changed careers when Hospital Corporation of America started to take off. He'd made good, or done well. I never know what to say about that. He was about my age, but dressed like a banker. Bob was in real estate. He had plenty of money too, but he never dressed above Lacoste and khakis. Though maybe that was a statement of wealth in itself. I wouldn't know.

"Got anything besides coffee in there, Jackson?"

"Funny guy."

"How do you know those folks?"

"We just came across each other. I was at the lecture they sponsored the other night."

"I never figured you for a Southern patriot, Jackson." Eddie wasn't smoking anymore, apparently. HCA must have a code.

"We're all just good old boys, right?" I drained the coffee and signaled for another cup. "Besides, what the hell's a southern patriot anyway?"

"You didn't just fall off the turnip truck, friend. You know damn well what a southern patriot is." Bob was grinning, like he'd heard a joke a long time ago and was rehearing it for the first time.

"He may not, Bob. You weren't much in the fraternity scene, were you, Jackson?"

"I was in the Housing scene. I was trying to keep you guys from committing stupidity."

"Still, you knew. There's a strain of it all through VU. How the South is the only true culture in the country. How the North is just a combination of melting pot crap. How you have to protect the culture."

"Doesn't that just mean you have to keep black people in their place?" I wasn't trying to fool the Pettibones now. I was agitated. I didn't know Bob or Eddie to be bigoted. But I didn't know where they were going with this.

"Don't get bent out of shape," said Eddie. "It's just that you were over there with a couple of pretty hard-core patriots. If you went to one of their lectures, you know how the line goes. They're out to restore the South. They don't want any Yankee interlopers. They don't want any people that don't know their place in society."

"That's not what I heard at the lecture. It was much more a history lesson than anything else. Weird, revisionist history, but history anyway."

"Then you got the acceptable version. Or the cleaned up one. Maybe the guy in the suit is more or less 'intellectual,' but the stocky one? He's pure bad. The sort you really don't want to hang out with."

"Then how do you know him, Bob?"

"Sucker bought a house from me. Out in Brentwood. He's not a friendly cat, and he doesn't hang with friendly people. I've seen them out at the range, shooting. He can get presentable, but the rest? Rough crowd."

"Not the guy in the suit," said Eddie. "Don't know him. But I like his looks."

"So you guys are just telling me this because you like me."

Eddie looked at me with what I've learned is pity. I don't care for pity. I don't get it much. But there it was. "You're up to something or else you wouldn't be anywhere near these people. Unless you're just trying to get into the girl's pants, which I might not blame you for, but that isn't you either. I'm just telling you to be careful."

"And," Bob added, "if the gossip is true, cut back on your drinking. If you're about to get in harm's way, you'd better be sober."

I stood up. They meant well, and they might be right. But I didn't need pity, and I didn't need anybody telling what I needed to do. "Thanks, guys." As I headed for the door, angry as hell, I said over my shoulder, "That coffee's paid for."

Chapter Sixteen

A LONG TIME AGO someone told me, "The way you think is the way you are." I wanted to know how Grace thought. Actually, I wanted to know how her father and Hanna thought too, but I didn't have access to anything like that for them. But with Grace? I had her research activity. And if I could ever find him, I had her boyfriend, Raines.

I walked from Hillsboro Village over to the JUL, and made my way to the back of the building where Special Collections was housed. At the desk was an oversized man in his fifties, reading glasses on a cord around his neck. He had sandy hair, the color that would turn gray before anyone noticed and a pronounced overbite. His name tag said that he was Grayson Greer, and he looked like he was the guy in charge.

But I knew him as Gray. He used to be in microforms, and that's where my undergraduate research always took place.

"Hey, Gray."

He looked up confused then smiled broadly. "Are you a ghost? You look just like someone I used to know."

He came out from behind the counter and gave me a bear hug. "Jeez, Gray, you're gonna bust a lung."

His laugh rang out and a couple of students looked at us, one with a particularly nasty stare that didn't go away until Gray returned it.

"Come sit back here and tell me what you've been up to, you scoundrel."

"You tell me. When did you come out from the darkness into the light?"

"About a year ago. Old Mrs. Bird, who had run Special Collections for at least twenty years, had a stroke. Otherwise she would have been carried out of here. Well, actually, I guess they did carry her out because she had the stroke here."

"That would have caused a scene."

"Oh, I hear that it did. Anyway, the job was posted, and it should have been Ann Tyler who got the job, but she decided she would rather be the head library priestess at Belmont, so off she went. And that was all the full time staff there was."

"And nobody else wanted it?" I said it as a question, but I really meant it as a statement. I couldn't imagine anybody wanting it.

"Au contraire, my missing friend. Half a dozen of my colleagues wanted it."

"And Mr. Microforms was the best qualified?"

"Indeed, I was. Not so much on the collections part, though micro is a collection. But more because of my peerless reputation for helping young researchers become professional researchers." He put his reading glasses on his nose, looked at me, and put them off. "Except for you. You are my one great failure." And then he laughed loudly again.

This time the nasty stare just got up and left.

"So you have found me, Jackson Trade. Now what?"

"Wasn't looking for you, Gray. But I'm glad you're here."

"What, then?"

"I'm interested in one of the young researchers you'll turn into a professional. Grace Pettibone."

He drew back a little and looked hard into my eyes. "I'm sensing you have more interest in dear Miss Pettibone as a young woman than as a researcher. No, no, that's fine. If I were thirty years younger, so might I." He looked like he might laugh again, but he didn't. "Well, that's not true, thirty years ago she would still have been out of my league. But you?"

"In fact, Gray, I am interested in her research. I saw her at a recent Southern history lecture, and I saw her coming in here twice."

"And you've not been in to see me, haunting the library? You are a ghost."

I ignored him. "I came in to see what she's working on so intently. I don't think it's the usual thing for undergrads to be in here doing research."

"True enough, and more's the pity. You know how I feel. Research is our homage to the past, our duty to the future."

"Spare me the homily, man."

"Ok. I can tell you that Miss Pettibone is a specialist already, so young into her career."

"She's an undergrad, Gray."

"Exactly. And she works like a doctoral student. She is organized. Knowledgeable. Precise in her searches. Fiendishly clever in the way she deduces where to go next."

"What's she looking for?"

"That would be a bit of a guess. She's never divulged what exactly she's looking for, if in fact she is looking for a particular thing. Her interests center in the Civil War, especially the last bits, and I think I can see developing an interest in the actual fall of the Confederacy."

"Appomattox?"

"No, I think not. She seems to be concentrating on the fall of Richmond. Appomattox Courthouse is simply the denouement."

"And you've got plenty of that in this collection?"

"Jackson, we've got more than you can get through. Hundreds of linear feet of documents. We have some rare daguerreotypes. And letters? Oh, boy, do we have letters. By the bushel basket."

"But you don't know exactly where she's going with all this research?"

"Listen, at one point I thought she was writing some killer paper for an upper-level history course. If you told me she was writing about what it was like to be a sharpshooter for the Confederacy, I'd have said, that's going to be something. But the longer she's gone at it, the more I think she's really looking for something. Something that isn't articulated."

"What does that even mean, Gray? Something that isn't articulated?"

"She's connecting dots. I think she may not know what she is looking for. Or she may know, but not know that she'll find it in one place. You know how research is. You look for the pattern."

I know that. Connect the dots. Look for the pattern. I'm not having much luck with it. But I do know the idea.

I gave Grayson a handshake, and exited the library. I still needed to find Raines Durst. Maybe he could tell me about his beautiful girlfriend, the researcher.

Just as a sunny day gives way to a thunderstorm easily in the summer, so October in Nashville can quickly become fickle. Somewhere a cold front had lost its baby, and the baby was stomping around middle Tennessee angry and ready to make some noise. The sky had turned the kind of gray that usually portends something unusual, with a greenish tint that would make you expect tornados.

Except that it was October, and the temperature hung in the 40s. Too cold for tornadoes, too warm for any kind of winter precipitation. What it would be, I could not tell.

The sky inside my head was pretty dark too. For reasons I couldn't quite explain, I'd been drawn into a back and forth with people who seemed cultured, seemed reasonable, but probably weren't. I was chasing student behavior that, while completely like every other undergraduate in intent, was so unlike it in reality that I had trouble comprehending it. And of course, one of them was dead. That didn't usually happen. Not even on a bad day.

And why was I letting myself get distracted into wandering around after Grace Pettibone? Yes, she was the girlfriend of one of the planners, but he was sick that night and didn't even go. Yes, she showed up as I talked with Howell Parsons, but that was simple coincidence. And yes, her father was impeccable and yet somehow borderline offensive, while his--whatever Hanna was--was entirely objectionable. And their Institute was penniless. Maybe it was bogus.

And there was something in it all that made people who weren't exactly friends of mine worry for me, and warn me off.

Plus, Grace was playing the vamp a little.

Just a little.

My skies were really muddied.

I made my way back to McGill just before the clouds opened up and rain fell sideways. Standing in the lobby was the kid in the robe from yesterday and a couple of other stoners. The one I'd roughed up stood on the third step to the parlor and squinted at me, as if he were trying to make me out through a haze. I figured he was a little hazy.

As he squinted, though, his eyes grew apart, then larger, until finally he recognized me. "Whoa," he said, and turned on his heel, first stepping quickly, then breaking into a run.

"What's that about?" the speaker was a red headed kid with a red bandana headband. He clashed with himself.

"I don't think he likes me." They nodded in agreement. "Either of you know Raines Durst?"

The red head ignored the question, but his buddy, who looked not at all like the usual McGill resident, said, "Sure." He looked more like a trucker: jeans, jeans jacket over a black t-shirt, a Mack Truck ball cap. He wore what looked like steel-toed work boots, and his belt buckle said "World Champ," thought what he was champion of was left unsaid. He was short, but he had a solid look, like it'd be hard to push him around.

"Raines is a jerk, but I know him. You a friend of his?"

"More like a friend of friends. But they told me to look him up."

"Yeah? Which set of friends? Raines pals around with a lot of folks."

Considering my long hair, beard, and jeans, I gave the South a shout out. "Sons of Shiloh."

"So you're not part of his brainiac crowd." He gave me an approving look. "Good. That bunch annoys the shit out of me. So you know him, his girlfriend, all that?"

"Grace? She's a looker."

He paused, then smiled. "Yeah, she's prime. How she ends up with Durst is beyond any of us, but maybe he's got talents we don't know about."

He nudged the redhead in the ribs and the redhead snorted. "Talent." And snorted again.

"If you're looking for him, though, he's not in." He looked beyond me at the deluge. "My guess is that he didn't get where he was going before he got soaked."

"He won't melt," said the redhead. "He's got talent." He snorted again. Stoned people amuse themselves.

"Know where he was going?"

"Who knows where any of us are going, brother?"

Chapter Seventeen

THE RAINSTORM STOPPED AS suddenly as it started, leaving the sky a mottled blue and the air pleasantly chilled. Not cold, but cooler, more seasonal, and brisk. My mind was also cleared a bit, though the continuing problem with catching up to Raines Durst was annoying.

I found myself at Hannigan's. Sometimes I wonder if I really mean to be there or if I'm just unconsciously working toward what I want or need. When I walked in, I remembered that I need to pay something on my tab to keep Mrs. H from demanding payment.

The reason I have a tab at all is because of the money pinball, a feature only found in Tennessee and South Carolina. The way it works is simple but hard to execute. The machines don't have flippers. You have to have enough touch, and enough skill in bumping the machine, to cause five balls to fall in the correct holes. You know the correct holes because the scoreboard shows you. And getting the correct pattern wins you games.

You can jack up the payout any given pattern will earn by putting quarters in the machine. And you can change the patterns you can shoot for by adding quarters as well. The most games I've ever won was 3200.

The trick with money pinball is that you can cash out those games. 3200 games is good for $800. And that's more than is usually in the cash register, for good reason.

See why Mrs. H lets me run a tab?

It's easier than paying my winnings.

I handed over a ten and asked Charlie for a roll of quarters, then took it to the Casino Royale machine. I jacked the odds up pretty high for a first try, and hit the pattern in red. Good. Off to a solid start. The machine clicked off 320 free games. Eighty bucks. About a third of my tab, probably.

I reloaded most of the free games to make the odds soar. If I hit another good pattern, I might be able to pay the tab completely off tonight. I nestled the first ball gently off the top bumper into the number one hole.

As I pulled the plunger back, I felt someone lean against my hip, in the sort of way you get in a crowded bus before the leaner pulls back. This one didn't.

"You mind?" I said, as I turned.

"I don't mind at all, as long as you don't." I smelled the light fragrance of a musky perfume at the same moment I saw Grace Pettibone smiling at me. She turned toward the machine and kept her hip in contact with me. "Are you good at this?"

"I'm very good at this."

"I bet you are." She put her hand on the plunger, above my hand but brushing it. "Show me."

"You'll have to give me a little room."

"I can do that, but show me something." I could feel her warm breath near my face, and then she removed her hand and her hip. "Let me see how a pro handles it."

I'm no rookie. But when a tall, gorgeous girl is playing her game, and you respond, if you know what I mean, it's hard to concentrate. I ended up junking the second ball, before bringing three and four into play on the green line. I needed the twenty-six to land, and I did. But for minimal gains.

"I think you were going easy for me," she said quietly, near my ear. "Go ahead. Go for it. Show me what you got."

I turned to face her and she leaned into me, from her legs to her breasts. "It might go a little over the line," I said. "Sometimes you have to pop the machine a little harder, give it a jerk at just the right time."

"Sounds about right," she whispered. "Do whatever you need to do."

I pumped in the reminder of the quarters and had the odds in a place where, if I hit the yellow or the blue, I probably made back my tab. The first two balls were easy nesters, dropping right where they needed to. The third ball had to hit the seventeen hole, and my shot didn't place as precisely, which meant I had to pop the machine gently with both hands, then once a little harder with my right, before it did a 360 and fell into the hole.

"Very nice," Grace said. "I like the way you took control of that."

The fourth ball clipped the twenty-two, but I saved it with a quick nudge when it hit the bumper below. The fifth ball, the money shot, had to hit the twenty-three, a harder shot and the one I saved for last. The plunger sprung forward with authority, clearing the upper part of the board twice before settling in a back-and-forth, slow and methodical descent. There wasn't much to do. It was perfectly placed, and I kept my hands on the machine, letting gravity bring it where it needed to be. As it got close to the twenty-three, it veered just a little left, and I let it find the bumper, then gave a sidelong pop, which caused the rebound to sink dead in the hole.

There was a moment of silence, and then the counter began clicking free games. Click by click, stroke by stroke, until it his 1786. Over $400.

She leaned into me, her front to my back. She was shorter than me, but her boot heels made up most of the height. She put her arms around me, pressed into me, and said, "That was impressive. You use your hands very well."

"Thanks." I stood still for what felt like a long time. Did I want this?

Well, hell yes.

Should I want it? And if I did, what should I want it for?

I don't think it was that long a pause. It didn't seem to register with Grace if it was. I finally said, "Do you want to try?"

"I don't want to try pinball," she said.

"Want to tell me what you'd like to try?"

"Cash out your games and come with me. I'll show you."

"You not going to turn me over to Hanna, are you?" I smiled, as if it was far from my mind.

She smiled back. "Oh, no. I'm going to turn myself over to you."

Charlie gave me a dirty look when he saw the games count. He took out a pad and figured the damage, then pulled the notebook with my tab in it from under the register. "Looks like I owe you about a hundred."

"That'll short you for the night. Just give me a twenty and carry the rest forward."

"We're never going to get even, are we?"

"Just depends on what you mean by even. Far as I'm concerned, the books are right."

The whole time, Grace was leaning in, her hand inside my back jeans pocket. The jeans were tight, but she still managed to give me a little squeeze.

Charlie gave me a twenty. "You kids have a good night."

"Going to." Grace sounded certain.

As we crossed onto campus, her arm snaked inside mine. "It's chilly."

"You came looking for me, didn't you?" I hastened to add, "I don't mind."

"You're not that hard to find, Jackson Trade. People know you. They know your habits. If I hadn't found you there, I had a couple of other places to look."

"And you came looking because?"

She burrowed in a little closer. "Are you that dense?"

"Maybe I just want to hear it from you."

"Ok. Fair enough. You are smart. I like that. You don't back down from Daddy. You clearly can't stand Rod Hanna, and, just in case you wonder, that counts as a gold star in my book." She matched my steps, her right to my left, with precision. "Plus you fill out your clothes nicely."

"You fill yours nicely too."

"I just knew you noticed." She had both hands on my arm now, making herself just a little smaller than she really was. "How'd you like to see the rest?"

I told her I thought that was the point of our walking now, toward Cole Hall, at the dinner hour on a Thursday night. "You're sure your roommate won't mind?"

"A Pettibone girl doesn't have roommates. I'm too much a princess for that."

"Ok, Princess. Let's go get you out of your crown."

***

The sex was enthusiastic and satisfying. I can vouch for my part. I think I know enough to say she wasn't any less happy. But who knows? People lie about everything anymore.

We lay there in her bed, me on my back and her cuddled inside my arm. She drew the cigarette from my hand and took a drag. I leaned to the nightstand and stubbed it out.

"Was it what you wanted?" she asked.

"It was. You?"

"Actually, a little better." I rolled my eyes and she slapped my chest lightly. "Stop it. Seriously. You're the first older man."

"I'm twenty-six, Grace. What are you, sweet sixteen, never been kissed?"

"I'm twenty-one. But you know what I mean. I've only been with guys my age." She leaned in again, snuggling. "You know what you're doing."

"When it comes to this, Grace, everybody knows what they're doing. They're doing what they want to do, what they're built for."

"And you were doing what I wanted you to do to me. That's different." She kissed my cheek, and then when I faced her our lips met and lingered, then became purposeful. She might be a little younger, but she knew how to kiss.

"Umm," she said. "That was nice."

We lay there for a while, and I dozed in and out a little. But after some time had passed, she roused me. "Ask you a question?"

"Sure."

"You seemed interested in the lecture the other night. Are you? I mean, are you really interested?

"Define 'really interested.' I'm from the South. I don't understand the South. Dr. Elsey has a point of view. I'm not sure I agree, but he's got certainty on his side. I used to hang out with Bruno Prince, and he's got a point of view."

"Dr. Prince is pretty cool, but he isn't a true believer. Daddy is a true believer, but his reach exceeds his grasp."

"Or what's a heaven for?" She got the allusion. You could tell. Smart girl. Hot girl. "What is a true believer, Grace? That sounds a little ..."

"Unhinged?"

"Well, at least not as balanced as you'd like to think is right."

"Then you're not really interested. You're just trying to be an intellectual about it."

"And you? You're in the library all the time."

She sat up on her elbow. "You've been spying on me." She didn't say it quite the way you'd want. "I am different from Daddy. He wants to do things. I want to know things." She bore straight into my eyes with hers. "But you've been spying on me."

Now it was time to lie. "Not at all. I saw you coming out one day as I went to visit my old friend, Grayson Greer, in Special Collections. He says you're the best undergraduate researcher he's seen in some time."

She went silent for a moment. "That's sweet. He's a nice man."

"So what are you researching? Is it something a true believer looks for?"

"It's actually pretty cool." She looked in my eyes, maybe searching for a sign that she could tell me.

"I'm game."

"Did you know that, at the end of the war, General Lee proposed taking a force into the mountains, and mounting a guerilla campaign against the North? Lee was a brilliant general. If he had done that, he might have been able to harass the Union troops into a negotiated settlement. He could have forced a stalemate."

"I know a poem about it. Or rather, a poem about Lee in the mountains as president of Washington and Lee."

"I know that poem too. One of the Southern Agrarians wrote it. But it's not just a poem. It was a serious plan."

"What went wrong, then? Lee didn't do it."

"The history books say, if they talk about it at all, that Jefferson Davis overruled it. He didn't know if he could give it enough resources to work."

"Makes sense. As I understand it, the Confederacy was out of cash."

"But that's not true at all. The entire treasury of the Confederate nation was shipped out before the fall of Richmond."

"Then it sounds like Davis just didn't want to do it."

"But here's the mystery, Jackson." She was warming to her tale. "The treasury disappeared. Gold and silver. Vanished.

Except for a pittance that was found later, when Davis was captured."

"Where did it go?"

"I don't know. But somebody back then knew. And that's what I'm looking for."

She had a vacant look in her eyes for a moment, then looked at me and laughed. She kissed me and threw herself on top of me. "Let's make love again, Jackson. All this talk about history gets me hot." There was a look in her eyes that said she was telling the truth.

"I don't know anyone that gets hot over Confederate talk."

"Any old excuse will do, Jackson." She rubbed herself against me. "Do you need another one?"

I didn't.

About halfway through, I thought about how it was good she didn't have a roommate. And about how she did, after all, have a boyfriend. Then I didn't think again until much later in the night.

Chapter Eighteen

When you hear a phone ringing in your sleep, it's at least possible that you're imagining it. Or dreaming it. But by the second ring it was clear to me that it was a phone actually ringing, and it was only when I reached for it that I realized I was not in my apartment. Grace reached over me and took the receiver from my hand. She gave me a look. An annoyed look.

"Do you know what time it is?" She put her finger over her mouth, signaling me to keep quiet. She needn't have bothered. "Oh. Well, I was asleep. What's up?" She nodded as she rubbed herself against my leg. "Ok. Well, that's fine. Give me a few minutes to get presentable."

After she hung up, and after I gave her a quizzical look, she said, "Raines. My boyfriend. You haven't met him."

"Should I?"

She smiled and hopped off the bed. "Not tonight, I should think. He's down in the lobby."

"Then it might be tough not to meet him."

"Well, there are options. I could just leave you here. You could be my personal toy."

"That's not an option I like. Sooner or later I'll have to have food."

"I can bring you food."

"Sooner or later I'll have to use the bathroom."

"Ok. I could handle that one too, but you'll eventually have to shower. So there is option two."

"Which is--"

"Which is I'll take you down the south stairwell, where you can wait right by the double doors. Then I'll go back and come down the north stairwell, and take Raines up that way. You'll just walk out."

"And the desk clerk won't be suspicious at all that an unaccompanied male is leaving?"

"You'll figure that out. You're very good at figuring things out."

And that's the way we did it. When I left, I waved back as if someone was there. "Thanks, Darlin'," I called to nobody. The desk clerk looked up from an organic chemistry textbook, briefly, then back down. Nothing to see here.

Once outside, I saw that a crowd had amassed. They were milling around, waiting for something. I walked to a short couple, a man and a woman with alligators on their shirts, and asked the natural question.

"There's a rumor going around that there'll be a mass streak on the lawn tonight."

"Isn't that so three years ago?" I asked.

"Vanderbilt never gets it until later," the girl said.

"I don't know," the boy said, "That means Auburn probably won't be streaking for a couple of years yet."

The crowd grew and I continued to walk around its perimeter. I saw Wendy Williamson and she confirmed the rumor. "I just hope it happens soon and we can all go to bed. I need my beauty sleep."

Undergraduates don't, however, need sleep. They can exist on coffee, then beer, for days on end, as long as there's goldfish crackers in the mix somewhere. This crowd was more on the beer part of the cycle, and there was a fair amount of yelling, laughing, and general merriment. It moved, amoeba-like, without really changing its location. From the air, it would have looked like a large sentient being with no purpose.

I'm not sure that's not exactly what it was.

At the edge of it I found Don Mercer, looking pissed.

"I hate Thursday nights," he said. "The start of the weekend for students. Just another long weekday for the working stiffs who protect them."

"Are you protecting them from streakers? Why?"

"For what it's worth, public nudity is against the law."

"And you're going to run down these outlaws?" I examined Don. All 5-7 and 220 pounds of him. "You'll need a head start."

"Very funny." He continued to talk without looking at me. I couldn't tell if it was because he really was looking for something, or because the reason he was pissed was me. "Why are you here tonight?"

"Just here looking for coeds to date."

"You sure 'date' is the correct verb?"

"Date is always the right verb, if you're in public."

"You should stay in public then. Your track record isn't all that good."

That's true enough. Let's hope Grace wouldn't prove to hew to that rule. "Can't be more public than this, right?"

The amoeba had spun a little on its axis, and a new set of undergraduates were now in view. Just to the right of my line of sight, I spied the young lady in question. She had pulled her hair into a pony tail and had not bothered with makeup. She didn't really need to. She had on the same jeans and boots from earlier, and she'd put on a heavier coat. Suddenly she focused on me, laughed and winked.

Next to her, looking away, was Raines Durst. My first impression of him was that she was way too much for him to handle. That would have been my impression even before tonight. Where she was tall, he was shorter. Where she was sophisticated, he appeared awkward. He was short, but long-limbed, skinny but with a paunch around the middle. He had light brown hair, left long over the ears and parted on the side. He had a fuzzy goatee that either was just beginning to grow in or never would.

He turned to her and said something, and she shook her head no. He shrugged, and they kept moving with the crowd as it spun slowly, waiting for the streakers, and drinking. As they moved just beyond my field of vision, she turned and, over her shoulder, made a kissing gesture with her lips.

"Was that girl blowing you a kiss?" Mercer finally looked at me.

"What girl?"

He looked back to the crowd. "Never mind. Probably blowing it at me. Happens all the time."

The full moon gave enough light to see everyone pretty clearly, added with the lights from Sarratt behind and the sidewalk lighting. On crisp nights like this, it was fun to be out, among a crowd. I remembered that from my undergraduate days. And then I remembered, from my Assistant Dean days, how something like this, so pleasant and collegiate, could turn. One moment you were quietly riding the energy of all those students, the next you were racing to some sort of emergency. Mercer was right to be on his guard. These days, I didn't have to be.

So I let him do his job, not that he wanted me there anyway. "See ya, Donnie."

"Stay out of trouble, Jackson." Still not looking at me.

"Too late," I wanted to say. But I just moved toward the west side of the crowd, closer to the residence halls.

It was slightly darker on that side. There was a young man in a flannel shirt, puking. The smell came as a piercing acidic burst, then it was gone as his friends dragged him toward the dorms. A girl nearby looked at her shoes and, satisfied he hadn't hit them, stepped gingerly around the mess and got on with her partying.

Inside the crowd, I spotted Howell Parsons with a group. They were pointing at Mickey on Kirkland and laughing. The prank had lasted, as it turned out Vanderbilt couldn't get a crane and crew to take it down for another month. Too bad they couldn't just hire Patrick Vincent to take it down. Nobody could hire him for anything anymore.

My mind returned to my brother and his predicament. It is probably a reflection of my general feeling of helplessness that I hadn't thought of him for a good twelve hours. Or maybe it was a reflection of how little he'd been in my life for so long. How the hell could I help him now?

There came a cry from the rear, behind me, and the crowd burst in my direction. Cries of "Over here. They're over here," came from various voices. Suddenly I was engulfed by a teeming crowd, swept almost without will along with the current. It was as if I'd been caught by a powerful undertow at the beach, but here the undertow was human powered. It wasn't as if it had a mind of its own. It was as if it had no mind at all.

I felt claustrophobia. Ever since combat, I'd been wary of enclosed spaces. It's not uncommon; veterans often feel that they're far better suited for the open air. I don't like small rooms, and I don't like big crowds.

This crowd was moving in the general direction of where a pack of streakers, which looked to be about a half dozen males in ski caps, tennis shoes, and nothing else, turning the corner at the Deke house and sprinting toward the Kappa Sig corner.

I moved with the crowd, knowing that I'd be trampled soon enough if I didn't. But there was no way a lot of undergrads with beers in their hands could catch young men properly motivated not to be caught. Surprisingly, however, the crowd gave it their best, reaching the Campus Ministry, halfway down the block, before the streakers split, half going toward West End and the other half toward McGugin, where cars waited with open doors to pick them us and, squealing tires, spirit them safely away.

I felt dizzy and nauseous, and I felt my heart pounding. The crowd around me roared approval at the escape of the streakers, and the noise, combined with the close quarters, made me short of breath. I felt like my heart would beat out of my chest. All around me, the crowd seemed to pulse with energy, drawing tighter and tighter around me.

I began pushing my way out. I knocked one guy's beer out of his hands as I flailed, and he tried unsuccessfully to grab my arm. He backed away when he saw my face.

I was frantic to get out of the mass of bodies. Almost at the border of the crowd, about to escape, I took a sharp breath as a shot shattered the night air. Then a second and a third.

The crowd seized and quieted, and I lurched forward, through the outer ring. I rolled on the ground, taking cover. When no shot followed, I got to one knee, had a look around, and tore across the lawn between the Chi Omega house and the Sigma Chi property, sliding under a chain fence, and across the back lot. I covered the ground between there and West End, moving in as serpentine a way as speed would allow. Faster was better.

I came to West End and darted into traffic, dodging the traffic until I was in the Krystal parking lot. Horns blared, and one guy screamed out an open window at me. By the time I was across Elliston and in my apartment, I was sure I was having some kind of heart attack. I raced up my stairs, unlocked the door, and took refuge.

I poured myself a tall bourbon and drank it down. The burn at the back of my throat threatened to come out, but I poured more and drank again. I stood with my hands on the counter, bent over, letting my breath come back to regular.

I went back and checked the door lock, then I slid the deadbolt. I poured another tall drink, and sat down. There would be no sleeping tonight. Not without a lot of help.

Chapter Nineteen

IT WAS MORNING. I unbolted the door and stepped outside. It had become much warmer, I thought. The air looked like morning now, the sun just beginning to rise, and there were puffs of fog, almost like little smoke bombs that had gone off.

Before I reached the bottom of the steps, I heard the sharp report of weapons fire, and I jumped the last two steps, rolled behind the boxwood shrub, skinning my face as I did. My heart was racing again, but I calmed myself, repeating as I always did in combat, "This is not your day. Today is not your day."

I scrambled, bear-crawl style, across the driveway. My Impala was parked close to the house, and I was able to take cover. I peered around the front of the car, trying to get a bead on whoever had taken the shots. I saw a body at the end of the driveway, about thirty feet away. The body had a weapon next to it. It looked like an M-16, but that couldn't be the case.

Could I reach it? The air was quiet. Nothing stirred. I stood slowly. No sound.

It was a horrible idea. I knew it then, but I couldn't stop myself. I moved as fast as I could from the Impala across to the boxwood, then down the side of the garage. No shots. The shooter must be on the other side of the garage. Maybe even down the street. Maybe I could get to the body and grab the weapon.

I raced to the dead man, grabbed the rifle and lay prone on the other side of the body, letting it give me what cover it could. The weapon was an M-16. Inexplicable. I looked toward the dead man's face, facing me.

Thompson! How the hell was Thompson here, dead in my driveway, next to an M-16? I checked the magazine for rounds, and pulled back the lever to see if there was a round in the chamber. It was loaded.

I ran to the other side of the house with the rifle, looked around and saw no one in the open. What should I do next?

I heard loud shouting to my rear and when I looked that way I saw a long line of men dressed in black with bushes tied to their backs. They had their backs to me as they followed two soldiers who were helping a third. The two GIs had him between them with his arms around their necks. His clothes were burned off except for his under shorts, which were a dirty white. I knew that I was cut off from the rear where the shots had come from and that I couldn't go toward Church Street with all the NVA there.

Where did that thought come from? There's no North Vietnamese Army in Nashville.

I decided to go back to the Impala. When I got there I spied a path that headed off to the right. I could see that the path led back toward Elliston Place. I started down the path very slowly, watching to the left and the right and checking the rear. Then I came upon a wounded soldier. He was badly wounded. He had burns all over his body and his face and could not see out of his right eye. I picked him up and put him on my left side with his arm hanging on to me. We walked very slowly. I had Thompson's M-16 slung over my shoulder and held on to it by the hand guard.

We started down the trail slowly and then I heard a sharp crack in front of us. I saw a man in black pajamas with his back to me aiming at people in front of him. I laid the wounded man down and lay down beside him. I waited a minute to wipe the sweat from my eyes and wondered what to do next. I was worn out and tired. The man in black shot again and it made me angry. He was picking off our men. I aimed at the center mass of his back and fired, hitting him. He threw up his right arm and tossed his SKS into the bushes to his right. Then he turned to face me. I shot him again, in the stomach. He sank to his knees, holding his belly with both hands. I took careful aim, and shot him a third time, right between the eyes. The bullet blew out the back of his head.

Then I picked up the wounded soldier again. We came to a small clearing and saw another man in black holding a Chi-com grenade. He was VC. How the hell are they in Nashville? I didn't see any other weapon. I let the soldier down to the ground and he started crawling away. I kneeled and took aim.

The VC was tossing the grenade up and catching it, humming to himself. He seemed to be considering where to toss it. I saw that he had a group of people in his vicinity, maybe they were students, maybe not. He didn't have a weapon. Just the grenade. I yelled at him. Then I squeezed off a round.

Startled, he began to run, zigzagging, so I waited for my second shot, aimed and fired. This one hit him, knocking him over sideways.

I rose and caught up with the wounded soldier. I put him under my left arm and we walked slowly onwards. I hoped to catch up with some of the other soldiers who were still alive. A little way down the trail I turned to my right, looking for more men. I walked around a bend in the trail and saw an NVA soldier about ten yards ahead of us. He was facing away from us and had an AK-47 in his hands.

Then the NVA turned toward me and I could see that he was putting a thirty-round clip in his AK-47. We looked each other in the eyes. I was surprised at how tall he was. I pointed the M-16 toward his chest and shot him. As he turned and fell, the wounded soldier and I went back to the trail we had been following. I still hoped to find reinforcements further down the path.

Several hundred yards down the trail, the path made a swing to the right and we came out of the bushes into the middle of a street I didn't recognize, next to a feed store. Had we really come so far? Two soldiers were sitting there. Both were wounded. A lieutenant, the forward observer, was further out in the street. I walked up to him, and said, "Man, what the hell is going on?"

His eyes were wide open. He was frightened. He took my hand from his arm and continued walking toward the middle of the street. I looked past him and saw some wounded men lying next to a storm drain behind a bunker of feed bags. I followed the lieutenant to where the survivors were and lay down at the far right side of the group.

I was lying there for a while when snipers opened up on the survivors from behind a small building across the street. I was on the end and could hear the bullets whack into their bodies with loud thuds. Thud. Thud. Each one was the sickening announcement of death. The fire was coming from the direction of Elliston. I crawled up to several of them to comfort them.

These soldiers were lying on their stomachs trying to get as low and as small as they could behind the makeshift bunker. A couple of sniper rounds hit near my head and I moved away from the soldiers. I was drawing fire as I moved among them.

I saw black objects flying through the air. Suddenly, a sniper was shooting at me and I could see rounds hitting close to my head. I looked to my rear to see if I could locate him. I saw a head sticking up above the dike. It looked like someone was waving his arms beckoning me to come to him. I thought it was a wounded soldier, so I got up and ran toward him.

A round exploded, hit behind my right knee, knocking my leg out from under me. I fell hard.

I got up again and another round tore my wristwatch off, but I kept running toward the soldier. When I was near I leaped.

I felt a piercing pain in my chest. Instead of diving down next to the soldier, I kept going and slid into a watering hole.

Down I went, further and further. I had lost the ability to swim. Nothing worked. My arms wouldn't move. I couldn't make my legs kick. And as I fell, I passed the faces of dead men. Dead Americans. Dead Vietnamese. All dead in this pool, this pool I was falling into. I was alive, trying to cry out, but all that floated past me were the dead. I was sinking, falling, into the blackness of death. There was nothing I could do about it. I felt the water go cold, as if to take my blood and chill it to death's temperature.

"This is not my day," I screamed. The faces went past in solemn procession.

"This is not my fucking day," I screamed. "Not my fucking day, mother fuckers." I could feel the bubbles coming out of my mouth.

"This is not my day." And I sat upright, out of the water.

In my bed. Cold as ice.

Chapter Twenty

WHEN I FINALLY ROUSED myself, it was after noon and my throat felt like I'd screamed most of the feeling out of it. I hadn't drunk enough for a real hangover, but I was hungover anyway, having tromped through my own memories and having spent my night ready to kill until they stopped. If anyone had presented themselves to me last night, as friend or as foe, I wouldn't have given you a plugged nickel on the bet that they escape unscathed.

I hadn't. Why should they?

I peeled myself off the bed, grabbed a handful of Bayer and a glass that had yesterday's water in it. I refilled the glass, took the aspirin, and noticed the bottle of Beam sitting there. Why not? Hair of the dog, right? A little something to settle my stomach. To clear my head.

Thirty minutes later I had showered, brushed out my beard, and changed into clean clothes. It's not true that I felt like a new man. I felt like the same sorry dipshit who couldn't make his life work right.

I walked out into bright October sunshine, feeling like the night hadn't yet ended.

I made myself walk over to the Steak and Egg to have as huge a breakfast as I could stomach. As it turned out, the bacon and egg special was about all I could handle. The waitress brought me a pot of coffee, which was done by the time I was.

I took the bus downtown and got off after the second transfer in front of the jail. Inside, I signed in and waited until they took me to the visiting room. In short order, Thompson arrived.

"You look like hell."

"Thanks, Thompson. You actually look a little better."

"I'm finally sleeping some."

"You're getting clean a little. Can't be easy, doing coke and drinking."

"Speaking of which, that is what you look like. You look hungover."

"Let's leave me out of it for now. I want to ask you some questions."

"Go ahead. I don't know any answers."

"When you came into Kirkland that night, what exactly did you see?"

"The back door was propped open with one of those little wedgie things, you know?" I nodded that I did. "So I went up--"

"Because you thought I might have an office in the building?"

"Yeah, that's right. So I went in, looked around on the top floor and didn't see anything that looked like it might be your office, and I did this for all the floors. Finally I went down to the bottom floor. That's where the other door was open."

"And it was just standing wide open?"

"Let me think." He bowed his head, searching his memory. Thompson was always the smart one, and his demeanor now was someone who couldn't remember anything. "I guess it was just sort of open. But it was the first door that had been, so I pushed it completely open and walked in."

"And what did you see?"

It was mostly just dark. There was a little light from a flashlight. I remember that.

"Who was holding the flashlight?"

"Nobody. It was just there on the floor. Shining."

That was strange. Somebody must have been there. "But you didn't see anybody."

"Right."

"And you didn't think that was strange?"

"Hell, Jackson, I was a little lit. Besides, I wasn't awake much longer."

"You just lay down and went to sleep?"

He touched his chin. It's something he's always done when he's thinking. As a kid, I remember that gesture. Something interesting was always going to come out.

"I guess."

Not that interesting after all. And I guess my aggrivation showed.

"Do you remember everything you saw and did last night?"

I could have said yes, I remembered way too much. But I said, "Nobody got killed where I was last night."

We sat there, two brothers with nothing to say to each other. I'd been through a war I couldn't quite shake, and he had his own war, one I think he started, maybe with himself. Either way, he was losing.

"What are you doing back here, Thompson? God knows, we all stopped waiting on you years ago."

"Would have been a great homecoming, then, even without all this."

"You made your bed, man. But you know that. So why are you here? In Tennessee again? After ten years?"

"I was out west, Jackson. You know that. I drifted a lot. Started in the Bay Area, ended up in the Central Valley. Worked some there, but didn't really like it. Wandered down the coast and ended up in San Diego."

"Where it's always 75 and sunny. Good pick."

"Especially when you're just drifting. Sometimes I had enough to rent something short term. Sometimes not. Sometimes I'd have enough to rent something cheaper in Tijuana, and sometimes not. But the dope was good and it was usually cheap. So I wandered."

"Nice travelogue. Still doesn't tell me why you're back."

"I got rousted in a bust a few months ago. As part of booking they strip you down and search you, then do a health check. I had sores on my back, just a couple at first, then they spread. They're pretty ugly, Jackson. Well, they didn't like the look of it."

I saw where this was going.

"One thing leads to another, and I get out, but the health guy is pretty convincing that I need to check with public health services. So I do."

"And it's bad."

He touched his chin again. "Yeah. It's bad. And it's spread. They say it's called sarcoma."

"What is that, Thompson? Cancer?"

"Something like that. It's some new strain of herpes causes it." He looked at me, his eyes suddenly sunk in his face. Now knowing his news, he looked weak rather than skinny, beat up rather than tired. "After I knew for sure, I told them I was going home."

"What's the treatment plan?"

"There's no treatment plan, brother. Oh, they could do a lot of stuff that would stretch it out, but the end is the same."

"You can't know that."

"You know. If you ever get this, you'll know."

There's not a lot you can say in a conversation you never imagined having. We sat there in silence for a bit. I don't know what I wanted to do. Hug him? Cry with him. Curse the universe with him. I watched my aunt and mother say good bye to my grandmother, but that at least you can wrap your head around. My worthless brother was 28. He was young enough still to be stupid. He was too young to die.

"I got to get you out of here. You can't stay. Not with, with--this hanging over your head."

"It's ok, Jackson. I feel the same in here as I do out there. In here, for now, I'm sober and pretty clear headed. Didn't think that would be a thing I want, but there it is."

"You can stay clean outside. I'll help you."

He laughed and looked down. "Look, Jackson, you can't even keep yourself clean. I'll be fine in here."

The jailer came and took him back. I tried to say something kind, something reassuring, but I don't have that language anymore. So I just gave a cautious wave as he left. The kind of shy wave you'd give an older brother you didn't know anymore.

I don't know how other people deal with that kind of news. I cut over to Broadway, and stopped in at The Oscar. I started with coffee, but after two cups I had a bourbon. By then, the place was starting to fill with the lunch crowd, such as the lunch crowd is at a strip bar, and rather than looking at the ladies' shiny suits that would come off a piece at a time, I paid up and walked down to the Dusty Road.

I spent the balance of the afternoon having a drink, then walking it off on the way to the next one. In every place, I began the drink with the same thought: "How young is too young to die?" I knew that I was pretending it was all about Thompson. But it was about Patrick Vincent too. And yeah, I knew I was talking about me, and every grunt I'd known, too.

By the end of every drink, as I paid up, as I walked out the door and walked toward the next spot, I came to the same place. Life isn't fair. People get sick. People are in the wrong place at the wrong time. And some people, like me, are in the wrong place at the worst time to be there, or they just got luck. Bad luck. Things suck, and there's no way to fix it.

By the time I got to Hannigan's, that conversation took about thirty seconds to get to the "things suck" part. I was there before Katie even brought the drink.

And she saw it. "I'm bringing you food. Right now," she said. "Special tonight is meatloaf." The look she gave me told me that I'd better take it when it came."

"Sounds lovely." I don't think it sounded like I thought it was lovely, but hey, I wasn't trying to be charming.

The plate came full and went empty, and I turned my attention back to the bourbon. I made it last until almost eight, and then I paid up to a surprised Charlie, and began my further stroll down my personal pub crawl.

The two hours I'd spotted myself in Hannigan's, plus the food, and combined with the now cold air, gave me at least the illusion of sobriety. Not that I had any illusions about how much I'd put away. But I recognized the feeling as the one where you've reached a steady state. Relaxed. Maybe even a little sleepy. But still all the cognitive cylinders firing, all the speech neurons on approximately the right settings.

If I could just keep steady at this level, by the time I got home I would fall asleep. And I would not dream.

I worked my plan through the evening, and as these things go, the plan worked. A beer here, a bourbon there, a walk in the night air. By the time I got to Linda's, it was two a.m., and by my reckoning I was about one beer away from goal.

Bobby nodded across the crowd and set a draft at the bar in front of an empty stool. The place was loud, even for a Saturday night. It was a local crowd, it seemed, an amalgam of cowboy boots and construction steel-toes.

"What's with the crowd?" I asked Bobby.

"Willie and Waylon played the Exit/In tonight." He handed a PBR tallboy over my head and took a dollar from a disembodied hand. "Half of them are here, I think."

"Guess they're still worked up."

"I'd say." Bobby left to fill another order. One thing you could say about him. He rested up on the slow nights because one man behind the bar on a night like this could take it out of a younger man. But Bobby seemed to be up to it.

As I nursed my beer, I felt a tap on my shoulder. When I turned I saw a man, about forty, in a captain's hat. He wore a jean jacket with the sleeves cut out over a red plaid flannel shirt. He was what we used to call a fireplug, and he probably was about as wide as he was tall. He had a long beard and shoulder length dirty blonde hair.

"Man back here wants to see you," he said, motioning over toward the pool room.

"If he needs a fourth for pool, I'm not very good," I said, turning back toward my beer.

He put his hand on my shoulder and left it there. "Man wasn't asking if you wanted to come back. Telling you to come back."

I spun around slowly to face him. "Look, friend. I've had a long day. I'm just having a beer, and then I'm going home. I don't need any trouble."

He leaned toward me and pulled my shirt so that I was face to face with him. "There will be trouble if you don't come with me." He stood back and put his hands on his hips, parting his jean jacket. I could see on his belt a hunting knife in a sheath. "You catch my drift?"

I wasn't armed and, even if I was, I wasn't dumb. I gave him a look that said, "Whatever, asshole," I hope, at least more than it said, "You win for now."

The walk back was one I'd made before. Through a big outer room, through a small entryway, and then into a room with three pool tables and enough seating to cause a ruckus. Once, I'd watched a giant man run the table three times without batting an eye. Now, there were too many people in a room designed for comfort. Some were frat guys. The others seemed to be Sons of Shiloh.

The fireplug guided me around the pool table to the left and back toward the back entrance, where you only went if you were about to puke. There, standing with five other men, was Raines Durst, looking every bit the jerk. His little sneer looked like the face of a bad prep school dream. His hair was moist. His eyes looked just a little drunk. Like everyone else's.

"You been looking for me, Trade? I hear you have. I hear you've been beating up on my friends."

"If you're Raines Durst, I wanted to talk to you. That's right."

"Wanted to talk to me bad enough to tail my girl?"

I held up my hands. "You and me don't have a beef about that. You want to talk to her, go talk to her."

"I'm talking to you," he said, and he lunged toward me.

I know my hand-to-hand skills, and I kept myself steady. I slipped his lunge and turned. His crew was behind me, but the entire room was filling now, ready for the fight of the night.

"Fine." I stayed on my toes. "I don't want to fight you. I got nothing against you"

"But I got something against you." He tried a kick, which I blocked, and then tried again to rush me. I caught his shoulders in my hands and spun him into the pool table. His momentum carried him halfway across before he caught himself. Then he held his hand out toward the man in the captain's hat, and in it the fireplug placed the knife.

"I just don't have any use for you at all," he said, and rushed me.

I had located the pool cue on the table behind me and I blocked his thrust, then whipped the thick end hard across his face, his eyes going cold and snapping back in his head. He fell to the ground, barely missing the knife he held in his hands.

I looked around at the crowd, who had come for a longer fight. The air came out of the room.

One guy said, "Aw, shit."

"I'm sorry, folks. The show's over." I kept the cue in my hand as I moved toward the door. "There never really was a show."

The captain's hat grinned in the corner of the room. "Watch your back, buddy. Next time you might need a gun."

A gun? I had a brother dying. I had a war that wouldn't quit. You really want me to worry about undergrads who hang with bikers, who can't even fight their own battles?

Is that what I'm worrying about?

I need to worry about getting my brother out of jail.

I walked back to my apartment, put out the light, and slept. Without dreaming. Without guilt. And without knowing what was coming next.

Chapter Twenty-One

I WOKE UP TO a knock on my door. It's a basic problem with a one room apartment. The world can knock on your bedroom door.

Of course, you can always turn over and shut your eyes again.

I tried that, but the knocker wasn't having any of it. A voice I didn't recognize said, "Open up, Trade. Metro police."

That did change things a little. "Hang on."

I slid into last night's jeans and pulled a cleanish t-shirt out of the pile near the hamper. I didn't bother with the pony tail, so my hair was on my shoulders, my beard was skewed a little to one side, and my breath wouldn't get any better until I brushed my teeth.

I opened the door. Two Metro cops stood there, both looking serious. To their rear was Don Mercer, looking peeved too. "Gentlemen," I said, looking from one to the other. "To what do I owe this visit?"

"May we come in?" The shorter one seemed to be the senior of the two. He had closely trimmed sandy hair. It wasn't hard to believe he had a buzz cut under the cap. He led the way as the three entered the apartment. I tried to catch Don's eyes, but he marched in with the other two, looking around the apartment.

"Please, sit," I said. "I'd offer you something, but I was asleep," I gestured toward the empty bed. "When you knocked."

"We'll stand," said the shorter one. "Can you tell us where you were this morning, about four a.m.?"

"Right where I was when you knocked, officer. I was here. Asleep."

"You live alone?"

"Yes." I looked at Mercer who was carefully avoiding me.

"When did you arrive?"

"I'd say 3:15, maybe 3:30. I wasn't really paying attention."

"Anybody see you get here?"

"Not that I know of. The Buckets, that's the folks in the house, are in Florida. Too chilly for them here." It was pretty chilly right now for me too.

"Where were you before that?"

I lit a cigarette. "I was bar hopping. All night. The last place was Linda's, up West End."

"And did anything notable happen there?"

I narrowed my eyes at Mercer. "The question makes me think you already know what happened there."

"I'm just asking you a question."

I considered my options. I hadn't done anything except protect myself. I didn't have any particular reason to protect Raines Durst. So far, I was just telling the truth. So I kept on telling it. "A Vanderbilt student named Raines Durst was in the pool room. He took a couple of swings at me, then got a knife and rushed me. I hit him in the face with a pool cue. He was stunned enough that I was able to walk away."

"Who can confirm that?"

"About thirty people. I don't know any of them. Some were students, I think. Some were bikers."

"And you knew Durst had something against you?"

"Look, I didn't even know Durst. I'd heard of him. I've met a couple of his friends."

"But no reason he'd be upset with you?"

"I was completely surprised."

"You know his girlfriend?"

"That's one of his friends I've met."

"She's good looking, I hear."

"If she's your type. Of course, that's true with everyone."

"She your type?"

I raised my eyebrow. "Why don't you ask what you want to ask, Officer."

"I did. Is she your type?"

"Long, tall drink of water. Very pretty. Yes, she's a lot of guys' type."

"Rich too, right?"

I motioned around the apartment. "Clearly rich doesn't appeal to me."

"Maybe you'd like to get out of this place, though?"

"I don't know that she's any richer than any other Vandy girl. Some are. Some aren't. Some strike a good pose. Anyway, doesn't matter."

"You sleep with her?"

There was the question. If Raines was after me for making him look bad, that one wouldn't have come up. He would have kept that tidbit to himself. So something else was going on. Something that gave me a motive for something. Still, no reason to hide the truth, right?

"Once."

"Durst knew?"

"No idea. Like I say, I never laid eyes on him before last night."

"I think maybe you should come downtown and talk some more, Mr. Trade."

"You arresting me? Because that's what I'd expect if you're taking me downtown."

"Why would you expect that? You do something?"

"I've told you what I did. But you are fishing for something else."

"Just go with them, Jackson," said Mercer. "You don't need to make this hard."

"I'm not making anything hard. I'm helpfully answering questions. I'm telling the truth. I don't see what going downtown accomplishes. Unless you're arresting me for something." I looked at the taller, silent one. He had his mouth set in a thin line, as if he didn't approve. The shorter one tapped his foot a couple of times.

"Raines Durst was killed last night, Mr. Trade."

"And you are starting with me?"

"You did deliver a fairly efficient beating earlier in the evening."

"It wasn't a beating. It was a smack in the face with a pool cue. And I was defending myself from a kid with a knife."

"Pretty scary. Sort of thing you'd want to clean up. Make sure he didn't do it again."

"Scary is a night patrol in the jungle, Officer. An undergraduate who can't handle himself is not scary."

The taller one scowled. Mercer looked like he wanted this field interview to just be over. The shorter one said, "Vietnam veteran?"

"Combat Infantry."

"You know your way around firearms, then."

"You ever been in combat, Officer?" He shook his head. "So it goes like this. Some come out and they need their weapon. It's something they trust. Some of us, though, come out and never want to see a weapon again. That's me. Mercer can tell you."

"That true, Mercer?" The taller one finally spoke.

"I have invited him to the range. He wouldn't go." Mercer said it as if it was being pulled out of him.

"And the reason," I said, "is that I did my share of carrying a weapon in Vietnam. I don't need any more of that. Tell them, Don. I have nothing left for that."

"Fair enough," said the one in charge. "If we got a warrant, then, we wouldn't find a firearm of any kind in here?"

"Not a firearm. Not a knife. Not a weapon of any kind, brother," I told him. "I spend my time trying to be peaceful. If someone attacks me, I fight back. But measured force is the best."

"What's that mean, Trade?"

"It means that Raines Durst didn't rise to the level of killing. He was just a kid with a pissy attitude." I looked at the three policemen in the room. "The kind you guys pass over ten times in a weekend."

"Call this a courtesy call, Mr. Trade. We may be back. We might want you downtown."

"I know. Don't leave town. Et cetera."

"This isn't Hawaii Five-O. We're not saying that at all."

"Don't worry. I ain't going nowhere. I got work to do."

"What kind of work?"

"Hadn't you heard? My brother is in jail. And maybe you didn't know. He's dying. I have to find a way to get him out of jail."

"Bond is good."

"Yeah, I know. Thanks."

Chapter Twenty-Two

I STOPPED AT THE Krystal for coffee and two square burgers, I guess because heartburn makes me think better. And I needed to think. Two of the three pranksters were now dead. My brother looked good for the first one. Metro thought I might look good for the second. They were all wrong about me, and I suspected they were all wrong about Thompson.

They were thinking like cops, which is no real surprise. They are cops. They work with other cops. They talk to each other. And the one thing that unites them is the way they think. Guy's passed out with a murder weapon in hand next to a corpse. Fact, meet fact. Inescapable.

In my case, I'd slept with the dead kid's girlfriend. Humiliated him, violently they would say, in public. He turns up dead. I'm a combat infantry veteran. Fact, meet fact. If they found the gun in my apartment, that would be fact, meet arrest. I fully expect that warrant to be issued. That's why I put a strip of cellophane tape between the frame and the door of my apartment. If it's disturbed when I get back, I'll know to look for a planted gun.

But I'm not a cop. and to get to the right answer, I needed to tack a different current, and it would be a path no self-respecting cop would appreciate. I was going to have to find out who had killed the two, and then I was going to have to find the facts that proved that.

My brother's life, or what was left of it, depended on it. Mine probably did too. So first, I had to get inside the living space of the last prankster living, preferably without him there.

I went outside to the phone booth with my burnt Krystal coffee, and dialed Art Blake's office where I got Dot, his secretary. After some idle chat, and her kind wishes for Thompson, she gave me what I asked for, the number of the Registrar's office.

I asked for Penny DiMello, one of the Assistant Registrars. Penny had been helpful a half dozen times when I was trying to locate students who were being really good at staying away from an Assistant Dean looking for them. Vanderbilt students will avoid their rooms with a good reason; they rarely avoid their classes, though. There's too much at stake.

"I can't, Jackson."

"We've always worked on this before," I said, a little confused.

"FERPA, Jackson."

"Is that kind of like eff-off, Jackson?"

She laughed. "No, but that's pretty funny. FERPA. Family Educational Rights and Privacy Act. It's been in force at least three years now."

I had heard something about it, but I didn't know about it. Penny explained that, unless a student had granted a waiver to me, specifically, I couldn't have any of his educational records. That included his schedule. Not even his parents could get the info unless he'd granted a waiver.

"So," she concluded, "I'd love to help, but I can't."

I considered how much to tell her. "Can I tell you something confidentially?"

"Not if it's going to make me feel bad," she said. "Feel bad because I can't help you."

"I know I can trust you, Penny." I waited just a beat. "You know the Mickey Mouse on the tower?"

"God, yes. What a hoot." Then she caught herself. "Too bad about that boy."

"Well, three students did that caper." I waited again. "Two of them are dead. Not one of them. Two."

There was a long silence on the other end of the line. I took the opportunity.

"My brother is in jail for the one. Someone's trying to frame me for the other one."

There was still silence. Then she said, "It must be awful for you. For you both."

"It's awful because we're innocent. But somebody's guilty. And unless I can find out who it is, the third prankster is in danger. That's why I want to know his schedule."

"You should tell the police, Jackson."

"The police aren't listening, Penny. They think they already have the answer."

She was thinking, I guess, if you can hear thinking on a phone line. Finally, she said, "Who's the student?"

"Howell Parsons. He's an engineering student."

She found the schedule and gave me the run down. I scribbled on the napkin that had the little Krystal logo on it. "Thanks, Penny. You're the best."

"Just don't get hurt, Jackson."

That would be the idea.

I took a quick pass through Rand first to see if he'd slept late and was just getting to breakfast. But he wasn't there, which meant he'd probably made this first class at eight. He had back to back classes before a break at 11:30. I wanted to check first if he was indeed there.

Olin Hall was a ten-minute walk if you were casual about it, so I was there in no time. I went up to the third floor, where he should have been in the first class, Hydraulics. I made myself inconspicuous and surveyed the class through the door glass. Parsons was there, leaning over a set of papers with two other students, absorbed in thought. He probably didn't even know about Durst yet.

I retraced my steps and ended up in Barnard, second floor, where Housekeeping had not yet arrived. Maybe they just avoided it. I think I would have. There were beer cans strewn here and there, an empty bag of Lays, and what I assume was the debris of a game of hall hockey, including a cracked window at the end of the hall.

There was nobody stirring. Those who had classes were already out, and those who didn't were still out cold. I heard snoring somewhere, loud enough to escape a closed door.

Parsons' door was cracked, and I pushed it gently, in case a roommate or visitor were still in, but the room had the haphazard feel of an undergraduate male's kingdom. The concrete block walls were painted an insipid yellow, but so long ago that they mostly just looked faded. The floor was host to a collection of books, albums, papers, and clothing, such that there was not a lot of the tile floor showing. I picked my way through the litter, and acknowledged that, except for the tile of the floor, it was enough like my place to make me consider cleaning my apartment.

I didn't know what I was looking for, but I decided that, whatever it was, I didn't want to be interrupted. I made my way back to the door and turned the deadbolt.

I gave the room a light toss first. Whatever else he was, Howell Parsons clearly was a serious student. The one neat and organized thing in his room was the material related to the current semester. Notebooks were categorized and classified into sections. Highlighting marks demonstrated a commitment to re-reading and learning material, so that it could be built upon as new information came in.

I hadn't been an engineering student, but I knew more than a few when I was an undergraduate. I recognized diligence, if not brilliance, when I saw the evidence of it.

But the rest of the room, the part of his life that was not academic, was on par with the grungiest of animals. His mini-fridge was stocked with two Schlitz beers, still in their plastic rings, an almost empty Mateus bottle, and an assortment of molded things that had once been food but were now antibiotic projects. His closet was about to run out of clean clothes, but that might not matter since it seemed he was recycling jeans, shirts, and maybe, though god forbid, underwear. It wasn't a pretty picture, but I didn't see a laundry hamper anywhere.

On the other wall, he had fashioned a bookcase of sorts from cinder blocks and reclaimed boards. On it were a 10-inch television set with rabbit ears, a pretty expensive Pioneer component set with KLH speakers, and two wine bottles of indeterminate origin with candles stuck in them. He cared about his academics and his music, it would seem.

On a second pass, I found nothing that made me take a second look. I was beginning to get used to the clutter, and recognized the pattern. And as much as I didn't know what I was looking for, I knew that the academic matter, with its disciplined organization, was far more interesting to look at.

He had a system. He bought wire-bound 8 and a half by 11 notebooks, pre-punched for a 3-ring binder, then he carefully lined each page, front and back, in half vertically, so that he essentially had two panes of notes. The left pane appeared to contain reading notes from his textbooks. The right pane looked like class notes, collated on the fly and put next to the appropriate section of text notes. He had underlined questions about extensions of the information, or questions about where lecture and text didn't seem to agree.

I was an ok student. I guess if I handled my business this way, I would have been more successful.

There were also drawings illustrating various mechanical concepts. The binder I was viewing, the one for his advanced materials science course, had all manner of precise drawings to illustrate load bearing and solid-state physics. I liked the pretty pictures. I didn't understand much of it.

He was in hydraulics class and in manufacturing processes this morning. He had a notebook on material science, and I knew he was taking an advanced thermodynamics course, and that notebook was there. He had apparently put off his humanities requirement, because there was a notebook for a lower level philosophy course too.

There was also a set of notebooks on the upper shelf of his desk, no doubt ones from prior courses to be used in case he needed to review.

I was impressed. No wonder he was vital to the Mickey caper. He was super smart, and super organized.

That's when the light bulb went off. If he was smart and organized, and if he collected it in binders, was there a Mickey binder?

Among the binders on the shelf above was one with a blank outside. The inside cover page, the first on the three-rings, was titled simply: Mickey.

Inside was a fascinating set of drawings, measurements, and photographs. Howell had taken his reconnaissance seriously. He had even managed to photocopy an original architectural drawing that showed the grade of the stairs and the number of steps, including the last part which appeared as a ladder rather than a stairway. Calculations were precise and entered into a timeline that demonstrated the exact amount of time the ascent would take.

Further inside the binder was an inventory of tools and materials, together with mock ups of how the two interior pranksters, Patrick and whoever had gone up with him, would bear the materials upward. There was also a schematic showing the top of the tower, and the angle at which the one who went over the side would have to work.

As an illustration of planning, it was marvelous. As an undergraduate's rendering of a classic prank, it was a virtuoso performance.

As I contemplated this brazen and yet meticulous operation, I heard the doorknob turn, and then heard the bang of a shoulder against the outside. "The hell?" I heard what could have been Howell. I needed to move, no matter who it was.

I took the binder and stuck it between my shirt and my pants. The casement window was open. A winding mechanism rolled two half windows outward. I looked out and saw very little traffic on this side of the building, facing West End. The other side, the side facing Alumni Lawn, would be heavily trafficked this time of day, so I was lucky.

I let myself out the left half of the window, worked my feet down the decorative grate and got my feet to within about eight feet of the ground. All of us, probably, had done this more times than we would admit as undergraduates. Certainly, the whole McGill crew had exited that way a few days ago. I let go, and landed with my knees bent to absorb the shock.

I scurried down the length of the building, found an opening in the hedge and crawled through it. Just like that, I was out on West End, across from the Methodist church, in possession of the pranksters' bible.

Chapter Twenty-Three

I MUST BE A homing pigeon because I always end up back at Hannigan's. Of course, it could just be that they have my favorite pigeon food, and they bring it to me as soon as I sit down.

This time I sat with a fresh bourbon, neat, and the three-ring binder the pranksters had put together. Or rather, the bible that Howell had penned. It was a masterpiece of precision. Every contingency was covered. From what would happen if it rained, if it stormed, if the VUPD happened on the scene, if Patrick's carabineer had failed—every contingency was taken care of. If Howell had been of a military mindset, he would have been leader of the ROTC on campus. I can tell you that I could have used that kind of mind in combat. He was precise, and he was thorough.

Howell's handwriting was also precise. His printing was all right angles and dashes, as if he had little use for a comma, as if even that was a flourish that he didn't need. But there was another hand in the binder, toward the back. That hand was the work of what I'd call a scribbler, the sort of writing that was not writing because it already knew what it was going to say, but instead was entering a voyage of discovery, doubling back onto itself recursively, searching out one true nugget of fact.

And in fact, that was what the writer appeared to be doing. If writing could be considered a doodle, this writer was creating a kind of mind-doodle, a doodle not in pictures but in words.

Think of the river. They would have been so far from home, some of them. What that river must have felt like! Frightening. Scary. You could be taken down and never resurface. The time of year. And the situation. You can't get any worse than that. Far from home. Scared. The night before.

That's why it was so important. The first rise of morning, they were all to get ready. Silently. How could that many be so quiet? But that's what was needed. When something is vital, things that are not normal become possible.

The river was at their back, sitting like an angry wall, pulsing at three in the morning. In the pitch black you could hear it, and you knew from the day before that it was snot yellow, ready to rage. Somewhere out there, there were boats. Somewhere, out there, danger lay.

This time of year, the flooding could be expected. This year was no different, even though in every other way it was completely different. Silent, cold, mud everywhere, the year was no different and completely different. This was not the mud of the past. This was the mud of conflict, sucking boots off your feet, making a sound that told you that no matter how you wanted to move, silently and quickly, you would move the way the mud allowed, the same as the river allowed what it would allow. And what it would not.

They named them after rivers. We named them after states. There, there is the blunt of the matter. States are arbitrary things, political units. We knew as much. Rivers, though, are natural things, mighty things. A river can rise up and make you regret you tangled with her. States? Well, I suppose that states are only as frightening as what you think they are. Ours rose up. See the good it did?

There are myths about this. The myth of total surprise. There was no surprise. The advance knew exactly where they were. We knew exactly where they were. But one of them and one of us got too far out in front. When that happens, what are you supposed to do?

It was an odd ramble. It felt like I should know what the writer was talking about, but it was a little too indirect. The river was alive, somehow, and something was named after the river. And states rose up.

Something triggered in my mind. We named ours after states. The Army of Tennessee. That was Confederate. As opposed to The Army of the Tennessee. Named after the river. That was Union.

So this was a musing about the Civil War. But what? A myth of total surprise? Something where one or the other army took the other by surprise?

This was about Shiloh! And the only one of the prankster group who could have done the research was Grace. The doodle-master had to be Grace Pettibone.

Grant didn't want to fight, not in April, not with the river so high, and not with Buell yet unarrived. But they knew where Johnny Reb was. There was no doubt about that. These were West Point trained generals. They all knew the battlefield. They all knew.

What they didn't know was that Peabody would put a patrol out, too far out in front. It allowed Grant to mobilize, Sherman to be ready. Myths. There was no surprise at Shiloh. There was a pitched battle.

Grace was deliberately puncturing the general belief about Shiloh, the one expressed by Art Blake. The battle was regarded as the moment when the South had the Union on the run. If only Beauregard had pressed his advantage. If only Johnston hadn't been killed on the first day. If only. If only. The Song of the South.

Prentiss was at the Hornet's Nest, as the area adjacent to the Sunken Road came to be called. But he was not the hero. His started the day with 5,000 men, but by 9:45 that morning he only had 500. When Prentiss took his position in the Sunken Road, he had lost almost his entire division, and could not have held his second line without the veteran brigades of General Wallace's brigade. It was Wallace's who held the Hornet's Nest.

But the victor is the one who tells the story. The winner is the one who writes the history. In this case, it was Prentiss who was captured, who languished in prison, and who lived long enough to tell the story of his heroics, longer than the other combatants. He became the Hero of Shiloh, the defender of the Hornet's Nest, the one who held off the Rebs.

Such are heroes.

Grace Pettibone, the girl of the Lost Cause, was a researcher. Grayson Greer in the library had said as much. But here was proof, in her longhand, of an ability to connect dots that would have impressed professional historians. In her doodling, she was reconstructing a story of war that had animated an entire region for several generations. And it had animated them, apparently incorrectly.

They say that Buell saved Grant's ass. In reality, the Confederates probably had little hope of breaking Grant's last line. Grant had the high ground, situated on a tall ridge overlooking streams known as the Dill and Tilghman branches. Even battered, Grant's boys still had enough fight in them to hold their position. After all, they had over 50 pieces of artillery in line. They were massed in compact positions. Good interior lines of defense also helped, and two Federal gunboats fired on the Confederates from the river. Grant poured heavy fire into the Confederates from the front, flank and rear. It must have been miserable.

So the Rebs never actually assaulted the Federal line. Only elements of four disorganized and exhausted Confederate brigades crossed the backwater in the Dill Branch ravine as gunboat shells flew through the air. Only two of those brigades undertook an assault, and one of them had no ammunition. The Confederates topped the rise and faced withering fire. They were convinced. Orders from Beauregard to withdraw did not have to be repeated.

Grace was systematically destroying the myth of Shiloh, the great victory that never was, the first day that Beauregard wasted with his dithering. But why? To what purpose? And why was it in the prankster Bible?

But, oh, what about Johnston? Our dead prince? The great general unhorsed. Our Lost Cause personified.

Another myth. Johnston wouldn't have won Shiloh either. Didn't Johnston's death cause a lull in the battle on the critical Confederate right, which slowed progress toward Pittsburg Landing? And Johnston's death gave us Beauregard in command, and Beauregard, the Creole, ultimately called off the attacks. This pair of linked events led to Confederate defeat. Didn't it? Didn't it?

If you look at the memorial of Shiloh, the one the Daughters of the Confederacy placed in 1917, you see the deification of Johnston, the beatification of Confederate officers. You can see the careful mythmaking, the artillery man looking through the fog of battle, serenely prepared to rain death down. You note the infantryman, frustrated by the order to cease the advance. Each one represents defeated victory, or victory refused. They are an army who lost despite their cause, despite their natural superiority, borne out in that first day of battle. And yet the second day did happen, and it is only noted on the memorial by the vacant stares of the sorrowful. Where on the right you see the first day, with eleven young Confederate soldiers, on the left you see the second day, with only ten. A battle so nearly won, so narrowly lost.

Myth. A lost battle. A Lost Cause. The failure of an army apotheosized, the deification of a mistake. A foundation of air. The making of myth.

And the myth of a fortune to be won, something torn violently. His dying breath. The half breed, the final clue in his head. Like Faulkner's Charles Bon, without Henry Sutpen.

Just myth. That's all. But real enough. And there are things yet unknown more real than these.

I had finished the bourbon, and made the cheeseburger disappear. And like that, Grace had made the myth of Shiloh disappear too. It was a signal piece of writing, the kind that made me admire her. She was clearly more than just a gorgeous woman. She had serious intellectual chops. She might even be a poet.

But why was she so relentless in her takedown of one of the key episodes that make the Lost Cause so seductive? I mean, if the motorcycle boys of Sons of Shiloh could be made Southern Nationalists on the strength of a battle's mythology, why would she follow this trail that discredits it? Her father, for one, would not be pleased. I suspected that there would be a whole host of people who wouldn't be happy.

"Hey, Jackson," said Charlie. "What's got you so studious?" Charlie looked over my shoulder. I had closed the binder to the first page, the one with the tower sketched carefully on it. "Hey, man, there's Mickey's face, just like now. On the clock tower."

"That's right, Charlie. This is the how-to manual for that."

"No shit?" He sat down next to me. "Got to be pretty cool, right?"

"Pretty cool," I agreed.

"So that's what you've been studying, huh? Boning up on how the deed got done?" He grinned at me. "Somebody hire you to take it down?"

"Not at all. Actually, I was engrossed in another part of the notebook. It's about the Battle of Shiloh."

"Shiloh? Like in the Civil War?" He shook his head. "What the hell's stuff about the Civil War got to do with Mickey on the tower?"

Sometimes it takes a splash of cold water to wake you up. "Say that again, Charlie."

"If that's a notebook about Mickey, then why does it have Civil War crap in it?"

It was a good question. A really good question. I had started to ask it, and had been seduced by Grace once again, this time by her intelligence. But why this was in the prankster Bible was a good question, one I needed to find the answer to.

Chapter
Twenty-Four

THERE WERE MESSAGES ON my answering machine. Art Blake was wondering if I'd decided how to get Thompson out of jail. Don Mercer was telling me that the interim chief was on the lookout for any way he could cramp my style. Grace Pettibone wanted me to call her. She didn't sound like she was distraught, so maybe she didn't know about Raines yet. Don didn't need a call, and I didn't know what to tell Art. So I called Grace.

She wanted me to come over.

"I don't think I can make it tonight. There's stuff I have to do." Vague. Seems like everybody has used that one time or another.

"Sure," Grace said. "If it makes any difference, you could come over late." She purred. "I mean, late."

"I'll call if it turns out that way." I hesitated. "Could you answer a question for me?"

"Of course."

"I've been thinking, since I'm around you lately. And since I met your father."

"Yes?" The word came out like thick honey. If she did know about Raines, she was one cool customer.

"What's the biggest myth about the Civil War? I mean, your father talks about how history gets it all wrong. What do you think is the biggest lie?"

"History doesn't lie, Jackson. People tell what they know. The winners know one thing, the losers know another. But the losers don't write the history books."

"Ok." I tried another tack. "What's the wrongest thing—I know that's not a word—that people believe about the war? Your father says it's the lie about slavery being the cause. Do you agree?"

The response came quickly enough that I didn't doubt she'd already thought it through. "I don't." There was, however a pause before she said, "I mean, I think there's a bit of truth in that, but it's far larger than that."

"Tell me the biggest lie, Grace."

"It was really a war of conquest. A war of capitalist conquest. It was all about the money."

"Don't you think the abolitionist movement was sincere?"

I could almost hear her thinking, deciding what she wanted to say to me. I had no doubt that it seemed an odd line of questioning. It was odd to me, too. What did all this have to do with Mickey on the clock? Or with my brother? I wasn't sure myself. I had to admit I was flailing a little.

"It was the act of secession itself that provoked the North. It's the same effect that Colonial secession had on England. Lincoln was pretty clear. He was fighting to save the Union. What he didn't say was that he was fighting to save it for the North's moneyed interests—just like George III was fighting to save the Empire for the interests of England's merchants and bankers." She paused in her lesson. "So yes, there was slavery and yes, there were abolitionists. But the slavery question gave both sides their moral disguises to wear. The war was fought over who would control Southern production, the South or the North."

"It's been a while since I had my political philosophy course, but you sound like a Marxist." I laughed, hoping I hadn't gone a little too far.

"Really?" There was no edge in her voice, but her quick reply told me she had played this game before. "Because it would seem to me that I'm arguing that this was a war fought for capitalist interests, and the Northern capitalists won, with the result that we can see today." When we weren't in bed, she could sound like someone who was defending a Ph.D. "If you need more proof, just look at what they set about doing right after the war's end."

"And what is that, Grace?"

"Remember, the north emancipated Confederate slaves. Then after the war they enfranchised the freedmen, but interestingly not Northern ones. That's how you know that it was the North's imperialism, and not its moral compass, that dictated events. And once the North had realized its economic and political ambitions, it abandoned Southern blacks to the poverty and racial hatred the War had engendered." Her voice grew low and conspiratorial. "Then, with the South subdued, the North looked west, where all that stood between it and a transcontinental railroad was tribal land and outgunned tribes." There was a triumphant note in her voice. "All aboard," she crowed. "Time to go from sea to shining sea."

I had to give it to her. If she wanted to, one of these days she might make a crackerjack professor. I wedged the phone between my ear and shoulder, and applauded. "Gold star, lady. I am bowing, though you can't see it."

"So let me ask you a question?"

"Sure."

"What was that really about?" I didn't answer at first. "Why ask in the first place, Jackson?"

"Lately, I've been thinking a lot about lies that are treated like the truth. And it seems like the Civil War ends up being in the middle of some of it." That was true. And it wasn't just the war that didn't look like it should. Thompson being held for murder, for instance, was one thing that just didn't add up, even though there was no other explanation.

"Call me later if you want to get together. I can show you one thing that's true anytime."

"What's that, Grace?"

"You know what it is, Jackson. You damn sure know what it is." She purred again, but this time the purr ended with a little growl. "Call me." And she hung up.

There's no way she knew about Raines. Either that, or she was the world's worst girlfriend.

The stuff I needed to do, as it turned out, was on campus anyway. I walked over and felt the lingering darkness fall over me. I had been an older undergraduate, and I'd found my peace in a lot of unusual rituals. The gym at the Methodist Church. Lying on the grass in the sun, over at Scarritt College. Hiding myself in plain sight in the reserve reading room of the Joint University Library. Even in Hannigan's, now as in undergraduate days, I could disappear into the woodwork, or so I supposed, and no one could see me.

But there was nothing to beat walking the Vanderbilt campus at dusk or at dawn. It was then that the shadows that assaulted my soul at night became my friends. I could walk, without the caution I knew in combat, and feel safe, knowing no enemy would fire at me. I felt most free when I was half in the dark, one of the shadows myself. No one could see me. And I could only half see myself.

I was sitting in the shrubbery that fronted Neely Auditorium. I had just put out a cigarette and was breathing the air that was left when I heard a familiar voice. It had a rasp of anger.

"I don't have much time, dammit. If you want to tell me something, quit beating around the bush."

The nasal twang left no doubt in my mind. It was Rod Hanna.

"I am telling you that you need to cool it on the boys. They are worthless." It was an almost familiar voice.

I couldn't see who he was talking to. I tried to move a little closer, but the holly bush wasn't going to allow it. "They're not worthless to me, and they're not worthless to the boss. We've got a lot invested in them. Besides, they've got nothing on you."

"You're missing my point." The other voice paused, and I could hear an exhale of exasperation. "You're trying to create a diversion when you don't need to. This thing is over, Rodney."

"There is nothing 'over' about it, brother. This thing is just getting started."

"There's two guys dead already. You're going to get someone else killed if you're not careful."

I could imagine the sneer on Hanna's face because I'd seen it. And his voice betrayed it. "If somebody gets killed, it'll be his fault. I won't have any grief over that if it happens."

"Listen to yourself. You're saying it'd be ok."

I could hear the grappling of a leather jacket, as if one was pulling the other closer. I heard Hanna's voice lower in volume. "We've got a lot invested because there's a lot at stake. So yeah, you're damn right, it's ok. It better be ok." Hanna hushed the other. "Did you hear something?"

I quieted my already quiet breathing. Squatting, I could feel my calf starting to cramp, but I stayed still. No need to inject myself into this little spat. Whatever it was about.

"I don't hear anything except you," said the familiar voice. "And you ain't making a lot of sense. There's two dead boys. Thank goodness there's somebody on the hook for one of them."

Keep talking, I thought. There's something here I need to hear.

Hanna's lowered voice was reassuring. "Don't worry. I'm not talking about anything that will hurt us. Not if everything goes the way it should." There was the sound of a hand slapping a back. "But there can't be any half-ass antics. Once this thing gets rolling, it has to go all the way. Read me? If the cause is going to rise up, the boss can't go belly up."

The other man exhaled. "Yeah, I read you. But Rod," he hesitated, then completed the sentence, "this needs to end pretty soon."

"It'll end," Rod Hanna said, "when it's over." There was what seemed like a long pause, though I'm sure it was just the night, the darkness, and my own cramping calf. "If we're right, Hal, this changes everything. Every damn thing. The work. The cause. Everything."

Hal, whoever he was, didn't answer. They began to walk away, Rod toward the Barnard parking lot, Hal in the other direction.

"Everything." Hanna's voice became more distant. "Every damn thing."

I waited until I was sure they were out of earshot, then released my screaming calf. I limped from behind the shrubbery, looking south, where Hal had gone. He was already engulfed by the darkness. I looked north, and could just see a figure making a turn behind Barnard Hall, toward the parking lot. That was no doubt Rod.

I stuck my hands in my pockets and headed west, angling toward my apartment. It had been a weird night. Propositioned by the girlfriend of a dead guy, the guy whose death had brought Metro to my door at first light. Lectured by said girlfriend about the political economics of the Civil War. Overhearing the girlfriend's father's muscle, talking about something big that would change everything, something to keep the boss from going belly up.

And if I needed reminding, and I didn't, a brother in a jail cell for the death of the dead guy's friend. And that brother who'd be dead soon himself, if he could be believed.

I almost turned left to go down West End for a few, or a lot of drinks. I didn't. I almost stopped at Hannigan's for a nightcap, or five. I didn't. I walked up my street, went up my stairs, checked the undisturbed cellophane tape, and walked into my grimy apartment.

I locked the door and turned out all the lights. I fell onto the bed, fully clothed, rolled over and closed my eyes. And prayed that I'd sleep. I didn't need any battles in my sleep tonight. Not tonight, when there were too many uncertainties.

That was the problem with my night dreams. Too many certainties, and all of them terrifying. Same as my days.

Chapter Twenty-Five

IF I KNEW WHAT caused my paralysis, I'd do something about it. But the mind's sickness is different from the body's. The body carries its marks, like the scar on my right arm where I got caught on a punji stick in the jungle. A flesh wound, made by an implement that was designed to skewer me, to kill me. I'm lucky it wasn't one made to poison me. It's a scar that, every time I roll my sleeves up, perhaps metaphorically to get something done, reminds that someone left a gift for me that was meant to be my last gift, and that keeps giving every time I look at it.

That is the nature of the sickness of the mind. It reminds without remembrance, each moment captured inside a hell of escaped moments, a kaleidoscope that you move, winding the cylinder around your eyes, until a new pattern develops. Sometimes the color is the color of a firefight, sometimes the color of a landing zone under attack, the wounded bodies on the deck of a Huey, barely aloft. Sometimes the color realigns and you see the creatures of the night crawling up your leg. Sometimes the color is black, like the costume of the Viet Cong, and all you can do is be still.

All you can do is wait. And hope.

If I did not drink, I could not move. That's the way I feel most days. Some of my fellow vets got into drugs in country, in order to cope. I did not. It's not that I was more upright than they were. It was that I was more afraid of the drugs than I was of the situation. As bad as it got, I knew that I would not make it out alive if I was fucked up when the time came. So I stayed clean.

And if it was a good thing I did, then it became a better thing when I came home. Stateside, too many of us stayed latched onto the drug that got us through the days in country. Too many of us lived, whether in our own homes or on the streets, with the beast of war inside our heads, intertwined with the drab drug beast that lived there with us.

Me, I came back with what seemed a quiet mind for a while. I got my degree. I got married. I got a job and I was on the way up. And then my wife was unfaithful, and I snapped. They said I could have killed him. They were wrong. I only wanted to mess him up. I wanted to mess him up so that no one wanted to look at him.

And that's what I did.

But what I also did was end my marriage and lose my job. And that's when the beast came out. For the longest time, it seemed, I was stuck in neutral.

No, that's not right. My engine didn't even crank. I sat in my garage apartment and ventured out only to pick up a few groceries, then go back. But I didn't eat. And I didn't really sleep. The beast was alive in my mind. And nothing else would move.

Some nights I lived entire months in my head, seeing men cut down over and over, men who died once and now died every night. I saw the jungle incinerated. I saw villages decimated. I saw boys who would never live to become men, night after night, eyes open never to see again.

So when I came back sober last night, I expected that kind of night to happen again. That's why I drink, to keep the beast quiet, to make me go to sleep. In the day, I drink so that I am not overcome by paralysis, or at least inertia. I drink so that I can keep moving.

And I did sleep of a sort. That is, I dreamed of something else. For a change.

I woke somewhat refreshed, the sort of awakening that usually means I've gone easy on the sauce. My head was relatively clear and my mouth tasted only of cigarettes, not cigarettes and cotton, the way it did after a bender. I would have congratulated myself except it wasn't exactly an accomplishment. Besides, it'd all be out the window soon enough.

It took me a minute to remember the last thing I was dreaming, and then I realized I'd been dreaming it all night long, the kind of night where you wake intermittently and find you're re-dreaming, or maybe re-living, the same thing over and over again.

This dream was not complicated at all. It started with Thompson and me as kids, though we were strangely adult. We were down by the creek that ran through the back part of our farm. Maybe we were wading or maybe we were pretending to fish. I don't know. But out of the woods came a couple of boys we didn't know, and they were giving us the business about what we were doing there. When we told them it was our land, they laughed.

"You ain't got no land," the bigger one said. "Trash like you live on a farm, but you don't own it."

"Yeah," said the other. "Unless you stole it." He threw a rock across the creek at us. "Your daddy steal this land?"

There was no obvious threat in any of this. Thompson was completely silent, and I was mostly so, except for telling them they needed to get on their way. But it was more the feeling of unease, of being treated like we didn't belong. Like we would never belong.

The dream returned two or three times after the first time. Each time I was mildly conscious that I was having the dream again before rolling over and falling back asleep.

Other than the fact that Thompson was on my mind, and perhaps that in my childhood I had my fair share of inferiority, there was nothing that should have made this dream stick on play and repeat all night long.

I drank my Folger's instant and listened to the news on WSM. The morning crew was up to their hijinks, and I wasn't in the mood. I flicked to WLAC, and didn't find their patter any better. I turned the dial to off, and sat finishing my coffee.

The Vincent kid was dead, and Thompson was in jail for it. Raines Durst had managed to get himself killed, and Metro wanted to like me for it. If Howell Parsons bit the dust, it would be a trifecta, and they would probably just craft a double noose and get rid of both Trade boys.

And there was something going on with Rob Hanna and the mysterious Hal. It wasn't clear they were in on the boys' deaths. In fact, it was unlikely given Rod's closeness with the Institute and the boys' connection to Grace. But there was certainly something important going on, something important enough to make Hal pretty antsy about the boys.

And then there was Grace. Grace, who had been Raines's girlfriend, of some sort. Grace, who had taken me to bed enthusiastically before Raines was dead, and invited me over to her room after he was dead. Did that mean she didn't know last night? And if she did know, what the hell did that mean?

I didn't know who Hal was. I knew Rod wouldn't tell me anything. And I'd already tapped out what little Thompson knew.

It looked like Grace was my only play.

I called her room and got no answer, so I walked over to the Library Archives, where Grayson Greer told me she hadn't been in today. "You know where I've seen her, though? Over in Sarratt, in that lounge with the baseball glove chair."

"She sits in the baseball glove?" It didn't seem like her kind of thing.

"No. She sits in the corner. But everybody knows the baseball glove, so that's what I said." He had really light green eyes, the kind you see on a cat sometimes. But without the calculation of a feline, so he just looked washed out rather than cagey. "Bet that's where she is."

Sarratt was still new. It had been built because VU had gone so long without a student union that things were getting ridiculous. But when one had come, Vandy did it right, up to and including a bar/restaurant with a terrace on the top floor. The iconic piece, however, because it was just so bizarre, was a giant baseball glove that served as a chair in the big lounge on first floor. Everyone from the Chancellor to the janitors had their pictures taken sitting in the silly chair. And the room itself was a hit, in the sense that Vanderbilt students, when they have time and they're not drinking, actually study pretty hard. And so the lounge quickly turned into a place for study, and was usually quiet.

If I'd been looking for the Grace Pettibone I knew, the long, legged self-assured genius with a shock of model's hair and enough swagger to carry you along for the ride--well, I'd have missed her. That person was not in the Sarratt lounge. Who was there was a young, almost coltish girl in jeans and a white knit sweater, hair tied back, looking down at a book and not moving, not even her eyes. Unless I missed my guess, she knew about Raines. One question answered.

She was sitting with her foot on a little ottoman, oblivious. I nudged the ottoman with my foot, just enough to jostle her. She looked up with red eyes. It was easy enough to forget that she wasn't a hot-shot graduate student, that she hadn't even graduated yet. But one look at her--red eyes, no make-up, dressed like most every female undergraduate who's not intent at that moment on impressing anyone--one look at her and you could remember that she was at heart a lonely kid who'd now lost two friends, one of them maybe closer than the other.

She blinked. They might have been tears, or may have just been the blink of focusing and that focusing took a little more effort than usual. She stood and put both arms around me, and I let my arms envelop her. "I'm sorry."

She held on to me for a few more seconds, then put her hand on my cheek and looked at me. She was looking for a friend. She sat back down, and I sat on the ottoman, leaning forward.

"Daddy came last night and told me about Raines. I tried to get hold of you." She pushed her sleeves up over her elbows. "I didn't want you to show up in the middle of all that."

"I'd have showed up, and what? What was going on?"

She started to answer, then caught herself. She leaned forward toward me and whispered. "I don't know. Rod was there with Daddy. He was going on about you."

"About me?" I tried to sound surprised.

"About you. About how you and Raines had a fight. Over me."

Now it was my turn to lean a little more forward. And whisper. "It's true that Raines came after me. But I don't know how it could have been about you. I never said a word to anyone." I looked into those blue eyes, circled in red. "Did you?"

"No." It was a firm answer. It came quickly. I took it to be true.

"It's also a fact that Metro wanted to talk to me about it. But they lost interest, for now anyway."

She looked like she wanted to cry and was keeping the tears at bay only by trying to look as angry as she could. They came anyway. She looked angrier. She wasn't a girl accustomed to losing her battles, especially those with herself.

She took a breath and summoned something. She sniffed once, then wiped both eyes with the backs of her hands. She set her jaw. "I'm glad you found me. And I'm glad you told me about the fight. It makes some of what Rod and Daddy said last night make sense." She managed a smile through her composed face. "I'm glad you came. But given what all is happening, I think we'd better not hang around together, know what I mean?"

"I agree."

"So, could I ask you to sit here with my stuff while I go wash my face?"

Her backpack's contents was littered, as if in a small blast zone, around the chair. I motioned to it. "Want me to pack it up while you're in the ladies' room?"

"It's a mess, isn't it?"

I took her hand. "How about, when you come back, it'll all have been put right? Zipped up in your backpack and ready for you to leave?"

She squeezed my hand. "I don't think I could get a vote for this with Daddy and Rod, but you are sweet. I think you are even a gentleman." She stood up with me, and gave me the briefest of kisses on my cheek. "I won't be a minute."

And she wasn't really, not over five minutes. By then I'd put her materials back in her backpack, secured everything, and zipped it shut.

Everything except one thin file labeled "Night Train." What I saw there made me put that file down my pants in back where, covered by my coat, no one could see. What I could see was that Night Train had something to do with the Confederacy.

Chapter Twenty-Six

"Unless you wish the government should fall, all due speed must be exercised in this matter. Quit Richmond, and take the contents of the treasury with you. Take care that this be done urgently. There is no time to waste."

Jefferson Davis received a message such as this one from Robert E. Lee. Lee knew that the advancing Union troops were headed straight for the Confederate capital, and while there was an element of pure capture (after all, the taking of the enemy capital is the beginning of the end of wars), there was also the taking of the treasure of the enemy. Lee correctly saw that, if there was to be any hope of extending the war, the treasury must be protected. This would either be the beginning of the end, or the end of the beginning.

So began Grace's paper, still in draft, clearly but already bearing the mark of an intellect more than standard issue. In a moment she had caught the essential underpinning of this moment in the Civil War, and it might well be one that gave me something to think about beyond the mindless death of two undergraduates.

And so it came to pass that, late that night, two trains departed. Davis was in the first, along with other Confederate officials. They carried with them the most important documents and other archived materials of the Confederacy. The second train carried all the cash reserves of the failed nation. There was gold, silver and other coins, as well as the gold reserves owned by Richmond's banks and a large amount of jewelry donated by Confederate women to the cause. The wealth of the South had largely been in its human labor, the slaves who, now emancipated, diminished most plantations' "wealth" to whatever the land and animals could fetch on the barrel head. What pulled out of Richmond that night was really all that was left of the "wealth" of the South.

Later there would be rumors, both in the South and in the North, that this Confederate Cabinet carried millions of dollars as they fled. There would be demands from veterans that they be cared for from these missing millions. And some Union soldiers carried out atrocities, just to force from Confederate mouths the secrets of where the millions were. But those were the rumors afterward, after the treasure had disappeared. They were the rumors of desperation. As the train left the south, the North hoped to make the hunt for the fugitives more urgent. And so they said there were untold riches, on the way south, for nefarious purposes.

By the time May came, a month had passed, and the trains had reached Washington, Georgia. If it's unclear what they started with, it's clear enough that they had expenses along the way. A.J. Hanna, in his 1938 book, Flight Into Oblivion, recorded some of the expenses. $108,000 for troops who had escorted the trains. $40,000 for supplies in Washington and in Augusta, Georgia. One might be forgiven for wondering what manner of "supplies" could cost a fleeing train $40,000 in 1865, but perhaps it was paid to keep the train safe, a kind of war time protection racket. Whatever the cause, it is clear that the fugitives kept sacred about $450,000 in Richmond bank gold. That gold did not belong to the Confederate government.

She wrote with assurance and with an attitude. In her telling the fugitives were the beaten leaders of an insurgency, not the protectors of a superior but defeated culture. If her father's voice was the voice of the Lost Cause, hers was the voice of the dispassionate scholar. Hers was the realm of facts. Or rather, the realm of facts reclaimed.

On May 4, Davis and the advisers that remained decided to disband the Confederacy. Two Confederate navy officers were tasked with moving $86,000 of the treasury to England, for purposes that remain unclear. Whatever its purpose, the money never arrived. It would appear that this much, at least, was unaccounted for.

Jefferson Davis and his family continued south. How much money they still carried is open to question, but we know about the Richmond bank gold, which totaled a half million and had been deposited in Washington, Georgia, so it was accounted for. But here were also the jewels, and whatever was left of the Confederate treasury. If you take the lowest estimate, which is Hanna's, there was about a million to start with. Even taking into account some other "supplies," a conservative estimate might be another half million, though quite probably more. There should have been a million dollars, plus jewelry, still with this group. But on May 10, when members of the 4th Michigan Cavalry captured Davis' group near Irwinville, Georgia, they had only a few dollars with them.

What happened to the money? Did the Michigan Cavalrymen steal it? That seems unlikely, given the size of the treasure and the small group of cavalry. Did Davis and his group hide it? There are anecdotal reports of people in various Georgia spots, where Davis' party is known to have camped, where reports of gold coins turn up.

As for the Richmond bank gold, it fell into the hands of Federal troops, which occupied Washington within days after Davis left. Loaded onto wagons heading north, in the custody of U.S. government officials, the half million began its slow trek toward the North. But on the night of May 24, as the group made camp for the night in Lincoln County, Georgia, near Danburg Crossroads, some twenty armed men on horseback invaded the camp and carried off as much gold as they could carry.

Federal soldiers were eventually able to round up some $140,000 of what was taken. The rest disappeared.

It is the thesis of this project that the missing Confederate gold, sought as far north as Michigan and Ohio, believed to exist in some small family fortunes in Lincoln County, Georgia, and held by others to be in places as far west as the Mississippi River, is a fortune whose provenance can be precisely traced through the war journals of a few soldiers, each of whom knew part, but not all, of the plan. And once the leader of that plan was deceased, the remainder knew only part, and not enough to reclaim the treasury.

I read Grace's paragraphs again. Even in draft form, she sounded sure of herself, certain that she had found an answer to a riddle that might have seemed ancient, if the cause it was related to did not still seem so current. If the treasure of the Confederacy could still be located, what else might be possible? Would it be enough to kill two undergraduates?

And if it was, what was the role of this beautiful researcher, who was so torn up over the death of one of those undergraduates?

I left my apartment and went to Hannigan's, got a roll of quarters and a bourbon neat from Charlie, and started the dance of the money pinball machine. I know the drill. Get comfortable with the machine. See how tight the plunger feels. Will it let you baby the ball up, or will it insist you pull back harder, so that you sacrifice your feel? Is the sensor that tilts the machine sensitive tonight? And most important, are you in your groove?

There have been times I could have maxed the machine and walked away with hundreds of dollars, with my eyes closed. There have been some nights that nothing worked at all. And sometimes these were the same nights.

Tonight, I started slowly. I caught a break on the last ball of the first game, and the counter clicked off thirty-two free games. Not much. The equivalent of eight bucks. Enough for a cheeseburger and a night's worth of bourbon. But this was not the game I played.

I set up a couple of hard boards to make. Tried to make the yellow line with almost no chance to get my ball into the 16 hole. And failed. Tried to run a five in a row green line for one hundred sixty-four games, and failed.

I was keeping pretty much even, but I was just a little off. And I knew why. I was on that train with Jefferson Davis. Or rather, I was on the other train, with all that money. How had that much money gone missing when everybody and his brother was looking for it?

I was about eighty games ahead when Charlie came from behind the bar with another bourbon and stood watching me play. I cranked off all the games hoping for one big win.

"Not your night?" You'd think, since the nights where it really was my night cost him money, he'd be happy about that. But he said it like he sympathized.

"Every night can't be special. Besides, as long as I'm on the right side of zero, I'm not unhappy."

"Yeah, I hear you. But I know you, man. You don't want to play money pinball. You want to own it. You want to commune with it." He took the empty glass off the table and set the new one down. "This thing's like food to you."

"True enough, Charlie. It keeps me in food and drink."

"That ain't what I mean, man. You take it in. It nourishes you some way. When you're on a roll, Jackson, ain't nobody looks like you."

"That'd make me Tommy Trade, like The Who."

"Nah, you ain't no pinball wizard. Not like that. But you got the touch. Just not tonight."

He walked away. Then he stopped and looked at me over his shoulder. "Course, it could be the man came to service the machine today. Might be he adjusted her so she don't like you as much."

I worked the plunger so that the last ball curved gently across the top and slid into the 1-ball hole. Great shot, except I was trying to slide past the 1 to nestle inside the 7. I was at zero games. Zero quarters left.

"That must be it, Charlie. You can't beat a machine you don't know anymore." But I had nights and nights of leftover good. "Let me get a liver and onions plate. I'll just sit over here, and cry in my bourbon."

What I knew was that the man could adjust the machine all he wanted to, and I'd still make bank. What I didn't know was whether Jefferson Davis, or some Confederate, or some Yankee made bank.

Chapter Twenty-Seven

IT WASN'T JUST THE pinball machine that had been adjusted, throwing me off. It was the universe. Or at least the part of it that I inhabited.

I went to my apartment, checked the trap I'd set, in case anyone wanted to plant something in it. Nothing.

I walked down to The High Life. Nobody at the bar. Nobody in the back.

I peeked in at Linda's. Same thing. Deserted.

Same at the Top Hat. Just a lonely looking waiter sitting by the register.

Nobody on the street either. Just a few cars on West End.

I ended up back at Hannigan's, thirsty.

"You just missed, Art Blake." Charlie held up a glass and I nodded. He poured a bourbon.

"Just as well, Charlie. Art's not amused with me." I took the glass, lifted it in salute. "Where is everybody else tonight?"

"Slow night tonight. Suits me fine."

"Not slow up the street. It's dead up the street."

"Some nights are just like that, Jackson. Can't worry about it. Kitchen crew is using it as a chance to get some cleaning done back there. Katie is scouring the back."

It's the same as winter on a farm. You see to the livestock, but you spend the rest of the day cleaning your tools, tweaking a tractor's engine, fixing something in the barn.

I re-read the opening of Grace's paper. It hinted of a plan, but one that no one person apparently knew in total. That made no sense, however. One person must have been the generator of the plan, and others knew their part but not the whole.

That was the way it worked with the pranksters. Howell held the notebook, and had been the creator. Apparently, Patrick was the inspiration and the daring executor. Raines had been the crafter of Mickey parts. But it was Howell whose brain pulled it together.

And it was Grace who was the odd girl out. She knew all three, of course. And she was dating Raines, although nobody had prepared an adequate explanation why. "Talent" didn't cut it, even if it was funny.

Charlie came from the kitchen and freshened my bourbon. "Anything to eat?" When I shook my head, he went back to whatever he was doing. "Holler if you need anything."

I didn't need anything. I needed the one thing that would fix everything that was broken. I just didn't think that particular thing existed, and I wasn't sure I wanted it anyway. Why fix myself if the world is broken too?

Grace and the boys. Pettibone's Institute. Hanna and his bad attitude. The Shiloh gang. What was I missing?

Oh, and Thompson. Sitting in jail. Dying.

I didn't call Charlie. I just went behind the bar and grabbed the first bottle I saw. Dickel. Some bourbon drinkers won't touch sour mash and vice versa. I grew up on the Kentucky-Tennessee border. I'm agnostic on the subject.

The night stretched out like a dark country road. I drank some of the Dickel. I could feel myself getting drunker, but I wasn't paying much attention to that.

What I was paying attention to were my thoughts. I've heard it said that some Buddhist monks counsel that, in meditation, you should detach yourself from your brain, stepping aside to observe your thoughts come and go. If that's true, then I was getting pretty damn Buddhist.

I watched a medevac in a hot LZ go sideways and explode in a VC firefight. I watched two 18 year old cherries fall in punji stick traps within a day of each other, one skewered and dead immediately, the other dying on a poisonous tip that lanced his hand, a wound that would have gotten him out either way. He had to take the body bag way.

I saw the steamer trunk that Thompson sent home, Thompson not to be seen again until he was in a Metro cell with a killing sarcoma on his back. I saw myself hunkered in a rainy jungle, reading the letter that told me my sister, Swanson, had been killed in a Christmas Day car wreck. I saw Lynn, the woman I'd married, in bed with somebody else, and I saw her lover bleeding on the floor.

I walked around these thoughts without feeling much emotion. They were like mailboxes on a dark country road, briefly illuminated by my headlights, barely readable unless you knew exactly who lived there, then behind you in the dark, the same as they were, the same as they always are, but unreadable. Unreadable by you. Maybe unreadable by anybody.

And I drank. George Dickel was not a close friend, but as a silent companion he did all right.

I drank as the kitchen help left at 2 a.m. I said goodbye to Katie as she put on her coat, patted my shoulder, and went out the back door of the kitchen.

It was just me and Charlie. The clock said it was nearly 3 in the morning. He locked the door, pulled down the blinds. He drew a Budweiser off the tap, and motioned for me and George to join him in a booth.

"You've about done that bottle in, brother." He lit a cigarette and shook one loose for me. I took it.

"Seems like the night for it, Charlie. Nobody to talk to. Nobody to get cross with. Might as well do some drinking."

"You've been doing some drinking all right. You have friends who are worried about how much."

I took a drag and put the cigarette in the little channel of the ashtray, so the butt could sit on its own. "Why's anybody worried about me, Charlie? What'd I ever do to them?"

"I remember you when you were going to school across the street. You know what Mrs H said one time?"

"About me? Probably said, don't let that fool put any more quarters in the pinball machine."

He laughed. "Might have been a good idea if she'd said that. Then again, people see you winning and they think it's easy. We probably clear more on the losers than we lose on you."

"I'll stop feeling sorry for you, then."

"What she said, and this was before you started playing pinball, back when you were just one of Art's student assistants, she said, that one is different. That one is going places."

"And here I am. Looks like I went here."

"Something happened to you, Jackson. And now you use us as your night office. God knows what you do when it's light out. When we close, you end up down the street, drinking until whatever hour is too late." He watched me take the cigarette, flick the ash, and take another drag. "Art's worried about you. Your buddy, the cop, is worried."

"Art and Don aren't worried. They're mad at me. They don't like the way I'm handling this investigation."

Charlie stopped my arm headed toward the cigarette. "You don't have an investigation, Jackson. You're not a cop. You're a brother, and your brother looks every bit like a murderer." He took his hand off my arm. "We're all worried about you."

I finished the cigarette and stubbed it out. "Look, Charlie. I know I've not exactly got the world on a string right now. I've spent some time tonight reviewing why that might be. I don't have an answer." I looked at him. Friendly eyes. I don't think

I've ever seen Charlie mad in my life and he wasn't mad now. Maybe he did look worried.

"You're going to kill yourself. Or get killed. It ain't safe to be a drunk man walking the streets of Nashville."

"You know what? It ain't safe to walk the streets, drunk or sober." I got up and swallowed the last of the Dickel in my glass. "The good thing is there's not much street between here and where I sleep."

He unlocked the front, and I said good night. Just a bit over a quarter mile to the garage apartment. It was balmy again, an October that couldn't decide if he wanted to head toward winter or see how much summer it could squeeze out still. I squinted at the dull yellow light coming from the streetlights. The streets were deserted, even the bad boys and girls home and in bed for over an hour.

So Mrs H had thought I was going places. I wonder what that could have meant. If Lynn hadn't slept with Bob, and if I hadn't broken several of his bones, would we still be married? Would I have become a star on Art's staff? Would I have gone to graduate school, maybe even be in the process of becoming a Dean myself?

That was the road I was on, no doubt. And even when I was in school, and then when I was one of Art's Assistant Deans, were there the nightmares? Did I blanch in crowds? Was I paralyzed most days when a sound, or a taste, or a sight would stop me stone cold, and make me unable to function?

If it did, I didn't remember it. Lynn's betrayal made me snap, but before that I don't recall being in danger. Maybe I bent, but I did most certainly not break.

Once I broke it became harder and harder to do anything. The nightmares. The headaches. The overall paralysis. It was hard to move.

So they were worried about my drinking. I wasn't worried. Drinking was not my problem.

My real problem was how to connect this really messy set of dots. If I could.

Chapter Twenty-Eight

WHEN THE KNOCKING ON the door commenced, it had an oddly familiar feel, like the dream you're having the third time in a night. Except this dream had a couple of semi-familiar voices too. Good thing I'd gone to bed in my clothes.

The same two Metro boys who'd been here with Mercer before were back. This time Mercer wasn't with them, but a couple of buzz cuts in suits were. Metro Boy One cuffed me and Suit One, said, "Don't fight it." Suit Two held up a paper, called it a search warrant and he and both Metros started tearing up the apartment. Suit One pushed me down into a chair and looked me over.

I know the look. It's your basic "you're fucked, so don't make it worse."

"Is your warrant specific? If it is, I could tell you where it is." I tried to look helpful.

"Guy like you, who knows? You might have six or seven things of interest." He looked at the full ashtray. "Mind if I smoke?"

"Knock yourself out." I could see them looking into the full sink. Under dirty dishes. Really?

"Where were you last night, hippie?" He snapped the Zippo shut, got a lungful of smoke, and blew it straight at me.

"Drinking with a friend." Don't ask George Dickel to confirm it. He's gone.

"What time?"

"Most of the night. Stopped. Came back here. Fell into bed."

He surveyed me. "Fell in with all your clothes on, looks like. That happen often?"

The fact that it did struck me as coincidental rather than meaningful, so I shrugged. "Didn't seem worth the trouble last night."

The others joined him. Suit Two shook his head. "Nothing."

The two Metros pulled me to my feet. One unlocked the cuffs, the other pushed me back down, a little harder than necessary, I thought.

I rubbed my wrist. "Mind telling me what this is all about?"

Suit One gave me the run down without looking at me. He moved about the room, as if he believed something he wanted might suddenly jump from its hiding place and present itself. "The search warrant was granted this morning as the first matter before the magistrate. It calls for us to look for any and all weapons, weapons cases, ammunition, spent casings, and any other items or materials which are used in the care and use of firearms, including revolvers, pistols, shotguns, rifles, semi-automatic and automatic weapons." He looked at Suit Two. "I leave anything out?"

"That covers it."

"So that leaves several other things to do." He pushed his hat back on his forehead. "We're going to search your car out there in the driveway. That the only one on the premises?"

I nodded.

"Good. Then we're going to search the garage below this apartment."

That was fine by me. The Buckets had their car in Florida. All that was down there was a collection of yard tools nobody used and some Christmas decorations in boxes."

"And it'd be nice if you have a key to the house next door."

"I guess you want to search that too?"

"Warrant specifies all buildings, domiciles, and vehicles at this address, doesn't it, Simmons?"

Suit Two nodded. "All buildings, domiciles, and vehicles. That's right."

"So now that you know, anything you'd like to tell us we'll find?"

I know two rules when dealing with police. Rule one: be calm and don't provoke. Rule two: don't answer questions. You never know when an innocent answer will get taken the wrong way.

"You got to do what the warrant says, I reckon." That's all. Just a statement of fact.

I handed over the key to Bucket's house, made a cup of instant Folgers, sat down and let Metro One watch me, more or less balefully, while I turned on the set, adjusted the rabbit ears, and tried to watch the morning news.

"You know," I said to him, "to get a search warrant, somebody has to present probable cause."

He just grunted.

"So if somebody thought a gun was here, and it was used to commit a crime, somebody would have to make a case that I was a likely person to do something."

He looked sleepy, like he could not care less.

"A few days ago, we did this dance because a VU kid got killed. Now here we are. This about that? Or is anybody else dead, Officer?"

Chapter Twenty-Nine

THE NEXT DAY I had some breakfast, and then I called Don Mercer. He may be mad at me, but he's still the best cop I know.

"What's the chance I can get in to see the police report on my brother?"

"You're kidding, right?" I assured him I wasn't. "Anyway, there's nothing there that will help him. Trust me."

"Then it shouldn't be a problem for me to see it."

"It's a Metro sleeve, Jackson."

"You could see it. I could just be along for the ride."

"No."

There's no reason to push Mercer when he's saying things like "no" firmly. He's the kind who just digs in.

"Just so I'm in the know," he said, "tell me you're not doing anything that's going to get you in trouble."

"It's hard to tell if I'm getting in trouble. Metro searched the property. I guess they had to. They didn't find anything."

"And what else have you been doing?"

I could have told him that I was keeping an eye on Grace. Watching out for Hanna and whoever his midnight mystery guest was. Could have told him I had scored the Mickey binder, had seen an architectural drawing of the tower. I could have told him a bunch of Civil War trivia.

I didn't. "Nothing. There's nothing much to do." I said it as firmly as he had.

And he must have bought it.

"Let me know if you do anything that will get you arrested."

"Sure." I never do that.

We talked a few minutes, partly about Clint's insufferable way of taking command, partly about the possibility that the University could get a crane earlier than thought to pull Mickey off the tower. He wasn't mad at me anymore, I guessed, but he was talking like he was also filling out a crossword. I let the conversation run its course, then hung up.

I left my place on foot. The sky was mottled, the way it gets when it's between cold fronts. What do they call those clouds? I used to know. For the longest time I thought I wanted to be a weatherman. Every day, the first thing my parents wanted to know was the weather. To a farmer, it's the most important fact of the day. To be a weatherman, I thought when I was a kid, was to have possession of the knowledge of the world.

And now I couldn't tell you what kind of cloud was in the sky.

If that's not a symptom of something, it's at least a metaphor.

I hung a left on Elliston and headed for The Hideaway. It was empty except for the bartender and an old guy who looked like he might have been there overnight. The bartender poured me a double shot of I.W. Harper and slid a glass of water next to it.

I held the glass to the light, watching the cheap amber leave a little swirl near the lip of the glass. Probably not a good idea, I thought, to show up downtown at the jail with bourbon on my breath. On the other hand, with all the smells down there, who would notice?

I drank it and, in a nod to hygiene, polished off the water too.

Then under the cloud I could not name, I set off for downtown and the Metro jail.

When I got there, it was nearly noon. "You don't have to keep coming to see me, little brother." Thompson looked better. Scraggly, but better.

"You're right. I don't have to. What does that tell you?"

"You must not have anything better to do." He didn't look at me. But he said it with certainty. In his mind, there was no good reason for me to be there.

"Maybe I think you still know something that will help yourself." His fingernails were dirty, but he otherwise looked clean enough. Clean and sober too. Thinned out, but still resembling my brother. "Maybe I can shake it loose."

"I don't remember, Jackson." He finally looked at me. Yeah, there were my brother's eyes. They were sad, but you could still see the intelligence in them. The light had gone out of them, but the intelligence was still there.

"I think you know something. It may be hidden to you, but it's there. We just have to bring it out."

He shook his head and looked away again. "I don't remember a lot of things. I don't remember how I got from California to a truck stop outside Kansas City. I remember getting to Nashville on a Greyhound, but I couldn't tell you where I got on it. I remember my last couple lines of coke and that I bought a little bottle of Seagrams. I know I looked for you." He let out a breath. It was the longest he'd talked since I'd seen him. "And that's all I remember out of the last few weeks before I ended up here."

"Sounds like you partied the memory out of your head."

"It ain't partying, Jackson. It's life. You do it enough, and it's not a party. It's the way you live."

Maybe there was something to that. It had the benefit of sounding familiar.

"Let's try it this way. Where'd you get the Seagrams?"

He shut his eyes in thought. "I got off the bus and asked some old guy in the station which way Vanderbilt was. I kind of zigged and zagged until I got on Broadway, then there was a divide and I hung left."

"You should have hung right. That would have been West End. Instead, you were still on Broadway."

"It ended up all right. There was a little liquor store about a block or two from campus. That's where I got the Seagrams."

"What did the clerk in the liquor store look like? What'd he say to you?"

"What does this have to do with that kid's murder?"

"Work with me, Thompson. I'm trying to shake something loose."

He looked at me, the same way he did when we were kids, when I'd propose doing something he knew was stupid. But he would usually go along with it. "The clerk was a woman. In her forties." He shut his eyes again, trying to see her. "White blouse with a mustard stain on it. Busty woman. Blond hair. I remember thinking she looked like a country singer who'd gone completely to seed." He opened his eyes. "Good enough?"

"Very good. You were still on Broadway. Tell me where you walked to do the coke. Did you wait until you were on campus?"

"Well, I wasn't going to hit a couple of lines on a Nashville street corner."

"So how fast did you walk? Where did you enter campus?"

"I wasn't walking all that fast. I uncapped the Seagrams and had a couple of sips. It was in a brown paper bag."

"Of course it was." Stereotypical. Prudent. All at once.

"Then I crossed a street."

"21st. Did you cross at a light?"

"No. I dodged a VW beetle." He smiled at me. "It was orange. I remember more than I think I do, I guess."

"Sometimes it helps to slow it all down. You crossed onto campus by the law school. What did you do next?"

"That's easy. If that was the law school. Big building?"

"Big enough."

"I went in and found a bathroom. There was a little table in there, one of those stainless steel things? I did the lines there."

I didn't want to sound like our mother, but there was no telling what had been on that table. And you were sucking all that up your nose.

He seemed to be thinking the same thought. Maybe he was hearing the same voice. "Hey, I'm putting a controlled substance up my nose. What's a few germs?"

"Fair enough. What next?"

"Walked across this big field toward the building with the clock."

"That was Curry Field. Were you drinking?"

"It was a pint. I probably drank half of it walking over."

"Did you look at the clock?"

"It was after 3 by this time. Maybe 3:30."

"Liquor store closes at 2."

"That's right. She said I was going to be her last customer of the night."

I did some calculations. "So you got in on the bus, what about 1:30?" He shrugged. "That puts you in the liquor store right before 2. It was after 3 when you were walking across the field." I leaned in toward him. "That's a long time to go not even a quarter mile, Thompson. It doesn't add up."

"I had some other business to do in the bathroom."

"For an hour and a half?"

"Well, no. I kind of mellowed out in the lobby there. Sat down. Maybe I had a little shuteye."

"Did you or didn't you?"

"Sure. I caught a catnap."

"Anybody see you?"

"How would I know if I'm sleeping?"

"I meant, was anybody in the building? Did anyone see you?"

"One guy walked by. Stocky. Maybe 40."

"Ok, so once you got into Kirkland, that's the one with the clock tower, you went in the back?"

"Yeah, it was open. Mighty trusting place, Jackson. By this time, it's got to be nearly 4 a.m. on a Saturday night, and not a single locked door."

"You went up the stairs."

"I kind of walked all the hallways."

"Looking for me?"

"The guy I met out west said you were a dean or something. I thought this looked like the place."

"And you went all the way to the top floor, looking at office doors?"

"I started at the top, worked my way down. On the bottom floor I came to a door that was slightly open. So I went in."

"Because you thought, what, my office would be there? Seems like a leap to think that."

Thompson stood and walked over to the concrete block wall. It was painted an industrial gray. Next to it, Thompson had more color. But not much more.

He appeared to be deep in thought. It was a simple question. Did he really think I was behind that door? If so, why? If not, why did he push it open?

Finally, he opened his eyes and began to speak. "I heard something. The building was so quiet, you know, the way you'd expect it to be. It was so quiet I could hear the gin in the bottle as it went into my mouth. It was still, Jackson. Everything was still. I was the only thing moving. I was the only alive thing in the whole building. And I heard something behind that door."

"Go on." He had my interest now. But more importantly, he had his own."

"It wasn't a voice. It was more like a grunt."

"Like somebody in pain?"

"More like the sound you make when you're making an effort, like when you pick something up and it's heavier than you thought it would be."

"So you went in?"

"I sorta pushed the door open a little more."

"Any more grunts?"

"No. It was completely quiet again. I pushed it open and I may have said something."

"What sort of something?"

"You know. The sort of thing you say. Hello? Anybody here? That sort of thing."

"You were found passed out in a corner, Thompson. How do we get from here, saying "Anybody here?", to passed out in a corner with a crowbar?" I stood up myself and walked to where he leaned into the wall. He turned to face me, and I put both my hands on his shoulders. "With a crowbar that killed a kid."

His look told me he had no answer. "I think I passed out. I must have."

Chapter Thirty

HENRY HARRIS WORE A light blue Plant Operations shirt with his name in a little white oblong circle. The black baseball cap had the gold V in the middle, and the bill was furled downward, so that the sun wouldn't get in his eyes if it snuck up from the side. He had navy workpants on that were an inch too short and that rode up his legs when he sat down, leaving a gap between the white socks peaking above his work boots and the bottom of the pants. His arms were brown and leathery, but the legs, which never saw the sun, were a florescent white.

As long as I'd known him, Henry had looked the same. Days. Nights. Fall, winter, spring, summer. Good times and bad. Henry Harris was unchangeable. He was a shift foreman for the unit that made the University work. From light bulbs to plumbing, from light demolition to the light renovation that followed, Plant Operations made the place hum, and Henry was a shift supervisor, the one who rotated from days to nights to weekends. "Because I'm an old man with no family," he'd told me once. "Got to be somewhere. Might as well be somewhere they pay me to be."

And invariably, he'd turn and spit a brown stream from the Red Man that was constantly in his cheek.

Back when I was paid to work on campus, Henry and I pulled duty together lots of times. Once we'd even helped a mother birth her baby as she leaned on the back bench seat of a green Dodge Polaris parked in the loading deck area in married student housing, legs splayed as I played catcher and Henry played third base coach, coaxing her when the time came to push.

You might say we were pretty good teammates, at least before I got kicked off the team.

We were sitting astride two cane chairs, the sort somebody had decided were no longer suitable in a house, in the main shop, surrounded by the kind of scrap that accumulates anywhere that men cobble together solutions to mechanical problems. Wire and pipes and boxes of bolts, washers, screws—all the sorts of things that handy men were handy with. We were finishing our cigarettes in silence, the way people who are comfortable with each other do, completely at ease with complete silence.

"Ever been up inside Kirkland tower, Henry?" I ground the cigarette under my shoe, putting the butt out.

"Once." He flicked his toward the open overhead door, onto the concrete drive. "That's Sig Presley's area over there. He don't take to anybody getting up in his business."

"Bet he was fit to be tied over that Mickey Mouse business."

Henry whistled. "You don't know the half, boy. Shoot, if he'd caught those students, they'd have all been dead." He stopped his sentence hard. "Sorry about your brother, Jackson. I know he didn't do it."

I acknowledged his concern by patting his shoulder. "But you've been up there?"

"Didn't much like it. Stairs are pretty narrow. They're steep. I'm telling you, you better not look down if you got any fear of high places."

"It makes you wonder how those kids figured out everything, doesn't it?"

"I don't know about that. If you've got common sense, you can look at the outside and work it out. You might not know much about details, but you know it's got to be stairs.

You'd know about the options for load bearing, all the way up. There's not but a couple of ways it could be constructed. I'm just saying it's not for me."

"Do you think that there's room for somebody to hide something away there?"

"Like what, Jackson?"

I looked around the shop and spotted a case of what looked like faucets. "Something like that."

"Why the hell would Sig have a case of sink fixtures up in the tower?"

I laughed. Part of Henry's talent as a handy guy was his literal mind. That was some of the task in having a conversation too.

"I just mean something that size."

"Down on the floor? Sure."

"How about further up? Along the way as you climb the stairs."

He leaned back on the chair, tipping it onto its back legs. "I reckon there's a place or two. As you get higher, not so much. Of course, once you get to the top you're climbing a ladder. There's a little floor space there, but not much call for putting anything up there."

"Is there a trap door to put things underneath?"

"No. Not at all. You can see underneath that flooring as you climb. It's just a floor." He set the chair back on four legs. "What're you trying to figure out, Jackson?"

"To tell the truth, Henry, I'm not completely sure. And short of getting up in there myself, I don't know that I can even formulate my questions right."

"Well." He paused to put a wad of Red Man in his cheek. Cigarettes were the way he got his nicotine indoors, but when he could spit, he got it from chewing tobacco. Once he had the wad set, he turned to me. "It might be I could help. Ray keeps a set of architectural drawings in the cabinet over there." He motioned toward the little office of the head of Plant Ops, which was really more an elevated square platform. "I don't think there's any harm in you having a look at them."

I didn't think there was any harm in that either, but I was pretty sure Henry and I were alone in that belief. "You sure? I've seen one already."

He stood up and shifted his belt, like the sheriff would in the Saturday afternoon Westerns we watched as kids. "I'm sure."

"This won't get you in trouble, will it? I don't want that."

A long trail of brown juice lined the shop floor. "Looks like I'm the shift foreman right now. Let's just say that I'm going to have a look at a drawing or two. It might be you'd see something when I'm looking. I can't control that."

"Henry, you're an old dog." I stood, and just for good measure, adjusted my own belt too.

Hunched under the bare lightbulb of the office, Henry pushed a variety of older and newer papers to the side, one by one, looking for the Kirkland tower original. "It'll be in this mess somewhere. This is the folder for all the older ones. The Old Gym. Furman."

"I saw a picture not long ago, one of those panorama types? Four buildings. Three trees. It was taken in the winter, and it looked pretty damn bleak."

"Well, we're pretty crowded up out here these days. But it wasn't always like that." He kept pushing papers to the side, but only after inspecting each one. "Still, sounds like the VU of yesterday wasn't like this one."

Henry had that right. The landscape had changed. But some of the attitudes hadn't.

"Here we go," he said, holding a rolled paper aloft. "Let's get this puppy flattened out and we'll see what we've got."

We rolled it out and put a couple of ledger books on two corners, a paperweight from Beamon Pontiac on a third, and a broken piece of a brick on the fourth. The paper was yellowed and a little brittle. "You'd think they'd keep this in the library. I mean, it's a historical document."

"The original is up there. This is a copy."

"Sure looks like the real thing."

"Oh, it's real enough. It's probably the same age, roughly, as the original. See? College Hall. That what it was called in 1907 when it reopened."

"After the fire."

"The story that got passed down, over the generations of us Plant Op folk, was that the fire took down the north tower first, then took down the whole building."

"And when they rebuilt, they only build one tower."

"Yep. The south one."

"Kind of hard on the north tower."

"Well, it wasn't the one with the clock anyway."

I squinted to focus on the drawing in front of me. There was a drawing of the exterior of College Hall and its new tower, then a cutaway look at the tower itself. It was different from the one Howell had managed to get. "I don't know what I'm looking at here, Henry. Talk me through it."

He put his index finger on the lower part of the tower. "Mostly what you have down here are the specs for the tower, the trim and some venting information. As you come further up, you can see that how they were planning to integrate the tower into the roof. So far, not a lot of interesting stuff, right?"

"Maybe. It looks like there's an awful lot here about how to vent the tower. Why's that? Seems like that's maybe what made the original towers catch and burn so fast."

"That's not a bad thought, Jackson, but think a little more about it. If you don't have ventilation in a structure, all sorts of other bad things can happen. Not the least of which is you can't vent heat out of there. It'd be like having a hot core driven right through the center of the building."

"Save you on heating in the winter." I grinned.

"Which you'd spend out on cooling in the summer. Besides, you don't want an unventilated space where you have to do work."

"Like fixing the clock?"

"More like fixing the motor that runs the clock. Or the mechanism that strikes the bell. Not to mention the carillon that plays the music."

"I get it." I stared at the drawing. "I can't tell from this what I thought I would."

"And that was?"

"Are there places where you can store things, Henry?"

"Sure. There's tool bins at the bottom."

"That's not really what I mean. Are there storage places that could be hidden?

"You mean like a secret passage? I don't think so. Never heard tell of that."

"I'm not sure what I mean. But if I wanted to hide a big box, say the size of a steamer trunk, would there be a way to do it?"

Henry spewed a stream of juice off the platform. "Where there's a will, there's a way, I reckon. But you'd think it'd have come to light.

You'd have thought that, for sure. But had anyone been looking?

Chapter Thirty-One

I DIDN'T KNOW HOW to do the thing I needed to do, because I didn't know what I didn't know. That's basically what I told Thompson.

He looked at me with the sort of older brother stare that says, at the same time, you're an idiot and I don't care. "You talk like you're drunk, but as far as I can tell, you're sober." Thompson's eyes gleamed, the brown in them a shade lighter. He looked like my brother a little, not like a facsimile, a pale copy. "What's the part you don't know?"

"I know that a guy named Hanna works for a man named Pettibone, a guy who is a "South will rise again" kind of guy."

"Redneck? Bigot?

"Nothing of the sort, you'd think. Very cultured. Well spoken. So cool butter wouldn't melt in his mouth."

"I don't get it. I thought the southern diehards were good old boys with beer bellies."

"Some are. This one's not."

He brushed his hair back from his eyes. "How do you know these guys?"

"Mickey Mouse." He gave me a blank look. "The tower. The kids who put Mickey on the tower. The one you're supposed to have killed."

"I'm lost."

Yeah, I got it. But I needed to talk it through. And I hoped talking it through might shake something loose. For me, or for

Thompson. "Pettibone's daughter is the girlfriend of one of the guys who put Mickey on the tower."

"Ok, so you tracked down the guys who did the prank, you met the girlfriend, met the girl's father somehow. Who's got a guy who. . ." He paused, did that thing with his hand on his face that he always did when he was thinking. "They're all singing 'Dixie'." He laughed a mirthless laugh. "You sure you're not just stringing together a lot of unrelated things? I don't see where you're trying to go with this."

"That's a fact." I didn't know how it all fit. "But look, this girl? She's brilliant."

"So?"

"She's an ace at research. And she's researching the Civil War. They've all got a thing about it, but she's an intellectual."

"Got a crush on her, little brother?"

"Not exactly. But what I got is her research folder on a couple of Civil War soldiers, and her thinking on a pivotal battle in the war."

"You're getting further and further away, Jackson. What does any of this have to do with anything?"

"That's my question." I lit a cigarette and offered one to him, which he declined. "I believe that you came into the tower at a very bad time. For that matter, I think Patrick Vincent did too."

"He was there putting Mickey on the clock, right?"

"No. That had already happened. He was back, collecting something he'd left behind."

My brother was the smartest guy I knew growing up. We always called him the smart one in the family. My sister, Swanson, was the sweet one. And I was the one that could be counted on. To do the chores. To keep quiet. To follow along. I was the youngest but, not being the family pet, I had turned out to be the quiet one.

But my brother, the smart one, was thinking now. I let him.

"What's with the Civil War? What's this girl working on?"

I told him about the Battle of Shiloh and the Lost Cause of the South. I recited from memory what I could of the soldiers' letters. And I told him one thing he already knew: some southern folks are drunk on the Confederates.

"And you think the wild card in all this, the key to whatever lock you're trying to pick, is wrapped up in the Civil War."

"I guess I do."

"Then I don't know why you're in a jailhouse talking to me. Sounds like you need to be in a library somewhere."

***

I guess I'd been feeling a little of that too, but I was too proud, or too stubborn, to admit I needed more information. I found myself back in Special Collections with a different Chi Omega, this one a red head who apparently could not speak if she was looking you in the eye.

"I can bring you those letters if you have an ID." She was looking down at something behind the desk. When she was finished, she looked up at me.

I flashed my old student ID at her, but only so she could see what it was, not so she could inspect it.

She looked away, over my shoulder. I started to look too, but realized she was starting to talk. "Ok. I guess that's ok. You know you can't take them out of this room."

She looked at me. It was a little unnerving, the disconnect between speaking and looking at me. "That will be fine."

Then she turned and said, speaking toward the stacks behind, "I'll just be a minute."

This time she brought out the second box of the Artemis Williams papers, the officer, and the same box of Gilbert Adkins, the corporal.

"I think I've seen this one," I said, pointing at Adkins' box. "Is there another one?"

"I've got another of Williams. This is the only Adkins." She was looking at the clock on the wall. Then she looked at me.

"Ok. I'll take what you've brought."

It was a tough slog. If you've ever tried to do research, when you don't know the goal, when you don't really even know the question, you can imagine the pace of the work. You have to read everything. Twice. And half the time you have to go back and read something you read an hour ago to make sure you actually remember what you read.

I tried to make notes, but in the end I surrendered to the fastest possible way through. Read everything once, quickly. See if sense impression gave me anything.

I was in the Adkins box. He was not a prolific diarist, but what he lacked in volume he made up in substance. He was unsophisticated, but not unlettered, and almost all of his entries were addressed as if he was talking to his mother. As such, they were filled partly with the kinds of things sons tell their mothers if they don't want to tell the truth. In Adkins' case, he didn't want her to know how bad it all was in the field. I could relate. When I wrote home, I pretended I never encountered the enemy, much less death.

But halfway through the box, I finally saw something that made me smile. The regiment had been run out of Tennessee. The Army of Tennessee had splintered, and Adkins' group had ended up in north Georgia, somewhere around Reinhardt.

And there they'd been joined by a young Captain named Artemis Williams.

The same Artemis Williams that Grace Pettibone had been researching. And the author of the very same box sitting next to my elbow on the table.

I pulled the Williams box to me and stood to look down into it. It was packed with folders. I wedged a hand in to discover what kind of organization it had, saw that it was chronological, and pulled the latest folder out.

It was dated April 5, 1865, a letter to his father.

Do not be distressed, Father, with the news you are hearing. It is true that Richmond has fallen, and the great Army of Tennessee is routed. I remain with a splinter of that fine band of men. We are in a place, the name of which I cannot write for fear of enemy interception, but I can reassure you that a plan is afoot. No Yankee will anticipate, nor will any one of them be successful, if our cause is right and our execution is flawless.

And so went several other letters. Artemis Williams, marksman and scout, the sort of man I'd have got along well with, if only he'd been enlisted and not an officer.

I went back to Adkins' box, searching for a similar date. I found one written later in the same month.

The last weeks have given me new hope. While we are small in number, we are great in determination. When we reach the railhead, we will know more about how this ends.

Now I was alternating between the two boxes, sorting. There were growing clues that Grace's obsession about the Confederate treasury and the letters of the two men were cascading toward an intersection, one that would shine some kind of light about the tower.

There is nothing to fear. The train has arrived with its freight, and the delivery has been made. Now, we will test the will of the Yankee devil.

It could only be the train with the Confederate treasury, right? Why else would a cavalry officer and marksman, an expert scout, have joined with this splinter of the Army of Tennessee?

These are exciting times. I watch our officers as they plan, and I'm amazed by their daring. There is word that Lee might yet appear.

And if that happened, with a treasury at hand, the hoped-for campaign of Lee in the mountains might finally take place.

Except that it didn't. The history books told that story. Lee surrendered at Appomattox. He went into retirement, and became president at what would become known, eventually, as the College of Washington & Lee.

This was the paper that Grace Pettibone was writing. She believed that there was a half million dollars that had disappeared. That the money might somehow have been secreted all this time, waiting for the time when it would be used for some grand purpose, now seemed clear. It was enough for two young men to have paid with their lives.

But this was where the whole thing broke down, if the idea was that the gold had been hidden in the Kirkland Tower. It was a romantic idea, but it was impractical. The fortune, if it was hidden in the tower, would have perished in the College Hall fire of 1905. The tower that stood now was the new tower, not the old one that would have presumably held the fortune.

It wasn't a story that was going to wash.

And besides, who said there was gold anyway? Just Grace.

I returned to the Williams box. The letters did not play out in some kind of drama. In fact, there was precious little of great interest at all. The thing, whatever it was, that the train's delivery suggested, seemed to peter out like a dud shell, ending not with a bang but, well, you know.

Adkins war diary did much the same thing. There had been the buoyant moment of possibility—where General Lee himself might appear—and then, nothing. Adkins served his time well, it seemed, and came back home to Nashville when the war ended.

I pushed to the back of his box to see how the story ended. And end it did, with a signed commemoration of his 50 years in the employ of Vanderbilt University. Signed by Chancellor James H. Kirkland, it lauded him as the steward of Old Main, in which role he had served from the beginning of the University in 1875.

Corporal Adkins had joined the university at its founding, and had served as the primary keeper of Old Main, later Kirkland Hall, through the fire and rebuilding.

It was not the officer that was the most interesting, after all. I should have known. It was the corporal.

Chapter Thirty-Two

I WAS STARTLED WHEN Grayson Greer creased the box between his fingers. "You look like you've found something." His smile was somewhere between a grin and a grimace.

"I'm deep in Vandy history, and it's starting to give me a headache."

"You're deep in Grace Pettibone's research, that's for sure." He pulled a chair between his legs and leaned forward on the back, and peered over half-moon glasses. "What have you found?"

"Corporal Adkins was steward of Kirkland Hall for 50 years. That's really something."

"Indeed. Fifty years is a long time to do anything."

"But what else did he do? Is there any record of that?"

"I would bet that Grace chased it down. That's how tenacious she is."

"Any way that I could shortcut that? And find out what she found?"

"You could ask her."

"I'm not that kind of friend." I wasn't sure exactly what kind of friend I was, but I didn't think she'd give up her sources.

"I think you know that we could go through every sign out for the last year to see what she looked at. That wouldn't be very productive."

"What would be productive, then, Gray? Besides asking her."

"I would ask the young woman who works here."

"The one who won't look at you when she speaks?"

"I call her, the one who remembers everything."

What she called herself was Pansy Bolt, and she was perplexed when Greer called her over. "Who?"

"A tall undergraduate female. Interested in Civil War papers. Comes in about twice a week, usually during the day."

"Sure. She's nice."

"And smart." Grayson gave her a fatherly smile. "Smart is always good when paired with nice."

Pansy Bolt looked at me, and quickly looked away. I don't know if I didn't look nice or didn't look smart, but I kept my mouth shut.

Gray leaned forward, his elbows on his knees. "So, here is my question, Pansy. We know that Grace, that's her name, was interested in these two soldiers, Williams and Adkins. Do you recall any others she was studying?"

Pansy's face went blank. "I don't know, Mr. Greer."

"I completely understand. The question is out of the blue. Why don't you take your time? Think a little about it." He leaned back. "Something may come to you."

She nodded and stood, heading back to her station behind the counter. Her face was a study in concentration. First she wrinkled her mouth, this way and that, a face that would have told you she'd eaten something sour, if she'd been eating. Then, her nose went into gear, nostrils flaring and unflaring. She made a slight guttural sound in her throat. Then she shut her eyes and lowered her chin onto her chest.

I leaned over to Gray. "She always do that?"

"She's not a great researcher. But one day she could be a great archivist. I tell you, Jackson, she remembers things that are not memorable. That is, until you need them and you can't remember where they are." Gray leaned away and asked her, "Anything?"

She opened her eyes, rather like someone waking from a long nap. She pursed her lips. "Maybe." And she went back into the Special Collections stacks.

A few minutes later, she emerged with a small square file box, and set it down on the table in front of us. "She only asked for this once, at least while I was working."

I read the card inside the small, aluminum bracket: Papers of Sgt. Carl Bradshaw, CSA, Army of Tennessee.

I looked up at Pansy. "This is a much smaller collection."

She looked at me as if she still couldn't decide if I was nice or smart or just plain dumb and mean.

"I think what Jackson means is, is this the entire Bradshaw collection?"

"That's the whole thing." Pansy looked vaguely triumphant. "It's in the back on the bottom shelf behind battlefield photos. I had a devil of a time finding it for her."

This is the final report of Sergeant Carl Bradshaw, Army of Tennessee, Tennessee Regiment, Hull's Company. August 13, 1865

I joined the Army of Tennessee in November of 1862. Our company mustered originally at 100 men, of which 80 were privates, and was originally commanded by Captain Winslow Hull. We were an infantry company, usually supported by artillery from the Tennessee Regiment.

I was installed as First Sergeant, and my job was to write reports, take musters, keep records, and in general to run the company. I have served for all this time as the ranking enlisted man in the company, and I report directly to the Captain.

I will not rehearse the history of our company. It is the sad narrative of most companies in the Army of the Confederacy, being one of misery, despair, death, and finally surrender. We had our moment, to be sure, at Chickamauga, but all else was defeat. Thousands of men lie dead. Thousands more are maimed.

How our company came to be identified as the one to take this final, perilous assignment I know not. I only know that after the battlefield death of Captain Winslow, we were sent a new Captain from the Third Corps of the Army of Tennessee, Captain Artemis Williams.

I came to learn that my new commanding officer was an engineer, with an exhaustive knowledge of bridges and roads, and that his primary task in Third Corps had been to manage transport. But in the Battle at Stones River, he had displayed an uncanny ability with a Whitworth rifle, when he wiped out two Union artillery crews from his sharpshooter's location.

He was sent to us, Hull's Company, to separate from the Army of Tennessee for a secret mission.

I looked up from my reading. Gray was behind the counter, looking through what appeared to be a new set of acquisitions. Pansy was at her station.

"Pansy?" She looked toward my whisper. "Could you bring me the last Artemis Williams box?"

She hesitated. Apparently my being in good with her boss wasn't good enough to take direction from me. She didn't move until Gray glanced at her and nodded.

By this time, the mighty Army of Tennessee was reduced to about four and a half thousand men. Our company, now Williams' Company numbered only seven, including Captain Williams. General Johnson, now in command, was intent on rebuilding our force as we prepared for a campaign in the Carolinas.

At the Battle of Bentonville, we engaged the marauder Sherman, and gave as good as we got. It was not enough, though, and we retreated during the night of March 21 to an encampment near Smithfield. During our three-week encampment, the general reorganized our various forces into a single army. By the end of his labors, our total strength was about 30,000 men.

On April 3 of this year our company received a dispatch from none other than Jefferson Davis, addressed to General Johnson. I know because as First Sergeant I saw every scrap of paper concerning our company. The dispatch was clear: we were to meet a party which included President Davis in Washington, Georgia, a month hence, on May 4.

We left the next day, having provided ourselves with enough to get us started, for we would live off the land after a few days. We were Captain Williams, Lieutenant Hood, myself, Corporal Adkins, and three privates, Grand, Phillips, and Ward. All of us save the Captain original members, and all of us hardened and war-worn.

I looked up to see Pansy holding a box, and she nodded toward the empty spot on the table. "Yes, that's fine."

She set it down and turned as if to go. Then, she pivoted back. "What are you looking for?" It was said helpfully. "If you know, I can help you."

"I'm almost to the end of Sergeant Bradshaw's memoir, if that's what it is, and it doesn't look like I'm going to get the nugget of information I need."

"What are you looking for?" A simple request, repeated.

"I think that Grace Pettibone is looking for a pot of gold. Literally."

"A lost treasure?"

"Something like that. I'm more and more convinced she thinks it's here in Nashville, on campus." I looked at Pansy. If she was impressed by a lost treasure, she didn't show it. "I'm looking for a clue to that."

She stood and looked at me, expressionless, for two beats, then turned toward her boss. "I'll be back in a minute."

And with that she walked to the door, opened it, and left the Special Collections area.

"Give her a minute or two. She'll repay your patience."

I got up and stretched.

A few minutes later, Pansy returned with a large book. "This is the Birth and Death Register for Montgomery County, Tennessee." She opened it on the table and I stood next to her. "Here. Deaths in 1865. Artemis Williams. May 6, 1865."

I narrowed my eyes. "He didn't make it back from Georgia."

"Bradshaw did. Adkins did. He didn't." Pansy shut the Register. "I remembered that Grace had this book. That was the last time she was in here."

What the hell did that mean?

I paged to the last of Bradshaw's account.

This final mission was never completed. Captain Williams was killed when Corporal Adkins' musket discharged as he was cleaning it. The rest of us ran to where they were, and Adkins was standing over the corpse of the captain. We had all seen so much death, I suppose, that it was no surprise Adkins face was blank. He was perhaps in shock. His only words were, "All this for a slave." And I suppose that could be the epitaph on all our tombstones.

My epitaph will probably read, "All this for a clue." There was something here, nagging at me, but I couldn't pull it out of the dark.

And what it was, I was sure, was the one fact that would link them all.

Chapter Thirty-Three

I HAD CHASED A fried chicken plate with a couple of beers and a bourbon at Hannigan's, then walked over to Church Street to get a fifth of Dickel at The Southerner. I had to pay a couple of the dollars out in change, which earned me a scowl from the guy at the register. His look said something like, "Get a job." If he only knew.

By the time I was back in my apartment above the garage, it was growing dark and I'd lost a little of the edge that was making me want to drink. Instead, I sat in the darkness and thought, both hands around a tumbler that held an ounce of amber.

I had been sure that Thompson could remember something that would crack the door to that night just a little, kind of like the door to the tower stairs was cracked that night. I had counted on there being something just below the surface that I could tease out and illuminate.

But Thompson had crapped out on the last throw. The look on his face while he was reconstructing, remembering had caused a little of the old Thompson to emerge, but by the time he ran aground, the look was a worse version of the sad one he'd started with.

It was tough, ten years ago, to have a brother disappear into thin air, for no apparent reason. Now, it was just as tough to see him almost become himself, then fade at the moment of truth.

That's way too dramatic a way to put it. He almost remembered something. Except he didn't. And maybe there wasn't anything to remember at all.

And while the discovery that Adkins had been the steward of Kirkland was interesting, that bit of information had crapped out too.

And there was a group of men, yes, who'd been assembled for some purpose, but the purpose seemed not to have been served. There was a mission, and it disappeared into thin air. Did it disappear because Adkins shot Williams? And why did he shoot him? Was it an accident? Williams, Adkins, and Bradshaw shone but paltry light on it.

I put out a cigarette that had been burning in the ashtray since the moment I lit it. In the moonlight I could see the ash trail behind like a gray caterpillar. Or perhaps like the exoskeleton of some long, narrow bug. I set the tumbler on the side table, leaned forward, and rubbed my eyes. The night didn't feel like it was one for sleeping, and it didn't feel like one for drinking. And at two in the morning, that was an odd feeling indeed.

I heard the husky rumble of a Harley in the street. They have a distinctive sound because of the way the crankshaft is aligned, making the cylinders fire at uneven intervals, like some motor spirit saying potato-potato, over and over, loudly. Then, there was a second bike, also a Harley. At about that moment my only window lit up with a yellow flame and a crash of glass hit my floor. The smell of gasoline suddenly permeated the apartment and the flame became a small intense wash of fire.

I instinctively grabbed the blanket resting on my feet and used it with my body to stamp out some of the fire. I could feel the searing heat of the fire, the gasoline up my nose and causing me to cough. Every part of my body felt seared as I rolled back and forth over it, trying to deprive it of air. As soon as I got one part extinguished another seemed to flare. Back and forth, I went, as fast as I could.

I heard the roar of motorcycles as they departed.

I don't know how long it took to get the fire mostly out. But when it was, I ran to the cupboard under the sink where there was a dusty fire extinguisher. I sprayed the fire with it, sweeping back and forth, until all that remained was the smell of gasoline and the scorched hardwood.

It was only then I got myself to the window. Of course, no one remained in the street. The bikes had waited to see the flames, then had hightailed it out. I could guess the rest.

The idea probably had been to make sure I wasn't in any of my regular haunts. If I'd been in one, they'd have waited me out. But if I wasn't at High Life or Linda's, and if I wasn't at the Top Hat, and Hannigan's had closed, then it was a safe bet I was in the apartment. Asleep, if the lights were off.

And if I'm honest, probably passed out. At least, that's the way the thinking would go. A drunken, sleeping sitting duck.

But luck was with me. I'd stopped drinking at dinner, and I'd spent the rest of the time letting darkness grow around me. If I had known an attack was coming, I would have done the same thing, waiting for the moment when something unusual would be needed. That would have had a good result. I know enough from the past that being prepared when your attacker doesn't know you're prepared is a winning tactic.

The fact that I didn't know I needed to be alert just made it a miracle.

I pulled a change of clothes out of the closet, got the key to the Bucket's house across the driveway, and locked the smell of smoke and gasoline away. I could shower, sleep on the couch, and get a head start the next morning.

Chapter Thirty-Four

WHICH IS WHAT I did. I never did get the smell of gasoline out of my nose, but I did manage to get six hours of quiet on their couch. I didn't hear motorcycles in the night as I thought I might, but I did dream once, a dream of the motor depot at Fort Riley. That's probably what the gasoline does to your dreams.

I called Metro to make a report, and they sent out a guy who looked all of 16, a slightly built guy about 5 foot 6, who didn't approve of my waiting until the next morning to make a report. Then I called the Bucket's home insurance agent who said he'd be by in a few days to have a look. I thought they paid those guys to make sure no additional damage took place, but maybe they just assume everything's a fraud to begin with.

So I did my duty to the Buckets and set out to see what I could find about my enemies. The Sons of Shiloh seemed a certain bet, and a certain rotund biker seemed the right target.

Nashville on a work day morning gets going early, and by 8 a.m. the place is filled with the sort of traffic that demonstrates its importance to middle Tennessee. It's the region's retail center. It's a major medical center. It's a distribution center. And even though its manufacturing base has mostly migrated outside the city limits, the manufacturing base's banking needs are handled in the city. Everybody thinks "country music" when you say Nashville, and it's an industry, but there's more than that industry, and the others employ a lot of people.

I ended up at the IHOP, reading the Tennessean and scarfing down a stack of pancakes with a pot of coffee. Despite the scare in the night, I'd had a good night's sleep and now I had a clear head.

The experience of being bombed in my own apartment wasn't exactly edifying, but it was certainly clarifying. Someone wanted me dead, and they were prepared to be ruthless in making sure it happened. By now, no doubt, someone had driven by to see the results of their handiwork, and had been disappointed by the lack of result. I hadn't slept very soundly, so I think I would have heard a motorcycle. But I don't think a car even came down the street in the night.

Not that someone couldn't have found out any other way. No sirens and no firetrucks—that would have been a sign.

By the time I finished the short stack at the IHOP, it was close to 10 a.m. I called Art Blake's office from the pay phone at the restaurant.

I got Blake's secretary, Dot, and she put me through to the boss. "Got time for a beat down, former assistant dean, today?"

I could imagine the look on his face. The handlebar mustache would be lifting from side to side. "Are you in trouble? Because I warned you."

I interrupted him. "You're a Civil War buff, Art. I have a quandary I can't quite work out."

"Does it still have to do with your brother being in jail?"

I could see how this was going to go. "Yes, it does, but," I cut him off, "not in the way you may think. And with much larger stakes than we knew before."

"How much larger?" I could hear the suspicion in his voice, the way it rose when an undergraduate was hatching a false story to get out of some punishment.

"Large enough that someone tried to kill me last night."

Art Blake had made his reputation on being ever calm and always steady. It wouldn't do for a man his size to be anything else. But he failed to contain an urgent, "What?" that was shout-level loud, loud enough that I could hear him reassuring Dot, who had doubtless rushed into his office, that everything was fine.

"Tell me that I heard you right. Somebody tried to kill you? When?"

"Last night. A motorcycle rolled up, pitched a beer bottle's worth of gasoline and a lit rag into my place."

"And you escaped?"

"Not before putting it out. I spent the night on the Bucket's couch."

"I was afraid of this. Although I expected nothing quite like this. I knew no good could come of sticking your nose in the Vincent boy's murder."

"Well, too late now, boss. Somebody's got me on his list for some reason. And it's mixed up with the motorcycle gang, which is mixed up with the pranksters, who are mixed up the Pettibone Institute."

"And that's how you get to the Civil War? Tell me about that."

"Too complicated, Art. I really need to sit down with you, show you a few things, and see if you can connect a dot or two for me."

"I can clear my morning now, but I have a meeting with Dr. Word, the vice chancellor, at 2 that I cannot break. How soon can you be at my place?"

"I'm at the IHOP. Ten minutes."

"See you then."

It was the sort of fall day that all but guarantees that winter will slip up on you, unaware, and cold cock you into lethargy. It was an almost-spring day, except that the leaves were brown and gold on the sidewalks. When I got to West Side Row, Blake was standing in the door of his apartment, opening the screen door so I could come in.

"You don't look like someone who had a Molotov Cocktail last night. How many other cocktails did you have?" He was moving toward his office, where he held court most nights, before and after he went to Hannigan's. He wasn't looking at me. He seemed distracted.

"Funny enough, I was just sitting in the dark, thinking. Couldn't sleep. Didn't drink. Just letting what's in my head rattle around."

"Well, I wasn't trying to imply ánything." He sat down hard on the wooden banker's chair behind the desk. "I've seen you be pretty nimble even when you've had a few."

That was true enough. More than true enough. "What's bothering you, Art?"

He slid his considerable frame forward on the seat of his chair and leaned on the desk with both elbows, his face forward of his torso, at a forty five degree angle. He seemed to be looking for something on my face. "I don't like when people try to hurt other people, especially people that I like, people that I care about."

"I hear you, Art."

"No, I don't think you do. This isn't normal. This isn't right. This isn't the way Nashville is, with bikers trying to burn down people's houses in the night."

"Nashville ain't Nashville anymore, Art. Nashville's different. You're not out real late like I am. Not anymore. All kinds of things happen on the west side that you never heard happen. Other parts of town, it's even worse."

"It doesn't seem worse at all on campus."

"Campus isn't real, Art. Townies call it Vandyland. It's like a board game with safe challenges and lovely prizes."

"You're cynical. I've never heard you be cynical before."

"I'm telling you the truth. And your board game has two dead undergraduates now, and they're mixed up in some pretty bad things. Or at least with bad people."

Blake rested back in his chair, rocking it toward the wall and letting it stay there. His eyes seemed to trace the path of the crown molding. "I know. I feel old, Jackson. I feel like all this happened when I wasn't paying attention."

"You're not in charge of Nashville, Art. You can't stop this."

"I don't need to stop it. I need somehow to understand it. Our students are living in this world. It affects them. It's my job to understand it."

I got it. Art always believed his job was to provide a safe place for growing up. He had his doubts about some students, and whether they would grow up before they ruined their chance at VU. But he never had any doubt that he could rescue the ones who wanted to be rescued. That's why he was good at what he did.

I had my doubts about my rescuing anyone, want to or not. But I was pretty sure I was supposed to rescue my brother, if I could.

"Then help me, Art. I need to get to the bottom of all this." If I do, I thought, at least a little bit of the new mayhem would be contained.

"Tell me what you need."

"I need you to tell me what you know about a missing shipment of Confederate gold. It left Richmond right before the capital fell."

He raised an eyebrow. "Good lord. That myth?"

"You've got a pretty sharp undergraduate who thinks differently."

"One of the prank boys?"

"One of them had a girlfriend. It's her."

"What's her name?"

I knew that Art wouldn't be satisfied until he knew. "Grace Pettibone."

"Good looking girl." It figured that Art knew who she was. Often, he seemed to know everyone. And half the time he knew something significant about them. But not this time. "A Kappa Delta, I think. Never been in trouble that I know of. Does she live on campus?"

"Cole Hall."

He exhaled. "Can't say I know much more. Is she mixed up in this?"

"I don't think so, although I don't see how she didn't know about Mickey on the tower in advance. But she's working on a paper, and it's pretty damn well written, that there's a significant amount of unrecovered Confederate gold."

"That story has been around for a while. There's just no evidence that any of it is true."

I reached behind me and pulled out the file folder. "Have a look at this, and tell me what you think."

He leaned forward and took the file, looking at me with the same eyebrow raised as before. Art took seriously his own amateur scholarship. While he was an amiable and open-minded man, he also had a healthy regard for the opinions he'd already formed. It took more than a little to shake him out of certainty.

Blake took his time with the incomplete manuscript. He would read a bit, then turn back to the page before, or wait and look ahead for something. I'd seen him devour campus police reports this way, and incident reports written by Assistant Deans for that matter, but this seemed to occupy his mind so thoroughly that I believe he forgot I was there.

At last he put the final page down on his desk. He sat straight up in his chair. Art's 6 foot 6, and a lot of his height was, of course, in his legs. But as he sat up straight, I realized he had some serious torso length too. Of course, I was slouching in his upholstered visitor's chair, so I was shorter than usual.

"Well. What do you think?"

"You're right. She writes like she's a scholar. Very impressive prose."

"And her argument?"

"It's an old argument, and one that's been generally disproved by serious scholars. The suspicion, and it's one she pushes aside relatively quickly, is that the money got spent paying soldiers as they went. And as protection money too. The Union troops were never far enough away for them to feel safe."

"So they doled out a million dollars along the way. That's a lot of money, Art, even if it's Confederate money."

"Well, there's the problem, though I never really thought about it like that. This was not Confederate script. This was gold. And jewels. Kind of hard to pay people in gold if there's script in circulation. Especially," he laughed, "if it's worthless script."

"Pardon me, sir, but you seem to confirming the young lady's point."

"I do, don't I?" He picked up the pages again, and scanned. ". . . a fortune whose provenance can be precisely traced through the war journals of a few soldiers, some of whom did not know the elements of the plan. And once the leader of that plan was deceased, the remainder knew only part, and not enough to reclaim the treasury." He looked at me over the top of the pages. "It's an intriguing theory."

"You're my Civil War expert, Art. Give me something more than intriguing."

He rose and started for his kitchen. "Let me get us a couple of iced teas, and I'll think." He left the room.

I was half hoping he'd return with a couple of iced bourbons, but I knew he had a meeting with the vice chancellor in a couple of hours. Art was not the kind of man to contemplate going in with liquor on his breath to Dr. Word. Although Dr. Word would not have minded, even if he noticed.

Art returned and put my glass on a coaster, then returned to his familiar position, sliding a coaster matching mine, with the VU logo, under his own. He made a steeple with his fingers and scowled.

"Why would an upstart undergraduate be able to pick apart a well-known and established theory?"

I knew the game. Art and I had played it when I worked for him. He wanted to run what he called a "logic panel." It was his way of poking holes in things he didn't understand, to find out where it was his understanding lagged.

"Because she, too, is a Civil War enthusiast."

"Fair enough. What motivates this interest? Do we know?"

"Her father is head of the Pettibone Institute, which believes not only should the South rise again, but it must, if only to throw off the last of Yankee domination."

He had been leaned back, with his eyes closed, the picture of concentration. He opened them now. "Is that right?" He leaned back again and shut his eyes. "That would account for the interest, certainly. Do we suspect that she is trying to please Daddy? Or is it a more organic interest?"

"Oh, it's organic. Although Daddy is a feature. And his Institute is not quite a going concern."

"You seem quite confident. Is that because you have asked her yourself?"

I knew the surface question. I knew the deeper one too. I answered the surface one. "Yes."

"And if she is doing this research, in which she believes she can divine the location of a lost treasure, why is she interested?"

"I've thought about that. Part of it, no doubt is the intellectual challenge. But it wouldn't be hard to believe that the Institute could profit from an infusion of cash that size." He cleared his throat. "An infusion of cash from the sale of that amount of gold. What would it be in current dollars if it was a half million to a million in gold?"

"It would be a great deal. And how would she find the location?"

"I'm assuming she would discover it from further study of these two soldiers' letters."

"Then you would need to know these soldiers' names. I'm assuming, of course, they are in the library."

"They are. And I've seen some of them already."

He pulled himself slowly from his recumbent posture, took a sip of tea, and fixed me with his firmest look. "You wouldn't have read them late at night, all alone, would you?"

"It was night and I was alone. It's always quiet in the Archive."

He sucked his teeth. "Then I would suggest your next job should be to get back to the Archive and finish your research. If you already know where to look, I'd advise you to start looking."

"So you think there's something to it?"

"I think she thinks there's something to it. I think she's motivated to find out. And I think you're wasting your time asking me what I think after that."

I got up and left the tea, unsipped, on his desk. "You're saying I need to do what I know I need to do. You're right." I turned and headed out. Over my shoulder, I said, "Always good to spend time with you, Art. Always a treat."

He growled a little. "Let me know what you discover."

By the time I walked down West End to Linda's, I had lost the smell of gasoline. I looked through the plate glass window, the one that proclaims Linda's "West Nashville's Watering Hole," and could see a guy I recognized as a replacement bartender mopping the floor. From the looks of him, he had had a lot less sleep than I had.

He shook his head "no" when I tapped on the window. So I kept tapping. Finally he came to the door. "We don't open until 2." He looked at his watch. "Come back then."

I stuck my foot in the door. "I don't want anything to drink. I just want some information."

"Read the newspaper if you want information." He tried to kick my foot out of the way.

I put my hand on his chest and pushed. It wasn't a hard push, and it wasn't meant to hurt him.

"Hey, bud. What gives?"

"I want some information. I bet it won't take you two minutes to give it to me." I gave him a glare. "And I know it will take a lot longer than two minutes if you're going to mess with me."

He looked me up and down, trying I suppose to decide if I was likely to get rough. Or maybe he was just getting a good look so he could call the cops later. Whatever the reason, he said, "Ok."

"You know the biker club that drinks here sometimes? Sons of Shiloh?"

"Hard to miss them."

"It's hard to miss this short guy who's in the club. About as wide as he is tall. Wears a boat captain hat. Long beard. Carries a hunting knife on his belt."

"They all have beards and they all carry knives."

"Yeah, but this one is a ringleader. Times I saw him, he sat on that stool right at the door of the pool room. Got a raspy voice, kind of like he's been yelling a lot."

"Oh." A look of recognition crossed his face. "Wears a red bandana around his neck."

"That's the one."

"You don't want to mess with him. He's just a little bit of bad news."

"How do you know I'm not?"

He stepped back. "I'm not saying you are or you're not, buddy. I'm just saying he is a little crazy."

"How do you figure that?"

His mouth was a thin line, closed off like he wouldn't have anything else to say. But he did. "I remember you. You were the one that student went after."

"What about it?"

"You laid him out, then you said something to Road Dog."

"That's his name? Road Dog?" It was humorous, almost demeaning. "How do you get a name like that?"

"Guy who's been on the road too long. Taking a lot of rain and wind in his face. He comes in off the road like a dog. It's not a bad thing. Kind of a respect sort of thing."

"Know where I'd find Road Dog during a weekday? What's he do for a living?"

"He and his brother have a garage further down Highway 100."

"Brother?" That almost made a cylinder click in my head, the kind a combination lock makes when the first number is right. "What's Road Dog's real name?"

"His real name is Hal."

"It wouldn't be Hal Hanna, would it?"

"That's the one."

Click.

Chapter Thirty-Five

I DROVE OUT GRANNY White Pike and stopped once to ask at a Gulf station where Farragut Road was. It turned out it was just a half mile further. I needed to set something in motion. And now that I knew Hal and Rod were brothers, the clicking of tumblers began.

The pranksters and the Sons of Shiloh. The Hanna brothers and the conversation in the hedge. The motorcycles throwing Molotovs. Even the attempted frame for Raines Durst's death.

And at the bottom of it all: The Pettibone Institute and its cash problem.

No wonder the location of Confederate gold was important. I remembered Grace. "I want to know. Daddy wants to do."

Hanna's Body Shop was a concrete block building on a lot that sat between two houses, both of which appeared to be occupied. Hanna's lot was pretty scraggly, with isolated tufts of Bermuda grass trying to launch some kind of tacky lawn. The building was small but it fronted a larger building behind, presumably where the auto work took place.

Inside, there was a wood railing around a guy with a pencil behind his ear and grease on his fingers. He was looking through what seemed to be work orders. There was an old, beat up red sofa along the wall, also with its share of ancient grease stains, and a closed door that led to the shop in back.

The guy, somewhere in his twenties with straw colored hair, didn't look at me. "Yeah?"

I leaned on the railing, sitting one thigh on it. "I'm looking for Rod Hanna."

He put the papers down, leaned back in his chair and looked at me for the first time. "He ain't here. Maybe I can help you."

"You can't. Where would I find him?"

"I don't keep track of him, mister. How about you leave your name?"

"Home?"

"Beg your pardon? Is that your name?"

"Is that where he is?"

"Like I say, mister. . ."

"How about you tell me where he lives." I didn't like the way this one looked. He didn't look like he was going to be talkative.

"That's none of your business, buddy. Why don't you just hit the road?"

I tapped the railing with my thumb, the way a bass player might pop a couple of notes off. "You're screwing up." I looked at his name patch on the shirt "Billy. Metro's got a warrant."

He frowned. "What's that mean?"

"If you're lucky, it doesn't mean a thing to you. It might mean a lot to Hanna."

Billy hesitated. You could see the hamster wheel turning in his brain. "I don't think so. If Rod wanted to talk to you, he'd have said something. If he wanted you to find him, you'd know where to go."

"Maybe I do. Maybe that's why I'm here."

"Like hell. All you had to do is look in the phone book."

I'd had enough of this game. It was going nowhere. And the odds that Hanna was here was a good as the odds he wasn't. I moved to the side of the railing and walked toward the door to the garage. Billy shouted that I shouldn't do that, but the door on the railing stuck and by the time he was moving in my direction, I was already through the door.

There sat Rod Hanna and four men around a table. They looked to be playing cards. There was a small pile of money in the middle. From the cards on the table, it was five card stud, or some variation.

Hanna stood. His eyes said something murderous, but his mouth grinned something less ominous, though no less cold. "What the hell do you want, Trade?"

Another man stood. "Get out."

Billy came alongside me. "He just wouldn't give up, Rod." He reached for me, and tried to hook his arms under mine. "Outside, asshole."

I slipped his grasp and planted my knee in his crotch. When he doubled over, I punched down, hard, where his jawbone hinge was. "Stay down, Billy." He did.

The card players were all standing now. "You can't take all of us." That was a big, round man speaking. He was probably right.

"I didn't come to fight with you. I came for Rod."

"I don't want you here, Trade. You can go back out the way you came."

"Not until I leave you a message."

The men looked toward Hanna for a clue. Hanna looked not at them but at me. "What's the message?"

"Metro's got a warrant."

"For what? For who?"

I walked toward the door, keeping Billy and the card players in my sight. "You don't want to talk about this in front of all these boys, Hanna. Come with me."

"I wouldn't do that, Rod." It was the round one again.

"Why would I go with you?"

"You don't want these boys to hear this. It concerns the Institute. It might have to do with a young woman you know." I stood in the doorway. "It's a warrant, Hanna."

He stepped around the table. "I got this, boys. It's not the sort of thing you should worry about."

"What's an institute?" Billy was still on the floor. "That like a doctor's office?"

"Never mind." Rod was nearly to the doorway. "Go back to the game. Billy, put some ice on that jaw. I'll be back before you know it. Give me a half hour."

"If you're not back by then, we'll come looking, mister." This was clearly aimed at me.

"He'll be back." I was pretty sure he would be. But if he wasn't, that wouldn't be on my timecard.

We went outside, and Hanna pointed to a late model Lincoln, a big four-door that had the look of money to it. "Get in."

I did. I got in the back. "I want you where I can see you, Rod."

He started up the big V-8. "What's the matter, Trade? Don't trust me?"

I knew that he would take me down pretty hard if he had his druthers. So that's what I told him. I also had a small coil of rope in my coat pocket. It could go around his neck if anything got hinky. I didn't tell him that.

"That's good you don't trust me. You shouldn't. I don't like you one bit."

"Just drive until I tell you to stop."

We traveled south toward Radnor Lake. Hanna's business was just outside Belle Meade, so I reasoned he made good money being the go-to for some of the wealthy when they banged up the Benz. "Nice car you got, Rod."

"You know anything about cars, greaseball?"

"I know how to drive them. I can change oil. Replace brake shoes."

"Shade tree mechanic. Tinker, tinker. I mean, do you have any idea how to work with cars. Put the soup on one. Turn it into a work of mechanical art."

"Not my line of work, Rod. That what you do?"

"That's not just a body shop back there. My line of work is to take an engine and turn it into something special. There's as much art as science in it. Modify the engine so that there's more air, colder air, richer fuel mix." He grunted in a way that was half sensual, half bestial. "It's a metaphor for life, Trade. Nothing comes off the factory floor like it should. You have to make it come to life."

"That why you're hooked up with Pettibone? With the Institute?"

"What's with the warrant?"

"Pull over here."

"All right." He looked in the rear view mirror at me as he pulled the Lincoln to the side of the road. "So talk."

"Metro is working on a theory you ought to know about, Rod. They are looking for a gun."

"What's that got to do with the Institute? Or Grace?"

"I thought you might want to tell me."

He half turned on the leather bench seat. "Why would I tell you anything?"

"I know you, Rod. You didn't trust the boys. Patrick. Raines. Howell. Well, two of them are past tense, aren't they?"

"What're you saying? You think I had something to do with that? What about your brother?"

"Wrong place, wrong time. Metro is looking for a gun, Rod. The gun that killed Raines. My brother isn't in on that."

There were a hundred holes in this story. I knew that. I just hoped it sounded believable enough that Rod wouldn't think of any of those holes.

"Maybe you did Raines."

"Nice try, Rod. That's what Metro thought too. That's why they got a warrant." I wanted to put the rope around his neck and pull hard. I left it where it was. "But you know what they got? Zip. Zero. Nothing." I leaned forward and dropped my voice. "Because I don't have a gun. Because I got nothing against Raines, even though he tried to fillet me."

"All right. So you didn't do it." He pointed out at the night. "Why are we here talking about it?"

"I think you can figure that out, Rod. If it isn't me, who is it? The likeliest, to me, would be one of your Sons of Shiloh." He jerked all the way around to look at me. "Yeah, that's who would be on the top of my list. A bunch of wild-ass characters who think they're bad boys. Raines hung out with them. Hell, they were cheering him on to slice me up. My guess would be one of them."

"What's that got to do with the Institute?"

"Everybody knows the Sons of Shiloh do security work for you sometimes. You don't want Metro asking too many questions. Won't look good for your boss. Won't be good for Grace either."

"Why bring Grace into this?"

"I know you've got a thing for her, Rod. Easy to see."

"You son of a bitch." He turned back to look out the front windshield. "Why are you telling me all this?"

"Maybe I've got a little thing for her too. Maybe I don't want her tied up in all this. So if you can fix it, Rod, you should fix it."

We drove back to his shop in silence, returning about twenty-three minutes after we'd left. Billy and the round guy were standing outside the door, probably trying to decide if they should give us a few more minutes. Rod and I got out.

"There's something going on here, Rod, and Metro is starting to spin its wheels over it. They know it's not me now. I'm betting it won't be long before they know my brother's not in it either. Maybe you know something, and maybe you don't, but whatever is going on is happening on your side of the net. I just hit it back to you. Ball's in your court now, cowboy."

I turned on my heel and walked away toward the Impala. It wasn't souped up. It wasn't a Lincoln. But it was paid for.

Whatever else was paid for was not my business. For now.

Chapter Thirty-Six

I EASED THE IMPALA between two hot little red cars, one a Benz SLK and the other an MGB, in the Divinity School lot next to the library. Vanderbilt undergrads sometimes have very good taste in cars. Come springtime, the tops would be off both those beauties all the time. Maybe the Impala would pick up some charm sitting between them.

You could feel the chill coming in the air because the day's warmth had radiated upward, toward the moon, leaving behind only the sparest of moisture. The air had gone dry and lost its heat, and what was left would only need a ten degree drop and a bit of breeze to become cold.

It was nearly 10 pm, quitting time for the library on a Thursday, and because Thursday was the unofficial start to the weekend, the library would only have graduate students and hard-core pre-meds in it. Except for one hard-core history buff. I hoped.

I smoked outside the west entrance, waiting. As the lights began switching off upstairs, the door opened and several people exited, Grace among them. I waited to see if she was with them, but she wasn't.

She was lost in thought and, as I came nearer to her, I realized that I could have walked right past her and she wouldn't have seen me. "Hey, lady." I was standing right in front of her.

She took another step before she realized the words were meant for her. It took her another couple of beats before she realized that the words came from me. "Oh," she said. She still wore the outfit from before, the jeans and sneakers, but she'd exchanged the sweater for a sweatshirt that proclaimed Harvard the Vanderbilt of the North. "Hi, Jackson."

"Hi, Grace. We need to talk."

She just nodded. If she knew what we needed to talk about, she didn't say. If she'd asked, I was going to be vague. It worked out.

We went back to her dorm room silently. I offered to carry her book bag, but she just shook her head no.

Inside her room, she put the book bag and her purse on the bed. She pulled a hot pot off the desk, checked to see if it had water and plugged it in. "Tea?"

"No, thanks." I sat in the lounge chair, waiting for her.

She went about the ministrations of tea-making, then sat at her desk. She blew on the tea and took a sip. I imagined I could smell Earl Grey with its citrusy, oily tincture. She looked off into a distance I couldn't see.

"You doing ok?" I tried to sound like I meant it, and in a way I did. I knew what it felt like to lose a friend over something you had no control over. I knew that you felt at fault anyway, as if there were something you could have done.

"Sure." She took another sip, then put the cup down. "Patrick is dead. Raines is dead. Howell has moved back home to Johnson City for a while." She still didn't look at me. "He's scared to death, you know."

"The Merry Pranksters," I said. "But that's not the entire group, is it, Grace?"

"I don't know what you mean." She still looked away, but this time she looked away with a purpose.

"Patrick and Howell were there that night. But Raines had some kind of stomach issue. He was in the McGill bathroom most of the night. He was in no shape to climb anything."

She pulled her hand through her hair, and then repeated the procedure on the other side. Reaching for the cup of tea, she finally looked at me. "How long have you known that?"

I knew what she meant. Did you know that when we were in bed together? Did you take advantage of me, when I thought I was taking advantage of you? It was a good question. But she didn't ask it, so I answered the one she asked. "A while."

We humans do funny things when we're under pressure. Some of us freak out. Some of us get nervous and don't think clearly. Grace Pettibone was not of those types. Under pressure, she would think clearly and act decisively. I had no reason to believe that she'd do anything other than what she did.

She gave up the fourth Prankster. "It was Rod."

"That's what I thought." I sat, waiting for whatever would follow.

She drank some tea and perched on the side of the bed. "We had gone for dinner. Raines and I. Belle Chateau, the little French restaurant that just opened on Division?"

I knew it. Nice place. Not one I could afford.

"He had mussels. I warned him. He had bad reactions to seafood. But he wasn't worried." She put the mug down on the night table. "He should have been."

"And Rod was just standing ready?"

"Rod had been in on the prank all along. I told him and he couldn't get involved fast enough."

"Seems odd. Older guy. Not exactly a fun-seeker. Am I wrong?"

"I think it was about getting close to me. Impressing me, you know?"

"Did it?"

She finally looked at me with those unnaturally colored eyes. "Look. Rod works for Daddy. As far as I'm concerned, he's an oaf. But he's a useful oaf."

She reached again for her mug and brought it to her lips. As she sipped, I thought about how easily a man can be tempted to believe that, given the right circumstances, a woman with lips like those could want to kiss him. It would be complete folly. I knew that. "We're all useful oafs in our way."

"Rod is only useful in the coarsest of ways. He's useful if you want to send a message, or have him do something you don't want to do yourself." She seemed to have a moment of recognition. "Oh, God. You're thinking of?"

I nodded. "I'm sure I was useful. In some way."

"No, that's not true. I'm attracted to you, Jackson. I told you that."

A long moment passed as she thought, perhaps, if she needed to say more. I let her off the hook. "I don't want to stir things, so soon after Raines' death."

She ground her teeth a little, her face tightening. "What?"

"You'd agree Raines and you aren't very much alike. Physically or otherwise?"

"True."

"So what was your relationship? I don't mean your physical relationship. That's none of my business. But I don't understand the boyfriend-girlfriend thing."

"Nobody did." She gave me the briefest of smiles. "I've heard the comments. There's this whole 'what's she doing with him' universe at Vandy, and we were one of those little twin planets that no one understood."

"But you did. Both of you did."

"We grew up together. We're both from Oxford. His father was a professor at Ole Miss, and Daddy is—-well, you know what Daddy is. Anyway, same age, same street, same schools. He took me to my first dance, my first real dance. When I had my debut at the White and Gold Ball, he was my escort. Raines has always been there. Even as Daddy's star dropped in the sky a little."

"So there was a natural romance."

"No. Well, not exactly."

"I think there either was or there wasn't, Grace."

She held the mug with both hands, the mug on her knees. "He was the first boy I ever kissed. Same for him. But that never translated much beyond some parking and petting in high school." She fiddled with the mug, running her finger along its rim. "He was my friend, Jackson. And that made him my oldest boy friend. My oldest male friend. My oldest friend."

"And he was ok with that?" I recalled his fury with me at the bar. "Old friend" might not cover that.

"Not always." She got up and walked the mug back to the desk, where the hot pot was. She unplugged the pot. If she was deciding what to say, she was taking her time.

"Not always?" I primed the pump.

"We would always agree, when the subject would come up. When he brought up the subject. That it was best if we were friends, not lovers." She said this haltingly, each sentence harder that the last to get out. She continued to have her back to me. Her head was bowed a little, as if she were looking for something on her desk.

"But that's not what he wanted."

"No. That was not what he wanted. But deep down, he knew—we both knew—that we were too important to each other as friends to ever let the other thing happen."

"If you don't mind my saying so, it sounds like that's your view, not his. Your desire, not his."

She turned back toward me. The sunlight in the window outlined her face's shape, and obscured her features, the darkness letting me see just enough to see sadness, but nothing more. "That's true, Jackson. And it's my right to say that."

"You think it would ever have worked out differently?"

"No." There was no doubt in her mind, and none in her voice. And apparently, since she didn't elaborate, there was nothing further to say.

"And Rod knew all this?"

"The difference between Rod and Raines is that Rod is not a friend."

Chapter Thirty-Seven

I HAD STIRRED ROD'S pot at the body shop, and I'd tied off one loose end at Grace's. It was time to put the final act of this little play into motion. And that would demand that some panic be induced.

I hung out at Hannigan's, toying with a basket of French fries and staying about even on the pinball machine. I had waved off Katie's offer of a bourbon, and had nursed a draft until it was warm enough to bring tears to my eyes.

About the time it was dark, I began to make my way down West End. I didn't know how long I had to wait, but my guess was that Hal and his buddies hit Linda's after work on the weekdays. Given that I'd never seen them in there late, except on the weekends, that seemed a logical deduction.

I waited in the alley where most everyone, except for Don Mercer, parked their bikes. West End traffic could get just weird enough that you didn't want an expensive piece of equipment out there. I was back behind the dumpster where I could see anyone who came in.

I was right enough that some of the Sons of Shiloh were going to get their pickled egg or Vienna sausage and a beer or two before heading off to whatever pitiful place they called home. The fourth motorcycle to back itself in was ridden by a fire-plug kind of guy with long hair. No doubt, it was Hal Hanna.

He got off the bike, shed his helmet and put it on the handlebar. His back to me, he didn't see me, didn't hear me. I was within arm's length before I spoke.

"Hey, pardner. Got a match?"

He turned, probably expecting a wino, or a pan-handler. What he got was a surprise.

I learned in the Army that hand-to-hand combat was not Marquis of Queensbury rules. You wanted to disable, disarm, and incapacitate the enemy. If you wanted to dance around like Muhammad Ali, you were going to get your ass handed to you. Fight dirty, and be done with it.

So I drove the base of my left hand upwards through his nose and, as he tumbled backward, put my right fist square on his throat. He made a bleating sound as he crashed onto the alleyway, clutching his throat. I lifted my foot and used all the leverage I had with a downward stomp onto his right knee.

He cried out in pain.

I fell hard with my knee in his groin, and grabbed his collar, using it to choke him and digging my index fingers' knuckles into his Adam's apple.

He tried to rasp words. It wasn't working. I had his arms pinned, and he was having trouble getting his breath.

It had taken a shorter period of time that it would have taken us to dance around each other like we were going to box. It took about five seconds.

Then, in a flash, he recognized me. His eyes got wide, and there was a fleeting moment where he almost was able to gather a surge of strength and push me back. But I leaned in hard on his throat. He wasn't going anywhere.

"Listen to me, you piece of shit. You tried to kill me. If I hadn't been awake, I'd have died in a wall of flames." I pushed a little harder on his throat. "You meant to kill me and just ride away."

The look on his face told me he was pretty sure what I was about to do in retribution. And don't think I wasn't thinking it might be a good idea.

Instead I said, "I'm not going to kill you, Hal. It'd be easy, but I believe the police are pretty good sometimes. They'd eventually figure out that you threw your little fire grenade into my place, and that I must have paid you back."

I let up a little on his throat. No need to strangle him, and no need, at least right now, to bust his windpipe either.

"So that's not what I'm going to do. You didn't kill me. I'm not going to kill you. But I am going to mess you up some. And then I want you to take a message to your brother. Understand?"

He nodded tightly, his eyes still wide.

"You tell him that I know what's in the tower. You tell him that if anything happens to me, I've left an envelope with a lawyer that lays it all out." He was listening, but not with his ears. He was listening with his pain, and it was telling him a lot. "Tell him that I'm going to blow up Pettibone's little scheme, and that he'd better know his place. This is about over, and when it is you are all going to jail. Because I know who killed the boys."

I was on my feet before he could move, and I brought my boot hard on his other knee, then I stomped on his groin. Just for good measure, I took a swinging kick at his ribcage.

He rolled in agony. He bled from his nose, just a little. But both knees were going to be in bad shape, and he'd have a couple of broken ribs. And talking wouldn't be much fun for a while. If that didn't make his brother and Pettibone show their cards, I didn't know what would.

Chapter Thirty-Eight

I DIDN'T FIGURE IT would take long for somebody to find him, and I sure didn't want to be there when they did, so I walked calmly, given the moaning in the alley, down West End toward the Impala. I got in, started it up, and pulled out into traffic.

It would do me no good at this point to go back to the apartment. They'd already tried to hit me there once, and I had the definite feeling the hunt would be on for me unless I dialed the panic meter higher. That meant I needed to get out of town. Without getting out of town.

I knew just where to go.

About twelve miles out of town, down West End Boulevard and hanging a left at Highway 100, there stood a landmark, the Loveless Café and its lesser known, but for now equally important partner, the Loveless Motel. After twenty minutes of easy driving, I pulled into the gravel parking lot. It was still early, about 5:30, and I put the Impala in Park and pulled the emergency brake.

When I got inside the motel lobby, I could see a mousy brunette with a choker necklace behind the desk. It was a study in contrast: a country girl who looked like she could be anywhere between sixteen and thirty, wearing a tired plaid cowboy shirt with snaps, and a psychedelic print choker with a peace sign woven into it in front. She had a toothpick hanging between bright pink lips.She looked up and barely registered interest. "Restaurant's the other building."

"I'm here to get a room for tonight."

She looked up and scrunched her nose, which made her eyes take on a peculiar shape, at once quizzical and pained. "You want a room?"

"At the motel. Here. Yes." I didn't know how complex my sentences needed to be. It was a pretty easy concept. "You do have rooms for tonight, don't you?"

"Sure." She looked like there were other questions on her mind. Like, why wouldn't you go on into Nashville and get a room?

"How much a night?"

"Twenty for a single, twenty five for a double." She tugged a little at her choker. Maybe it was too tight. Or maybe her fashion crime was making her a little nervous. Probably hadn't expected anyone to see this particular experiment.

"Single's fine." I put a twenty on the counter and counted out the tax in change. She gave me the key to room 7, I pocketed it, and thanked her. If tonight didn't work out well, or if I needed to hide, well, now I had the place.

Then I went across to the real reason anyone drove twelve miles out, or didn't drive the next twelve miles in. Loveless Café.

There were a lot of places to eat in Nashville, and many of them were run by folks who remember what their mama or their grandmaw did with a chicken, or with a pork chop, or even with turnip greens and cornbread. They are the folks who came to the big city determined to give people good value cooking the things they grew up with, just the way they liked them.

I think I read one time that the Loveless family had started the motel and restaurant sometime in the 1920s or 1930s, and there had been several owners subsequent to that. But what always came out of the kitchen were the best biscuits, and the best fried chicken, that most people had ever had. Whichever mama or grandmaw in the Loveless lineage must really have been something.

I sat alone at a small four-seater and ordered up fried chicken, creamed corn, and fried okra, and asked for a little chicken gravy on the side for the big pile of biscuits that came with my glass of water. Meanwhile, I watched as big groups began to arrive, get seated, and order family style an array of chicken, fried catfish, and chicken fried steak. The noise got louder as people waited, talking, and then the whole din collapsed into a general clanking of forks and knives on dinnerware, as everyone chowed down.

I chowed down too, but there was no quiet inside my head. Too many things had happened in the last couple of days. I had a bead on the truth, but I couldn't see it yet.

The only thing I was sure of was that it couldn't be the Confederate gold. There was not space for it and, even if there had been, Adkins would not have been able to get it out during the fire, and get it back during the subsequent rebuild.

But Pettibone needed for there to be gold, and Grace had uncovered the clues. The provenance. The papers of a few soldiers. The one who died with the secret.

Captain Williams. Killed by Corporal Adkins. The dying voice. Killed for a slave.

I would need more information tonight.

I had a slice of apple pie that was very good and a cup of coffee way better than Folgers Instant. Then I went to room seven and dialed a number.

"Pettibone." He said it in his cultured way, not the way most people would say it, but extending the three syllables somehow into five. It was like falling into a pool of vowels.

"Hey, Mr. Pettibone. Jackson Trade here."

There was just the slightest hesitation. "Mr. Trade. I understand you've been busy the past few hours."

"I figured your boy Rod would let you know as soon as his brother crawled out of the alley."

"Ah. I see now. Rod thought perhaps you, ahem, did what you did because of some other matter."

"That means that Hal Hanna wasn't up to talking, because I told him precisely why he was getting the beating he got."

"Well, whatever the reason, you should know that Rod is quite angry. I should think he is looking for you this very minute."

"Yeah, well good luck with that. I'm where he's not looking. But tell me, Pettibone, do you have any idea why I'm calling you?"

"I can't imagine, Mr. Trade. You seem to have formed an animus toward Rod, or his brother. I know, of course, that both of them have tempers, and they can be impulsive, but I do not believe that Rod has ever done something to cause you to be so violent."

"Let's leave that aside for a minute, Pettibone. Let's talk about Grace."

"My daughter?" Mr. Impeccable almost snorted, but covered it expertly. "What on earth?"

"What on earth, indeed. Your daughter is an impressive scholar. No less a scholar than the head of archives in the library says so."

"Grace is quite intelligent. I'm aware of that, of course."

"Probably gets it from you, right? At least, she gets one interest from you."

"If you mean the South, then certainly."

"Actually, I am being more specific. Grace has a real bulls-eye on the Civil War, especially the end. Oh, she's up on it all, especially the campaigns in Tennessee, but she really has a laser focus on what happened around the fall of Richmond." I stopped to light a cigarette, then snapped the Zippo shut. "Do you know about that period, Pettibone?"

He was silent. I guessed that he knew where I was trying to lead him, and he was deciding whether to play along. "I have more than a passing knowledge of the period of the war, Mr.

Trade. But you surprise me. I would not have thought you and Grace would have met in the library, or anywhere else for that matter, and discussed the fall of Richmond."

"Trust me, Pettibone, we've had more than a few deep discussions, and not just about the end of that war."

He silence was the silence of a father who didn't know if he'd been betrayed in some way. So I let him off the hook.

"And I've seen her work. It's impressive. More than that, I've seen the original sources she uses for her research."

"I understand the reference to the archives now."

"Then you may know what I have discovered."

"I do not. And it seems we've come some distance from the mayhem you visited on Mr. Hanna's brother."

"We are closer than you think. But for now, let's stay with Grace and her research. You know the myth of the Confederate Gold?"

"Of course." His voice was less syrupy now, more clipped. "There was no gold. That's what everyone has always thought."

"And do you think they are right?"

"Certainly. It's a myth."

"Then you don't know your daughter is researching a different path, one that says there is in fact gold to be recovered?"

"I have heard her say that she has an alternate theory. But, Mr. Trade, my daughter has an alternate theory on many things."

"Well, this one has some legs." I could hear him breathing, ever so slightly on the other end. "She believes that she has uncovered a plot to hide the gold and use it at an opportune time. At first, it was to hide Lee in the mountains and prolong the war until a better settlement could be had. When that proved impossible, the gold went somewhere else."

"This is all impossibly unrelated."

"On the contrary, it is entirely related. One of the soldiers whose correspondence she has studied is a Corporal Adkins, of the Army of Tennessee."

"A beleaguered bunch."

"No doubt about that, Pettibone. But this one came back home. To Nashville."

"How is that of interest?"

"Because he became steward of College Hall. Now Kirkland Hall. Now the tower with Mickey Mouse's face and hands and body on it."

I wished I could see his face. While I might not have known what the secret was, I was sure that Adkins had been the keeper of it. And I suspected that Grace's research, expressed to her father as the certainty of gold, held another treasure, one that Pettibone had been willing to murder Patrick Vincent, and later Raines Durst, to get his hands on.

I had set the hook. Now he just had to bite.

"You seem to know more than I thought, Mr. Trade."

"And, to return now to Rod and Hal, what you thought I knew before was enough to make you try to kill me."

"I see." He wasn't giving more than that.

"This is the way I have it figured, Pettibone. Hal slipped back in to the tower after everybody left. Rod made sure it was still open. Hal was going for your little treasure, whatever it is. But Patrick came back for his tools, and Hal panicked. Fortunately, there was a druggie to frame for it."

"Go on."

"Raines Durst is smart too. He saw me hanging around with Grace, or somebody told him, and he was encouraged by Hal to have a go at me. Problem was, he had started asking questions, and not just about Patrick. About the tower. So he had a go at me, then somebody, maybe Rod, maybe Hal, killed him. Set up to make it look like me. That didn't take. So you firebombed my place."

"You are making this all about you, Mr. Trade. Why would the brothers take so much interest in you?"

"Pretty easy, actually. I wasn't satisfied with the first murder. Why would I be? My brother is being framed for it." I put the cigarette out. It had burned itself to the filter in the ashtray. "But you're amateurs, even your muscle. What would you call it, Pettibone? Dilettantes. Just a couple of meatheads and an overcooked Southern apologist. Probably you're a bigot. For sure, you're prejudiced against anybody who doesn't see things your way. But mostly you're a bully. And what I know is that bullies don't like to be bullied back. They usually run."

"Are you finished?"

"Not yet. I don't know if you and the Hanna brothers are going to run. Hal can't run too fast right now. But if you do, you better run now. Because I'm going to pick up the phone and call the press after I hang up. I'll tell them what I know. Then I'll call the police."

"I wouldn't, if I were you, Mr. Trade."

"See? There's that bully trait again. You don't have a thing on me. You can't do a thing to me. Hell, Pettibone, you can't even find me."

But I was willing to bet I'd find him pretty soon. As soon, in fact, as I got back to campus.

Chapter Thirty-Nine

I DID NIGHT PATROLS in the war. Not a lot of them, but enough to know the value of silence, the necessity of stillness. Sometimes, in the bush, you could hear things that made no noise, before they made no noise. In that still moment, you had the briefest advantage. You couldn't fail to take it.

I was wedged in the tiny space between the staircase and the wall. The staircase, that is, that was the public staircase in Kirkland Hall, the staircase everyone went up and down all day. There was a small space just big enough for me to hide in, while the door to the tower staircase, the one whose lock the boys had managed to defeat, was six feet to the left of the public staircase.

If my supposition was right, Pettibone knew he couldn't stop my going to the press or to the police. He didn't know where I was. So the proper thing to do, if again my supposition was right, would be to get to the Kirkland tower, break in, and go get whatever was so important that two students were dead, not to mention that I could have been dead. What it was? Who knows? That was what I hoped would be revealed.

And with Hal gone, Pettibone figured to involve Rod as well.

I'd been waiting for fifteen minutes, long enough to have to find a more comfortable position twice without being visible, when the back door to Kirkland opened. It was a glass door whose lock I'd picked on the way in. I didn't trust Rod or

Pettibone to have the requisite skills to do it, and I didn't want a broken glass door alerting Campus Police to a break-in. That too would kill the party.

And I'd been right, at least as far as I had thought that Rod would be involved. He was in the building. And he was carrying a crow bar.

It didn't appear he would be gentle with any door in his way.

When I was growing up on the farm, my father had a saying when it didn't much matter how you got the job done. He'd say, just be rough and ready. Which in his terms simply meant that you had to ready to be rough. It wasn't something that came out of his mouth too often. He was usually a precise and careful man. But when he went rough and ready, the task in front of him was demolished in short order.

Rod was rough and ready by default, and upon finding the tower stairwell locked, he looked around, needlessly, and began to attack the door. It was no gentle matter. There was no looking for a strategic place to pry. Instead, he began to drive the crow bar violently, something like a left-handed hitter in baseball sighting the ball and lashing it, over and over, sending one line drive after another.

But these were no line drives he was hitting. This was a man who had a door resisting him. And he was going to make it pay. Sweat came on him as if summoned. He stopped briefly once to push up his shirt sleeves. Then he resumed his destruction, making loud animal noises, something more like you'd hear in a really bad section of the woods, something you'd hear and believe that you wanted no part of that animal. It was manic, angry, almost possessed. If Pettibone had been holding him back from what he really wanted to do, and if this was an indication, it was probably best that Pettibone kept him on a short leash.

The door finally relinquished enough of its structure that Rod could get the crowbar in place, and pry the door loose. At that point he could probably had just opened it. But he wanted to be vicious, and he wanted to pound the door open in submission.

I stood up from my cramped space, and let my legs' feeling come back. Standing in the dark, I couldn't be seen, and Rod was wrenching the last of the door off its hinges. He was out of breath, and he had scraped his knuckles so that blood was seeping out. In the half light of the basement, he looked like a character from some hellish movie.

I stepped from the darkness and he caught my movement in the corner of his eye. He spun, holding the crowbar against an attack. Squinting, he took a moment to recognize me. But when he did, the moment was unmistakable. "You." A little spittle came from the corner of his mouth. "What you did to my brother, Trade. You're going to pay for that. You are a dead man."

I have known lots of guys like Rod. He's a brawler, a grappler. He's the short and thick sort who will swing wildly and, if they connect, you'll be out for several days. And you don't want them inside your space. They're strong enough that they'll wrestle you to the ground, and that'll be it for you.

And I was right. He rushed me, and I avoided him, pushing him off course as he went by. "Oh, it's going to be that way?" He was so angry he was wheezing a bit. "You want to stand still and fight. You don't want to run like a pussy."

I assumed a boxing stance, but not because I wanted to box. Most tough guys think they can box, so they'll take you up on it. Anybody with sense would see that I've got about six inches of reach on Rod, and he wouldn't get close enough to do any damage. But that's not the reason I wanted to set him up to box. If he thinks I'm going to box, he won't be prepared for what I'm going to do.

And what I'm going to do is pretty damn dirty.

He dropped the crowbar. "All right, you son of a bitch. Let's go."

He stepped toward me and threw a wild overhand right. I slid away, and he turned and ran toward me, trying to catch me with one arm while swinging with the other fist. I faked one way and went the other.

"Come on. Fight." The blood on his knuckles was coming in a stream now and he wiped his face with the back of his hand. It left his face smeared with his own blood. "I'm going to tear you apart, you stinking asshole. You're going to be sorry you ambushed my brother."

Then he forgot all pretense of fighting. He came hard as if he was going to tackle me.

I played halfback in high school. If he had played any defense, he'd have known you don't put your head down when you move to tackle. You keep your head up and drive with your body. But because he didn't I slid neatly to the side and drove my left foot into the side of his knee. I could see the knee fold at an untenable angle, and his roar told me I'd hit it in just the right place.

He rolled on the ground for a moment, in a particular kind of agony that was agony, to be sure, but which was also anger. He seethed on the ground, making a noise like a broken steam engine.

But this broken engine was too close to the crowbar. I saw that too late, and he saw it too soon. He scrambled to grab it, and used it as a sort of crutch to stand up. He stood, his knee broken in some way, and he smiled. "Let's see you fight this, son of a bitch."

He moved with more swiftness than he should have, and now had a reach advantage over me, with one arm the length of a crowbar. I was still more mobile, but he clipped me on the shoulder, and I winced.

"Do better, sucker." He roared his command as if he expected me to grow crowbars for arms, and duel him like a cavalier. "Let's see what you've got now."

He rushed again, and I took a shot at the other knee. I missed, and he got close enough to land a hard blow on my side.

I've had ribs broken before. You have a little trouble getting a deep breath. Yeah. That was the feeling.

"Not so much fun now, is it?" He was fatigued. The violence on the door, together with lunging after me with a bad knee, had taken some of the starch out of him. He was standing with his knee bent, his free hand on his thigh. He was trying to get his breath for one last try.

I had no intention of letting that happen. This time I rushed, surprising him. I got low and drove my head into his, at about nose level. I heard a crack that wasn't my head.

But whatever the crack was, it didn't take Rod Hanna down, He was stunned, but he was upright. "You shouldn't have done that."

He moved toward me with as much speed as he could muster. When he reached out to grab me, I took his right wrist and pulled him off balance, onto his bad knee. As he came down, I dropped to one knee, twisted the wrist, and broke his arm, right at the elbow, over my knee.

The crack was sickening, and he heard it before he felt it, and he felt it before he realized what it was. He cried out, but it was a cry of rage, the realization that he was no longer in control.

And for a man like Rod Hanna, that feeling of being physically broken, not in control of your body, not able to wreak the kind of havoc you wish—that is the beginning of the end.

The crowbar was at my feet, and I picked it up. "How you feeling now, cowboy? You about done?" I patted the crowbar into the palm of my hand. "I'd take a knee, if I were you." I laughed at my joke. "Get it? Take a knee?"

I turned away to walk to the destroyed door. Soon enough Pettibone would be here. I had to make a plan, since the original didn't really anticipate Rod and, well, all this.

But before I could begin my work, I heard a desperate scrambling behind me and, like some bizarre force of nature, Rod was upright and moving toward me with manic rage. He was screaming, the blood and sweat on his face glistening in the half-light. I put up the crowbar in defense, straight out at chest level, too late for him to change direction.

He hit it at full speed, and collapsed, holding his chest. His eyes looked empty. And he didn't move.

Chapter Forty

I ENTERED THE TOWER staircase. It stood as a sort of small lobby, an antechamber before what I knew from the architectural drawings were 108 steps, which led to the main roof. These were the first set to climb. The chamber had a musty, woody smell, the smell of old wood, trees first sprouted well before white men came. I reached into my front pocket and pulled a small flashlight, about six inches long, with the logo of Quaker States Oil. Where I'd got it originally, I didn't know, but the small battery and tiny bulb combined to make enough light to see. Barely.

I shined the dim beam toward the first flight. There I could make out a standing figure.

"Well, Mr. Trade. I would not have bet on you, but here you are. So that must mean that Mr. Hanna is incapacitated." Pettibone was frozen on the stair. "Have you called the police, and the press, as you promised you would?"

"Not yet."

"No, of course not. You are more interested in what you think is hidden in the tower." His smile was visible, even in the dim light. Good teeth. Very bright.

"What is hidden here cost two young men their lives."

"I can hardly be blamed for that. Mr. Hanna, I'm afraid, took matters into his own hands. Truly unfortunate."

"But you are both here."

"When I entered, I thought Rod had much more fight in him. I had hoped enough that I could go up the stairway and collect the prize, then be gone." He seemed to hold two boxes in his hands. I could just make them out. "But alas, you made shorter work of him than I would have supposed."

"What's in the boxes, Pettibone?"

"You've proved very prescient, Mr. Trade. Why don't you tell me?"

"I know that Hal Hanna was in the tower that night. I know he was here when Patrick Vincent came back."

"Indeed. How would you know that?"

"Your daughter told me, in a way. She got Raines Durst to eat some bad seafood. He was out. Rod was in." I kept the small beam on him. "Vincent came back and surprised Hal. Hal panicked."

"I am quite sure my daughter did not tell you all of that. But let's say that you are correct. What then?"

"My brother was a convenient frame."

"Yes, that seems to have been a moment where another choice might have been made. After all, we acquired you in that bargain. And you have been difficult from the beginning."

I heard a sound to my right, a dragging sound, and when I looked I saw Hanna. He clutched his chest. His eyes were wild, and he weaved toward me with purpose, but not with a meaningful purpose. He was moaning. As he came near, I grabbed his broken arm and spun him into the stairway pylon. He collapsed on it, moaned once again, and fell over.

The stairway was silent. I shined the light again and found Pettibone had moved a flight further up.

"You're going the wrong way, buddy. No way out up there."

"You may not know all that I know about what is above." He sounded confident. But he always did. "Now, back to your detection. What was the key, Mr. Trade? My daughter told you Rod was part of the climbing party. You leaped to a conclusion about Mr. Hanna. Well played."

"I also know your daughter's research. I have seen it. In fact, I have read the opening parts of it."

"So it was you. Yes, she confided to me that some of her work had gone missing. Naturally, with poor Raines death, I assumed she had misplaced it. They were quite close, you know."

"I know. She told me."

"You seem to have spent a good bit of time with my daughter. Mr. Hanna was concerned, but of course he carried a bit of a torch for her."

I moved a little closer to the stairwell.

"Stay there, Mr. Trade. I do not want to harm you if I do not have to."

"Why not? Hanna did his best."

"Mr. Hanna and I are not the same. I would prefer to convince you of my cause. After all, I did not kill those young men. Mr. Hanna did. And you have him precisely where you want him." He paused. "And besides, the bomb they attempted to kill you with—yes, I learned of that too late as well—was the project of Mr. Hanna and his brother. And again, you have taken care of that."

"What's in the box, Pettibone?"

"First, tell me what you think it is."

"Grace has been convinced, I suspect, that the gold is here. Somewhere. But she has misread Corporal Adkins letters."

"Then you know about Adkins. Very good."

"And Adkins was here during the fire that took down the original towers. He was Kirkland Hall's steward. But he could not have carried out a million dollars in Confederate gold. There were too many people, and too much confusion. He would have been spotted by someone."

"Never mind when he returned—whatever it was—to the new tower." Pettibone was enjoying himself. "But I interrupted. Please continue."

"But there was gold. Grace is certain of that. If it's not in the tower, what is here that relates to the gold? That's the question, as I see it."

"And what is the answer, Mr. Trade. Or as you say, what's in the box?"

"If there is gold, then what's in the box is a kind of treasure map. A set of instructions that were put in different places. Adkins had a piece of it. Maybe Lee had the final piece. More likely Williams. I don't know. But what you have is the collection of clues that sort out where the gold was put. Or at least the set of clues, absent the key. Which was held by Artemis Williams. Who Adkins killed."

"Bravo, Mr. Trade. An admirable, and only slightly inaccurate, set of suppositions."

"If when you follow a trail it leads to a conclusion that cannot be true, you have to ask, what is the most likely true thing. In this case, the most likely is that you have the treasure map, as it were." I could just see him. He was silently making his way higher. "How did you reach your conclusion, Pettibone?"

"Grace told me her conclusion. She had made it, certain that the gold could have been hidden in the tower. It's why Rod was so eager to be part of the climbing party."

"But he would be too busy that night to really look. That's why Hal came later."

"Correct. And all would have been well if the Vincent boy had not returned." Pettibone continued upward.

"I really think you should stop, Pettibone. You can't get out by going up. You can't get out going by me." I watched him continue to climb, step by step. He clutched the small boxes, roughly the size of shoe boxes but square. "Come down like a good boy and we'll talk."

He stopped to catch his breath. "There are two boxes here, Mr. Trade. You are approximately correct about the one. What do you think is in the second?"

I made my way to the stairwell, and the effort made me gasp. It was like a sharp stick was poked hard into my side. I bent at the waist until the pain subsided. "You can't get away, Pettibone."

Unless he had a helicopter ready to come sweep him off the roof. But Hanna would have been the helicopter pilot and he wasn't flying anything.

"Come now. Play the game with me. What is in the second box?" He was getting closer and closer to the main roof. "Surely you want to guess?"

Maybe an insult would get him going. "If it's important to you, it's some damn fool thing that says the South is superior."

"Oh, the South is superior, sir. And the rest of the country is ravaged by the disease of greed, the desire for more, always more. The natural culture of the South is refined and graceful."

"Not where I come from."

"That's only because it's become fouled by what we mistakenly call an American way of life." He continued to climb, one heavy step at a time. "The South could have saved the United States, had she won her conflict. Or at least, she could have remained herself."

"Maybe you're just a bad loser, Pettibone. Maybe you can't accept the loss. Maybe your Institute is so poor because it's hanging onto a bad idea."

"One hardly needs to accept the unacceptable." He was nearing the door to the stairs that went from the roof to the bell itself. "There is the answer to all who doubt the South can rise again." He passed from my sight briefly, then came back in view, this time as he crossed the walkway where the main roof was.

I took steps two at a time, pausing twice to bend over and catch my breath. The pain in my side was like an ice pick. I imagined I could feel the rib splintering with each deep breath. I tried to keep my breathing shallow, or at least normal. But there was no way to do that and climb the stairs quickly.

I was halfway up when a box of flames shot past me and landed two landings below. Pettibone had lit one of the boxes on fire and dropped it behind me.

The tower was acting like a chimney with the flue wide open. The door below was removed and now Pettibone had opened the door that stood as the only impediment to the free flow of air from the base through the top of the tower. I could feel a well-defined flow of air.

And with it was a billow of smoke as whatever was in the box produced smoke that began to fill the tower chamber. I fought to get higher, the smoke making me choke.

"There you are, Mr. Trade. I wish you the best. That can't be very pleasant down there."

I tried to go faster. My legs felt leaden. My rib felt like it would puncture my lung. My shoulder suddenly felt all the pain it had not felt when Hanna had glanced the crowbar off it.

"Damn it, Pettibone, you've got nowhere to go. You're trapped."

Whatever was in the box was not burning as much as it was smoking. I pulled myself erect and climbed the stairs, my forearm covering my nose.

I called after him but he had moved on to the next chamber, the part of the tower that led from the roof to the bell. It was almost as long a climb as the last section. The door that had barred entry to that section had been taken off its hinges, so there was no shutting the smoke on the lower level. Smoke continued to billow, and was beginning to leak out the small cutaways in the brick work. From the outside, it would appear that Kirkland Tower was on fire, with trails of smoke exiting the cutaways.

Good. Maybe someone would call the fire department and an engine company would show up.

I looked up. The second section of stairs were made of concrete, and they moved along the sides of the tower, always in contact, but moving in an M.C. Escher like way. To look up was disorienting.

I couldn't imagine what it would look like when you looked down. I felt my stomach turn a half-turn upside down.

"Where are you, Pettibone?" There was enough smoke to obscure everything in the dark. And the little flashlight was worse than useless now.

I pushed myself to climb. Ninety steps to the roof door, I remembered. I tried to take it second by second. Minute and a half, if I kept my pace.

Minute and a half.

I heard noises down below, back on the main roof. My eyes burned. I couldn't see anything.

I pushed open the trap door, and smoke blew past me.

Climb the ladder. Ignore the pain. Ignore the smoke. Climb. Get to the roof.

I got to the top of the ladder. I pushed open the trap door, and smoke blew past me.

And there was no Pettibone.

I looked back. A shaft of moonlight flooded the uppermost chamber of the tower. I could barely make out the outline of the bell in the smoke. I heard sirens, then saw the reflection of flashing lights.

I ran to the balustrade. To the north was Barnard Hall, west and further away, McGill. To the southeast, I saw the library. Then, as I located the fire engines and police cruisers pulling into the circular drive beneath Kirkland, I saw the small figure of Pettibone, his hands clutching a rope as he lowered himself from the main roof below. From the looks of it, he had put the box inside his sweater so that he could use both hands.

And as he lowered himself, his hands began to slip. There was a short moment of desperation, as he tried to get his legs up around the rope, but his hands were too far down. He lost one hand's grip, then the second.

He made no noise as he fell. You think people will scream, or cry out. He didn't.

The look on his face was curious, almost comic, as if he might laugh as soon as he heard the punchline of the joke.

The sound he made when he hit the front stone steps, and bounced up so that one of his legs straddled the metal railing, was a flat thud followed by the kind of iron twang, the sort you might get if you hit a gate with a baseball bat. He hung motionless. He would not move on his own again.

Chapter Forty-One

THE REST OF THE night was a slog. Metro Fire got the smoldering under control; Pettibone's box of fire had managed to catch part of the old timber of the landing, but there was enough moisture in the wood so it didn't blaze, just smoked. And Metro PD had a few questions about Rod Hanna and the state he was in. It helped that they'd seen Pettibone fall without me being anywhere near him, so when I said they'd find Rod and Pettibone linked, and they were both out to get me, I got looked at, but I didn't get arrested.

So that was a good thing.

I pointed them in the direction of Hal, told them I believed they'd find evidence somewhere, the body shop or the house in Brentwood, that would lead them to Durst's murder weapon. Maybe they could even lift prints from the crowbar that killed Patrick.

So that was good too

What wasn't so good was the quick look I got at the Vandy ER. The prematurely white-haired resident had a couple of pictures taken, then sat me down on the edge of an examining table. "Two broken ribs, contusions. I don't think there's anything wrong with your shoulder that rest won't cure. Anything else?" He was a skinny guy who looked like he'd had one too many twenty-four hour shifts.

"I've got a headache from inhaling too much smoke."

"Then don't do that." He tapped the pack of Lucky Strikes in my shirt pocket. "And don't do this either."

On the way out, I almost tripped over the Metro officers who had brought Hanna in. They were still there. "Broken arm. Broken sternum. Knee is ripped up. He ain't going any-where."

Good. Maybe he'll stay put until they get enough to put him and his brother away.

I had a couple of drinks back at the apartment, then fell asleep on the couch, remembering what the fire looked like in the apartment, and what the smoke smelled like in the tower. But I didn't dream of anything. Not of being firebombed. Not of feeling overcome in the tower. And not of heat, or smoke, or fire of combat. My engine shut down, and didn't rev all night long.

The next morning after breakfast I walked all the way downtown to the jail. The Nashville morning air had a crisp-ness to it, as if it had decided, finally, to turn toward winter. The sky was a pale blue, flecked with clouds that were more afterthought than necessary. It was cool enough that I put my hands in my pockets, and cool enough that the air seemed to cleanse my face. I stopped several times to fill my lungs. It felt good to be here, and alive.

Thompson's court-appointed attorney had already been at the jail, bearing the news that he was filing a petition to re-hear Thompson's bail, given the new circumstances. "He said there's enough confusion in the DA's office that they might just go for it."

"How much confusion does it take?"

"Who knows? Not my world." Two weeks in jail had done him a world of good, but it hadn't brought the brother I knew back to life. This one looked like him, but he was still defeated, even in this small moment of victory. "All he said was that a good defense attorney could take all the stuff you've set in motion, and sway a jury."

"That would assume the kid lawyer is a good defense lawyer."

"I guess." Thompson bit the nail on his thumb, trying to smooth out some unseen imperfection. "He seemed pretty sure I'd be out in a few days." He looked at the thumbnail, in order to avoid looking at me. "What went on out there, Jackson?"

"What did the kid lawyer say?"

"He said one guy was dead. Two guys, two brothers, were pretty bad off."

"That's true enough."

"That you were somehow in the middle of it." He finally looked at me. I'd never seen that look before. His eyes were wide, and his face sank into his neck a little as he shook his head back and forth, once, as if the tables were turned, and now he didn't recognize me. Maybe he didn't want to. "Little brother, I don't know what you did. I'm not sure I want to know."

I'm not sure I want him to know either. "Remember when we were kids, Thompson?"

"What's that got to do with any of this?"

"You said it before. The things I set in motion got you off. Things got set in motion a long time ago, Thompson. Before you left for college. Way back."

My brother, the smart one, the good looking one, stared at the other thumbnail. He didn't say anything.

"Can you remember back when I was six, you must have been eight? The summer Daddy decided he was going to lease Red Bailey's tobacco base."

"He decided to lease it that winter."

"Ok. Be precise. It was a half-acre. It was burley tobacco. We had a plant bed where we raised the tobacco slips. We borrowed Bailey's tobacco setter and put it behind Daddy's Farmall H."

"I remember. We had pails full of tobacco sets and wooden pegs. We replanted every single one that didn't take."

"And we were out there every week. Hoed the tobacco. Topped it. Suckered it. Wormed it. We were two little boys, Thompson, working a piece of land with our father."

"You loved it, Jackson. I remember that."

"And you didn't."

"No. My knees hurt from squatting for hours when we re-set the plants. My back hurt from hoeing. And God, the tobacco gum. It got on your hands and you couldn't get it off. If you touched your face, you had it there." He almost looked like my brother again. For just a second. "I hated it."

"What was it you hated?" It was a fair question. My brother could endure long hours of anything he liked, no matter the discomfort. "I've seen you sit in a chair for hours, cross-legged like some Buddha, reading. Don't tell me that didn't test your back and your legs at the same time."

"If you're getting ready to say I didn't like to work, don't."

"Not at all. I've seen you work. I've seen you buckle down and do things you didn't like." I reached across the table and touched his arm. "What you didn't like was doing this kind of work. Manual farm labor. On somebody else's land."

"It made us look like sharecroppers. And we weren't. We had our own land."

"You know better than that. It wasn't about land. It was about the tobacco base, how much tobacco you were allowed to raise. We didn't have one. Bailey was across the line in Kentucky. He let us have his for the year."

Thompson shut his eyes, either thinking or remembering. "You didn't get called that in school. Just a sharecropper, they said. It was humiliating."

I remembered my dream from a few nights back. Some-where, my subconscious mind was working this out. But it wasn't about being called sharecropper by some third grade boys. Something in this explained my big brother, but I didn't know what. "Why was it important, Thompson?"

Mama always said Thompson looked like Daddy, and for a brief instant I saw it. The shock of hair that wanted to fall, just avoiding his eye. The brown eyes that could be angry, then turn instantly kind, as if in apology. Even the jawline, thinner now on my brother than my father's ever was. If Thompson had a plug of chaw, he would have looked like Daddy. But that was for an instant. For a moment, he was a Trade. He was The Trade, the prototype. Smart. Perceptive. Able.

Not like me. Not like him either. Not now.

"I could tell, Jackson, after that, it was never the same. Maybe you didn't hear it, but I did. Everywhere I went. You're poor. You farm other people's land for them. You're white trash."

"You can't have believed that."

He raised his voice. "You can't have not believed it." He shifted in his chair, sideways, turned away from me. "You went to the same school, the same high school. We were country. Everybody looked down on us."

"Half the people in our class were country, Thompson."

"And they looked down on all of us." He picked at his coverall leg. "Maybe it didn't matter to you. You were going to stay, work the farm."

"Country is as country does?"

"That's not what I mean. You didn't have hopes and dreams. You didn't want to get away. Swanson and I, we wanted it so bad. Just to get away. Just to get into the world. And to stay away from home."

This is what had been set in motion, all those years ago. I saw it now. Thompson had decided that the things that caused him pain had a local cause, and that he could cure it if only he could leave. He had left. And his pain stayed with him.

I had to go to Southeast Asia to find my pain. "I got into the world, big brother. I got into the world and it tried to kill me. For three hundred sixty five days." I lit a cigarette, inhaled and blew the smoke into the sunlight that came through the narrow window. "And now, I can't come back from there."

"I'm sorry, Jackson. Sounds like we're both screwed."

"And here we are. You asked what I did, what I set in motion. People tried to kill me. I responded. Every action has an opposite reaction, but the formula isn't exact. It's not an equal and opposite reaction. Sometimes people make mistakes. They poke the wrong bear. And the bear bites back."

"You're the bear, I take it?"

"This time. Not every time. Not even most times. Usually the bear scares the shit out of me."

"You've turned inscrutable, Jackson. Not like you used to be. You used to be all on the surface, easy to read."

"You don't want me to be easy to read. You don't want to see what's buried deep." I put the cigarette out. Its red glowing center detached from the butt, and burned quietly out. "And I think that's true of you too."

We sat in the quiet of the visiting room. I heard the tick of the round, black wall clock. My brother, half turned away from me, hung his arm over the chair's back, put his head in his hand. He stroked each eyelash, shut over each eye, and wiped a tear.

At least that's what I would have said he was doing. Back when I thought I knew what he was doing.

"What's next? After you're out."

He took a deep breath and held it before pushing it out, a long slow exhale that seemed to empty him. "I have to go see Mama. I have to tell her what's coming. I have to tell her I'm dying."

"Sure." It would be the second death, the second time she would lose him.

"Will you come?" He looked at me from behind his eyes, a sort of unfocused half stare.

"No. Mama doesn't need to see two of us." I thought that Thompson was more than enough. And I didn't think she needed to worry with my troubles.

"If that's what you want." He stood and so did I. We shook hands, and it turned into an embrace. "Thanks, little brother."

I felt tears begin to come. And when they started, they didn't stop.

Chapter Forty-Two

I LEFT THE JAIL drained of whatever buoyancy I'd had on the walk down. The wind was colder. The sky was paler. And if it had seemed that we'd turned a corner toward cold weather, now it seemed that we were on a downhill street, careening toward winter sooner than we wanted.

By two o'clock I was in Hannigan's. The lunch crowd was gone. The kitchen staff was hard at work closing down the midday meal and prepping for the dinner shift. The front of the house was cleaning the tables and booths, making sure that whoever came in for dinner would have the feeling they were the first customers of the day. They worked around me, such as they had to. I sat in a booth halfway back, in the part of the restaurant that is always the darkest, day or night.

The coffee in my cup had long since gone cold. I sat in front of a Tennessean, looking at the Daily Jumble. I had found all the words in the jumble, but couldn't get the final: "he know he was going to be a priest before he was admitted to seminary because it was. . ." Who knew? Bad luck? That was too few letters.

I felt her before I saw her. And when I felt her I didn't want to look up. I knew it was Grace Pettibone even without looking. I could detect just the trace of her musky cologne.

"Jackson."

"Hi, Grace." I motioned to the bench on the other side of the booth. "I didn't know when you'd turn up. I just knew that you would."

She sat without making the squeaking sound most people make when sliding on the vinyl seat covers. Her amazing eyes, so deep blue, were surrounded now by little red streaks. Her whole face was somehow saved from its mourning by artful makeup. If you didn't know her, you would not jump to any conclusion, other than that this was a pretty, but unhappy girl.

I knew her, though. I knew how she could be full of sensual swagger one minute, and deep concentrated thought the next. And both of those Graces were beautiful.

This one was miserable. Her hair was clean but unstyled. Her makeup was plain, enough to get by. And her features, which could be animated by anything from lust to academic passion, were dead. Her mouth made no shape, other than the one made by sadness.

"I don't know what to say, Grace." That may have been the understatement of the year.

"I've cried myself out." Until she said it, I hadn't noticed a tissue in her fist. "It doesn't seem real."

"I can't imagine, Grace." I could imagine, of course. I saw him fall. But I couldn't imagine how she felt. My brother was dying, but he was not my father. And my father was dead, but he was not, I suspect, like the father figure in Grace's life.

"I heard what you did to Rod and his brother."

"They killed Patrick and Raines." For all practical purposes, her father did too. But that was for another day. "They tried to kill me." I could feel the weariness in my voice.

She could too. "I know. You know I didn't like Rod. And his brother was loathsome." She dabbed unconsciously at a dry eye. "So Patrick and Raines, they are avenged." She said it with a voice I could imagine Corporal Adkins, using.

"Vengeance is a tricky thing."

She looked momentarily surprised. "Why do you say that? Don't you believe in it?"

I looked into my coffee cup as if it held the answer. "Why would you? If honor demands it, who decides what's honorable? If tradition demands it, than whose? Like I say. Tricky."

"An eye for an eye." Her voice was stern, but it was more as if she was trying to convince herself.

"Let's call it self-protection. Patrick and Raines were not on my mind when I tangled with Hal or Rod. It was the same as when Raines came at me in the bar. No more force than necessary."

"Jackson?"

There was no sternness in the question.

"Jackson, how much force was necessary with Daddy?"

There indeed was the question. Some form of it was coming no matter how the conversation went. I'd been the last to see him alive. It stood to reason that, if I'd done what I'd done to the Hanna brothers, I had propelled him from the tower, no matter where I stood when it happened.

But it hadn't. "Your father's fate didn't depend on me, except as the one who was below him, then above him, blind inside the tower. Once the smoke got thick, I didn't see him again until he lost his grip."

"But you set the fire, right? To flush him out?"

"Your father did. Your father set fire to a box of worthless papers and they caught a timber. He kept the box he wanted." Her eyes creased in the corners. "The one you have, the one he wanted, unless the police still have it."

Her mirthless laugh was muffled inside her fist, inside the tissue. It stayed inside her fist, and she bit the index finger, locking the laugh away. "Two boxes?"

"Yes. He came to the tower for the Confederate gold. The instructions. Each of the men in Williams' platoon had a piece of the puzzle. Until Adkins killed him. You know all this, Grace."

When she opened her fist, the tissue silently fell to the table. "He burned the instructions."

"What?"

"The box he had was full of receipts. Adkins kept a set of books there. He was overcharging the University on maintenance, and he kept the real receipts in the tower."

"With his other secret."

"Yes."

Charles Pettibone had burned the wrong box. He had fallen to his death with a box of worthless papers. He had risked everything, then torched what he had risked it for. "Folly."

"What's that, Jackson?" She had lifted her head, and she looked at me intensely. Not even the red streaks could diminish the searing blue eyes.

"Folly. Adkins saved the box from burning, a century ago, and it burns anyway, a century later. Patrick and Raines. Your father. All dead. A burned box that may or may not lead anywhere." I met her eyes. "Worthless, misguided folly."

"The treasure does exist." Her voice belied the declaration. It was flat, featureless.

"Even if it does, was it worth all that?"

Her voice became smaller. "No." She threw the tissue into the corner of the table. "What I knew, what Daddy didn't, was that Williams was the creator of the plan. He kept one piece of the puzzle to himself, as nearly as I can tell the central piece. Without it you could get so far, but you couldn't get close enough to the final solution."

"Why did he kill Williams, Grace? Why make the treasure impossible to find?"

"Adkins somehow discovered that Williams' mother was a slave. That he was under command of someone he considered not fully human." She read my surprise. "If you look deeply enough, it's all but said. He said he would not submit to half breeds. He said he killed Williams over a slave. It's all there, Jackson. It's just not all in one place."

"So Adkins killed any chance of finding the treasure when he killed Williams."

"Not that he didn't keep trying. There's evidence that he used his vacation time every year to trace some part of the clues."

"That's in his box in the library? I didn't see that."

"Oh, not his war papers. There's an entire box just about his time as steward." She looked at her hands, her nails newly unpainted. "That's how I knew what his receipts were. His accounting didn't add up."

Three people died for this. A treasure that may not exist. With instructions that have a hole in the middle. Hidden by a swindler, who'd killed a man for who his mother was.

We said goodbye. There wasn't much else to say.

***

And then the day had ended, and with it all possibility of solace. Pettibone was dead. So were Raines and Patrick. Thompson would soon be dead.

And the rest of us were hanging around, waiting for it.

I sat with Don Mercer, at Linda's, at 11:39 on a Wednesday night. His bike was parked, as always, where he could see it and worry about it at the same time.

"Just don't park it on the street if it bothers you." I signaled Bobby to give me another beer. "You don't have to sit here and panic every time you see a car."

Mercer isn't the sort of guy who worries. But he doesn't like bringing his bike up West End. There's something about being in a biker bar that makes a cop/biker nervous, I guess.

"You don't ride, Jackson." He waved his plastic cup at Bobby for another draft. "You wouldn't believe the shit that goes on."

Bobby performed the necessary labors to top us off, and went back down the bar to his previous conversation.

I don't ride, but I get that it's different for a black guy who does than a white guy who does. And I'm a white guy who doesn't.

"Clint still got a hard on for me?" I could easily believe the interim chief would be looking for something to run me in.

"Clint's hard about everything. But you know what?" Don sipped his beer without looking over at me. He had his eye trained on a five gallon jar of pickled eggs behind the bar. "That's because he isn't hard over the right things."

"You making a joke, Donnie?

He gave me one eyebrow up, briefly. "I don't make jokes, Jackson. I observe life." He looked back to the pickled eggs. "Like now. If Clint was here, he'd be strutting back and forth, looking at the low life, judging them, deciding where to plant his flag."

"I swear you're making a joke. Like a pun."

"I'm not joking. He'd be strutting, back and forth, and he'd come across someone like me, staring at the pickled eggs."

Which is what he was doing. Staring at the pickled eggs.

I told him as much.

"Yes, but I'm really into the pickled eggs." He motioned back toward Bobby, who took his time. "Gimme two of those eggs, and a can of Vienna sausages."

He soon enough had a couple of pickled eggs, four Vienna sausages, a cellophane pack of Saltines, and a shaker bottle of Texas Pete in front of him. The eggs were on a napkin.

"What's Clint got to say about that?" I was asking an honest question.

"That's what I mean. Clint ain't hard for the right things, or he'd be all over a half drunk egg and Vienna sausages deal at midnight." He bit off half an egg and chewed it slowly. "You can't trust a man like that."

It struck me that Don might be a little drunk. It was more than possible that I was a little drunk. I'd started right after Grace, and while I hadn't gone hard, I'd gone steady. I studied

Don's face. He was somewhere between black coffee and milk chocolate, with a nose that had been broken a couple of times, and dark eyes that could stop people in their tracks. "What kind of man can you trust?"

He took the other half egg and poured Texas Pete on it, bit down and let the yolk sit on his lower lip before he licked it off. You could just see a sheen of sweat on his nose. "I trust you, Jackson. Know why?"

"Because I'm a damn Boy Scout? Because I have so much integrity that you admire me?" I took a sip of beer. "I'm being sarcastic."

He took a pull from the plastic cup and doctored the second egg. He put more Texas Pete on it than I thought advisable. "Because, when it counts, I can ask you a question and get a straight answer. It don't take much more than that." He nipped off the end of a saltine cracker and sucked the salt off the rest. "If you're a black man, that's all you need. I just need a fighting chance. If you tell me where you're at, I can deal with the rest of it." The second egg went in his mouth whole. You could gradually see the sweat sheen become a drop on the end of his nose. He chewed, then swallowed, deliberately. "I always have a fighting chance with you."

"And here I thought you liked me, Donnie."

"I like you all right. And I hate Clint. I think he's a complete asshole. But ya'll both just white guys. Not like you ever walked in black skin. It's not like you know."

"Know what, Don?" He kept looking forward.

"This whole thing. These boys. That girl. The motorcycle gang. All this stuff about white people. All this stuff about white people wanting everything like it was. Their world. The one they own. You know, when black people knew their place."

"And were kept in their place."

"Or died." He paused. "Yeah, kept in their place or died." He wiped the Texas Pete sweat off his nose. "You sorted through all that mess, Jackson. You figured their shit out. You made it so the bad guys got what was coming to them. You did good, right?"

I probably looked doubtful. "I guess."

"Naw, you did. But listen, man. It was just a puzzle for you to solve. It was something to get your brother off, but he'd have gotten off, maybe, anyway. He's white. It works that way."

"Maybe. Maybe not."

"But you did your job, right? And you never felt the fear. Do you understand what a black man in your place would have felt?" He moved his plastic cup toward me. "He would have been terrified. Just being around folk who think that way, and say it out loud. And willing to act on it, no matter what?" He shuddered a little. "That's some bad stuff there, Jackson."

"You ever afraid, Don?"

The Vienna sausages disappeared into his mouth, and he chewed slowly, almost comically. When he stopped chewing, he swallowed, then washed it down with the rest of the beer in his cup. "I'm always on some kind of yellow alert. Not a full-on red alert. But even now, I could tell you what every white guy in this bar is doing. And how much attention they're paying to me."

"Well, there's only me and Bobby and those two guys shooting darts in the back."

"Don't be a smart ass, Jackson. You don't have to worry about this kind of shit. You're white."

"It'd be the same for me in a bar on the north side."

"Damn straight it'd be. You'd better have your whole head on a swivel. But the world ain't the north side of Nashville. The world is just like this bar. And the South is its own little booth in the corner. A place you can't sit with any comfort. Not if you're black."

And we sat there. Two vets with Nashville in common. One a police officer, who knew that he had to be careful whether he had a badge on or not, who understood that every bigot dead and gone was really just one less of a never-ending number. The other a guy who couldn't get out of his head if he tried, and who was tired of trying, tired of fighting it.

"One of these days, though, Jackson?" Mercer kept looking toward the pickled egg jar. "One of these days the South is gonna be different. Nashville is gonna be a lot blacker and browner, and this tide will turn."

I looked toward the pickled eggs, to the mirror behind them, and looked into Don Mercer's eyes. He was between black coffee and milk chocolate, and his eyes were piercing through the mirror and reflecting back, all at the same time.

"And when the tide turns, Don, what will that mean? Will it be better?"

He held my gaze in the mirror. I waited, ten, twenty seconds. "It will be different." He broke the gaze. "That's all I'm saying."

Also By TJ Arant

Thanks for enjoying *One Trade Too Many,* book two of the Hardboiled Southern series. If this is your first Jackson Trade novel, click on books one and three below. They are exclusive to Amazon and you can also enjoy them as a subscriber to the Kindle Unlimited program.

Nashville Trade http://getbook.at/NashvilleTrade
Even Trade http://getbook.at/EvenTrade

If you would like to keep up with publication news and other information, plus receive a free novella about Jackson's first case, just head over to https://BookHip.com/CNFHFK for a copy of TRADER. All you have to do is tell me where to send it.